10/22

Also by Adam Oyebanji

BRAKING DAY

A QUIET TEACHER

Adam Oyebanji

SEVERN
HOUSE

First world edition published in Great Britain and the USA in 2022
by Severn House, an imprint of Canongate Books Ltd,
14 High Street, Edinburgh EH1 1TE.

Trade paperback edition first published in Great Britain and the USA in 2023
by Severn House, an imprint of Canongate Books Ltd.

severnhouse.com

Copyright © Adam Oyebanji, 2022

British Library Cataloguing-in-Publication Data
A CIP catalogue record for this title is available from the British Library.

ISBN-13: 978-14483-0942-9 (cased)
ISBN-13: 978-14483-0986-3 (trade paper)
ISBN-13: 978-1-4483-0973-3 (e-book)

All Severn House titles are printed on acid-free paper.

MIX
Paper from
responsible sources
FSC
www.fsc.org   FSC® C013056

Typeset by Palimpsest Book Production Ltd.,
Falkirk, Stirlingshire, Scotland.
Printed and bound in Great Britain by
TJ Books, Padstow, Cornwall.

For Barbara and Alex.

*And for teachers: without whom this book – or any book, really –
could never have been written.*

ACKNOWLEDGEMENTS

I am not always on Planet Earth. So to find myself typing an earthbound murder mystery was a bit of a shock. In fact, the shock was so great that, but for the support and feedback of people who had more faith in my writing than I did, this book would never have seen the light of day. Especial thanks to Rachel Whipple, ex-police chief and avid consumer of mysteries, and Claire Marmion, relentless seeker of good things, for assuring me that I had written something worth the reader's time; to my friend, Shelly Geppert, for her unstinting support; to my agent, the esteemed Brady McReynolds, his assistant, James Farner, and all at JABberwocky Literary for not laughing in my face when I told them what I was up to; to my editor, Carl Smith, plus the fine folks at Severn House, particularly Anna Harrisson and Sara Porter, for taking this on and making it better; and last, but not least, to my family: Barbara, Alex, Amina, Alima, Tom, Nadia, Max, Elliot, Henry, Becky, Harriet, Angus, Corey and freshly-printed Margot, whose cheers from the sidelines kept me going when it would have been so much easier to stop.

*T*raitor.

The word echoed through his dreams. Sometimes in English, sometimes Russian. Though it was difficult to differentiate between them. He was diving from the harbor wall yet again, and for the first time. The slap of cool seawater a blessed relief from Djibouti's night-time heat; a shield against the bullets spiraling after him, their fury spent against the effortless resistance of the ocean.

It was hard to swim with a broken arm. At least, he was pretty sure it was broken. It hurt. He couldn't move it. He kicked hard with his feet, bare and bloody, pushing deeper into the water, praying to the Almighty that he was headed in the right direction. That his SOS had gotten through.

He was more worried about his eyes than his arm. The right was OK – at least he thought it was – but the left was closed shut and burning, the sting of it far worse than saltwater against a bleeding eyelid.

Morosov had used battery acid.

His body was arching upward now, seeking the surface. He came up in the pitch black, maybe twenty-five meters from the jetty. A couple of torches were flailing wildly in the darkness, their beams too weak to pick him out, even if they somehow managed to find him. He rolled onto his back, breathing in the hot, tropical air, and kicked out like a frog, careful not to break the surface with his legs. This far out, his bedraggled body would be invisible to flashlights, but the frothy splash of water would not. He kicked on doggedly, heading to a scuffed, concrete jetty and the lee of a small cargo ship. There was a name for the way he was swimming, he thought, even if the style had never made it to the Olympics. He just couldn't remember. And his left eye was killing him.

The flashlights had disappeared. Polukhin and Morosov would

*be considering their options. They could run to the jetty far quicker
than he could swim, but they'd need to think to do it.*

Please, God, let them go the other way.

*He reached his destination, the stern of the cargo ship towering
above him; the name* Excelsior *stenciled across it in pale, rust-
pocked letters. He found a set of steps onto the dock, but he was
too exhausted, too injured, to pull himself up. His head dipped
below the water. Came up once.*

Twice.

*But not a third time. He was going to drown within a meter of
safety. It was OK, he realized. He was tired of it all, anyway.*

Please, God, don't let it hurt too much.

As if God had ever answered his prayers.

*And then, as if to spite him, a miracle. Someone grabbing him
by the shoulders, hauling him safely above the waterline.*

*'We've got you, mate. Don't worry. You made it.' The accent
was crisp and well rounded. Tea parties, and manor houses, and
red-coated palace guards.*

He remembered the name of the swimming stroke he'd been using.

Backstroke. English *backstroke. He couldn't help it. He started
to laugh. And once he started, he couldn't stop . . .*

'You're listening to *Morning Edition* on WESA 90.5 FM Pittsburgh,
National Public Radio. Today: city sanitation workers are out on
strike for the first time in . . .'

Greg Abimbola's right eye cracked open. There was sweat on
his forehead and his heart was thumping against his ribcage. He
forced himself to take slow, easy breaths, staring into the distance
until his brain attuned itself to reality.

It was still dark. Winter wouldn't start spending its tightfisted
allowance of daylight for at least a couple of hours yet, and the
inside of the apartment's dormer window was coated with ice.

A cold one, then.

He swung his legs out from under the duvet and sat on the edge
of the bed, bare feet sinking into the carpet. After a moment or two,
he padded into the living room, a loud yawn drowning out NPR's
cheerful recitation of municipal discord. The living room was spotless, hard surfaces gleaming with polish, soft ones vacuumed to a
showroom finish. Freshly painted walls hosted carefully curated
fine-art prints and several rows of books. Even though most of the

furnishings remained the same, his landlord, more accustomed to Pitt students than neatniks, would have had difficulty recognizing it. The thought brought a smile to Greg's lips.

This place, he reminded himself, was a real shithole.

Except the word he used wasn't 'shithole'. It was '*trushchoby*'.

'English, you idiot.' The words sank without force into the apartment's sloping wall/ceiling. The apartment was at the top of the building, an undergrad-infested rowhouse in the middle of Bloomfield, so either word worked. There was nothing on the other side except battered slate, and maybe some sleet. He could hear its gritty pitter-patter against the windowpane.

Retrieving a set of free weights from the landing outside his apartment door, Greg worked himself into a lather while NPR jabbered on in the background: political gossip, natural disasters, whimsical human interest, all mixed together in the usual perky burble. He stopped listening almost immediately, concentrating on his aching arms and legs, making them work far harder than necessary.

It was better than thinking.

He managed to avoid any meaningful thought until after he was showered and ready for work. It was always the same, this moment when he stood in front of the bathroom mirror and pulled the patch over the top of his wrecked left eye. What if, what if, what if . . .

What if I hadn't climbed the stairs that night? What if I'd been a better son – a better Christian? What if I'd had a fucking spine and done what I should have done? And lastly: why didn't I just suck it up and let Polukhin and Morosov get on with it?

He stared hard at the mirror. With the patch on, he was still good looking – dashing even. The jawline was still firm, the caramel skin smooth and unblemished. His one, good eye was a bottomless dark brown, gleaming with apparent good humor. And if there were gray hairs speckled through the close-cropped black, they were still too few to see. If he'd been fully white, they'd have gathered around his temples and aged him ten years at least.

A wry smile. *One for the plus column, then.*

He shrugged on a dark, knee-length coat, and headed out.

G reg stepped smartly up the broad steps to the main entrance, waving to the security camera as he did so. He was rewarded with a buzz and a click. The glass doors barring his way unlocked themselves.

'Good morning, Mr Abimbola. Warm enough for ya? Even colder than England, I bet.'

'Yes, but it's a dry cold.'

Stacey, the security lady, chuckled. Although she was her usual, cheerful self, she was standing behind the front desk instead of sitting. And she was still wearing her outdoor gear, right down to the fleece-lined galoshes she'd used to stomp her way in from the bus stop. The faint reflection from a bank of TV monitors glimmered on the shiny quilting of her coat.

'What's up with the heating?'

'Furnace is out. Custodian's had an earful from the principal and is swearing fit to burst.' Stacey's voice dropped to a conspiratorial whisper. 'I'd steer clear of both of 'em if I was you.'

Greg shot her a quick smile.

'Will do.'

Keeping his coat buttoned, Greg headed past the front desk, crossed the opulent lobby, and skipped up a wide marble staircase, passing beneath Calderhill Academy's ornate coat of arms as he did so.

Calderhill Academy, pre-eminent among the private schools clustered in the city's Shadyside and Squirrel Hill neighborhoods, would not take well to the indignity of being without a furnace. As a child, Greg Abimbola had spent more than his fair share of winters in unheated classrooms – and on days far colder than this one. But then again, his mother had not been a member of Pittsburgh's one percent. He was not the son of some financial guru, or tech whiz kid, or prominent doctor. Calderhill's parents, who paid their five-figure school fees with little outward complaint, expected an Ivy League placement, excellent alumni connections, and something approximating an outstanding education. A properly heated building was so far beneath their expectations it wouldn't even register.

Until tonight, anyway. It was all too easy to imagine the fuming regiment of emails that would be lining up in the principal's inbox. He didn't envy her in the slightest. But that, of course, was why they paid her the big bucks.

'Greg?'

Emily Pasquarelli, the registrar's assistant, was waiting for him at the top of the stairs. She looked anxious. Leather-gloved hands meshed together like ill-fitting gears.

'Good morning, Emily. Elegant as always, I see, even when bundled up for the cold.'

He meant it, too. At Calderhill Academy, the faculty's fashion vernacular was best described as 'rumpled'. Lots of natural fibers and not quite matching outfits. Emily bucked the trend, though. Bobbed, strawberry blonde hair topped a petite, boyish frame, which she had wrapped in a red cashmere coat, brightly colored complementary scarf, and luxurious looking brown gloves. Brown calf-length boots completed the ensemble, their tops hiding coyly beneath the hem of her coat.

Emily smiled at the compliment, touched a brief hand against his wrist.

'The principal would like to see you. Soon as you get in, she said.'

Greg pulled a face.

'What have I done now?'

'No idea. But Lindsay Delcade is with her.'

Greg tried to ignore the sinking feeling in his stomach.

'I'd best be getting along, then. Oh – before I forget – how's your mother? Better, I hope?'

The shoulders beneath the red coat shrugged stoically.

'Physically, much better. And thanks for asking. Doctor said it was just a mild sprain and she's recovered fine.' Emily tapped a gloved hand to her temple. 'But she's starting to lose it up top, you know? I swear, she gets more absent-minded by the day.'

Greg nodded sympathetically.

'Watching your parents get old is no fun. It was good of you to take her in.'

'The dutiful daughter, that's me.' The words were said lightly, though, with no trace of bitterness. Emily glanced at her watch and looked pointedly down the corridor. 'Your nemesis awaits.'

'So she does. See you later – assuming I get out of there alive.'

Emily's tinkling laugh rang in his ears as he turned left instead of right and headed to the principal's office. Or, more accurately, the principal's *outer* office. The door to Elizabeth Ellis's inner sanctum was closed, though the amount of privacy this afforded was minimal. The office was glass-walled. On the far side of the partition the willowy figure of Lindsay Delcade, mother to Vicki and Chandler, and royal pain-in-the-ass, was leaning over Ellis's desk. Her porcelain-pale skin and mane of bright red hair were in sharp contrast to the principal's ruddy cheeks and gray-flecked auburn bun. It was easy to hear her, too. Greg sank into a brand-new leather sofa and listened.

'This is ridiculous,' Lindsay was saying, voice raised. 'Absolutely, goddamned ridiculous! We need a few more days, that's all. I don't see why my daughter has to suffer because of your stupid, arbitrary rules, and I won't stand for it. I won't!'

'They're not *my* rules, Ms Delcade. It's how this admission process works. The deadline's passed, I'm afraid. But next year is still a real possibility. It will give you time to—'

'I'm not waiting another goddamned minute for this, never mind a year! You fix this, Elizabeth. Fix it right now!'

Ellis's hands spread themselves placatingly on top of her desk.

'It's simply not fixable, Lindsay. I'm sorry.'

'Sorry? *Sorry?* You will be if you don't get this sorted. I'm not kidding. I'll bring the whole school down on top of your goddamned head if I have to!'

Delcade turned on her heel, ready to storm out. Seeing Greg through the glass, her expression darkened even further.

'You!' she screamed, opening the door. 'How do they even let people like you work here? Go teach in the ghetto. It's all you're fit for!'

'Ms Delcade! That's enough!' Ellis's words bounced pointlessly off Lindsay Delcade's back. The doors to the outer office were already closing behind her. She stomped off down the hallway, high-heeled boots click-clacking on the gleaming hardwood floor.

Ellis, with a resigned wave of the hand, signaled for Greg to come in.

The principal's office, even when he wasn't in trouble for something, invariably made Greg feel uncomfortable. It was riotously untidy in a way that only an academic could manage. Stuffed bookcases, too full to cope, spilled their contents onto the floor; photographs and mementoes from a dozen different conferences clung crookedly to the walls and littered the windowsills; unsteady piles of paper, held down by a motley collection of objects, encroached upon every available surface.

It offended his sense of order.

At Ellis's invitation, he sat down on an incongruously sleek office chair. It tipped slightly under his weight.

'I'm sorry about that,' she said. 'Lindsay is . . . excitable.'

'Not a problem,' Greg said, equably. The lie was second nature by now. Besides, his curiosity had been piqued. 'What was all that about?'

'Oh, you know. College stuff. You know how parents get at this time of year. Lindsay is absolutely fixated on getting her daughter into Stayard.'

Greg couldn't quite stop himself from smiling.

'Stayard? I know I'm not completely up to speed on American colleges, but that's a bit out of Vicki's reach, don't you think? That's Ivy League territory.'

Ellis sighed. There was a cup of coffee hiding on her desk. She took a sip and grimaced. Cold, presumably.

'It is, and you're right. Stayard would be a dream school for Vicki. But we have a great record of placing students there. Outstanding, actually. So some of our parents have, ah, *expectations*.'

Greg grinned at her.

'I don't envy you your job.'

'Really?' Ellis didn't smile back. 'Then I'd appreciate it if you didn't make it harder.'

The sinking feeling returned to his stomach.

'Problem?'

'Lindsay Delcade is complaining to me that you've got it in for Vicki. That you've got something against her because of so-called white privilege.'

Greg's eyebrows almost hit his scalp.

'Her words, not mine.'

'If I had an issue with white privilege, I'd have it in for every kid in this school.'

A small hiss of exasperation escaped Ellis's lips.

'That's not fair, Greg. We're pretty diverse these days.'

Greg let it slide, the decision reached so quickly he was barely conscious of making it.

'I like Vicki,' he said. 'Good kid. Works hard. Not the brightest, academically speaking.'

'And that's the problem right there,' Ellis replied. 'You can't tell parents that their kids are dumb.'

'I never said she was dumb. I just said she wasn't the brightest. There are cleverer children in my class, that's all.'

'You gave her a B in Russian Language III.'

'I can't give Bs, now?'

'No. You can't give Bs and then tell a complaining parent that their child is "not the brightest". You need to say something like, "Vicki works really hard, and I love having her in my class. She shows a great deal of promise. If she could just work on a couple of small things, I'm sure her grades will improve."'

Greg found himself snorting with exasperation.

'So you want me to mollycoddle some preening, entitled parent? Because their perfectly OK child got a perfectly respectable B? Give me a break.'

'No,' Ellis snapped. 'Give *me* a break. Is this an English thing? Do teachers routinely denigrate students over there? I know you haven't been here long, but you've got to get with the program. Grade the kids firmly but fairly – and be *gentle* about it. These people pay your salary, you know.'

Greg's eyes narrowed.

'They don't, actually.'

Ellis had the good grace to look abashed.

'Look, Greg. I know we have you pursuant to a . . . er . . . *special* arrangement. And we're glad to have you. Really. We are. But you've got to help us out here, OK? Ease off with the parents. I know Lindsay Delcade is difficult, but there are plenty of good moms and dads whose noses are going to be put out of joint if you keep going on like this. Do you understand what I'm saying?'

After a moment's hesitation, Greg nodded.

Different country. Different rules.

'I'll do better,' he promised. His face, he knew, was a study in contrition.

Ellis, apparently satisfied, broke into a smile.

'Look,' she said. 'English schools are harsher. You need time to adjust. I get it. But look on the bright side. You don't have to be half as diplomatic as the rest of us. With that accent of yours, you can say *almost* anything you like and get away with it. Just don't abuse the privilege, that's all I'm saying.'

Ellis's backhanded compliment ringing in his ears, Greg took his leave, glanced at his watch, and hurried back down the stairs to the main lobby. Emily Pasquarelli was standing by the front desk, still in her red coat. She was delivering the bad news about the heating to incoming staff and students.

'How did it go?' she asked.

Greg grimaced.

'Well, I still have a job, so best to look on the bright side, eh?'

'It'll pass,' Emily assured him.

'Until my next screw up, anyway.' Greg grinned at her to assure her he was joking and headed down another flight of steps to the basement.

It was noticeably chillier down here. He half expected to see his breath misting up in front of him. The corridor he was walking along, being in the bowels of the school and not much used, was significantly less grand and a lot less well-lit than the floors above. Perhaps if the lighting had been better, or if he'd had two working eyes, he wouldn't have stepped on it.

Reeeeeeeooooowwwrrrr!!!!

Greg stepped back, startled. A blur of black hurtled off along the passageway.

'Really, Mr Bimbo, why would you do such a thing? What has *Señor* Sanchez ever done to you?'

'He exists,' Greg growled. 'Isn't that enough?'

Andrea Velasquez, the school's assistant custodian, was at the far end of the corridor, her head poking out of the door to the custodian's room. Sanchez, the semi-feral cat whose tail Greg had stepped on, slipped past her and into the workspace beyond. But not before spearing him with a reproachful, green-eyed glare.

Greg sneezed.

'Aw, *c'mon!* You didn't even touch him!'

'My shoe touched him. It's enough.'

'It's all in your head, you know that, right?'

Greg grinned. 'Probably, Maybelline. But that doesn't make it any less real.'

'Don't call me that,' Andrea pouted. 'You know I hate it. It makes me sound like a make-up commercial.' She stepped fully into the corridor, her mountain of black hair hidden beneath a woolen Steelers hat, the rest of her bundled up to the nines, like everyone else today. Sanchez reappeared, rubbing himself against Andrea's patent leather Doc Martens.

'"Maybelline" is the name your parents gave you. You should show them more respect, young lady.'

'Uh-huh. And *you*, Normal Name Guy, should think carefully about insulting someone you want a favor from.'

Greg's grin grew wider.

'Whatever makes you think I want a favor?'

'Oh, I don't know. You're a teacher. And you're down here.'

'Fair enough . . . *Andrea*. I was wondering if you had a space heater or something in your cave of wonders. Something to stop my class from turning into an icebox.'

'Like the rest of the school, you mean?'

'Exactly.'

Andrea leaned against the battered entrance to the custodian's room and gave him a long, considered once over. The sort of stare that made it clear she liked what she was looking at, even though, God help him, he was close to twice her age.

'Come on in,' she said. 'Let's see what we can do.'

The custodian's room, like janitors' rooms everywhere, Greg figured, was a confusing mélange of scavenged domesticity and architectural engineering. A grimy, glass-brick window allowed in a faint approximation of daylight which, in turn, fell upon a threadbare sofa and two mismatched armchairs. The three pieces of furniture lounged comfortably around an oak coffee table that had seen better days. There was a small kitchenette with a couple of mugs upended on the draining board, and an old-style TV on the top shelf of a rickety bookcase. The bookcase did, in fact, have actual books in it. In addition to a handful of worn paperbacks, there were some IT textbooks and a ring binder to go with them, the latter emblazoned with the insignia of Pittsburgh Community College.

Greg, looking at the textbooks, found himself gripped by a strange churning of emotions. Nostalgia, sympathy, pity, anger. Andrea Velasquez might only be an assistant custodian, but the textbooks confirmed what he'd long suspected: that she was determined to make something of herself. Greg knew what *that* felt like. To be young. To have potential. And then to fight every fucker from Archangel to Vladivostok for the chance to use it.

In contrast to the room's domestic elements, the metal hulk of the school's furnace rose like a surfacing sea monster from the scarred concrete floor. It was cold and dead now, the warm roar of burning fuel completely absent. Metal shelving and half-open cupboards, full to bursting with vacuums, mops, spare parts, and cleaning fluids, ran around the whitewashed brick walls. The walls themselves were decorated with fading pictures of scantily clad women. Greg, not for the first time, raised an eyebrow.

'Where's Mr Szymanski?' he asked.

'Vern?' Andrea shrugged. 'Checking out the classrooms, I guess. Figuring out how cold it is.'

'And when he does, can he do anything about it?'

'Nah,' Andrea giggled. 'But it makes it look like he's doing *something*. Keeps Principal Ellis off his back.' She patted the furnace's broad metal shoulder with something like affection. 'Choked up with dust and crap is all it is. Open it up, clean it out, good as new. But we have to wait for the contractor to get here. Until *then*, welcome to Alaska.' She fished about in one of the shelving units. Tugged. Tugged harder. There was a small clatter of displaced objects. A dusty portable radiator was wheeled into the middle of the room.

'How's this?'

'Looks great,' Greg said. 'Thanks. But . . .'

'But what? I just got you a freakin' heater out of the goodness of my heart, man.'

'Yes, I know. And I'm truly, genuinely grateful. But what about you? It's freezing down here. Do you two have another one? Something to warm this place up?'

Andrea looked at him thoughtfully, as if surprised by the question.

'Nah, take it. We're not here much during the day, and it wouldn't do us much good even if we were. It's not big enough, and all the heat would go straight out that door.'

She was pointing, not at the door Greg had come through, but a different one. Battleship gray and metal, with a hint of rust on the hinges and a giant lock that looked like it belonged in a medieval dungeon. There was a key for it, too, also enormous, hanging from a nail banged into the nearest bit of wall. Hints of daylight peeped through the small gap between the door's chipped bottom and the concrete floor. Andrea was right. He could almost feel the cold seeping through it. Just looking at it was making him shiver.

'Why don't you just board that thing up?' he found himself asking.

'Because we need it to get to the loading bay. We bring the smaller stuff in through here sometimes. Saves the hassle of having to open up the big roller door. The drive chain on that sucker keeps coming off the cogs. It's a total bitch to get it back on again. And guess who gets to do *that*?'

'Not Mr Szymanski?'

'Right in one. No wonder you're a teacher.'

'Yes, I am.' Greg grinned. 'And thank you for this.' He tested the heater's weight. It was heavy, filled with oil or something probably, but not so heavy that lifting it wasn't easier than wheeling it along bent double. Using both arms he heaved it up against his chest, letting the power cord trail behind him on the floor. The dustiness of it tickled his nose, but it was nowhere near as bad as a cat.

As he headed out, he took one more look at the walls.

'You know, Andrea, I'm pretty sure you don't have to work surrounded by naked women these days. Last time I looked, the year began with a two.'

Andrea's response was a derisive snort.

'Some of these thots been up there longer than I've been alive, man. No point moving 'em now. It'd just make Vern more of a pain in the ass than he already is.'

09:06 A.M. EST

Greg was more rattled by his encounter with Principal Ellis than he cared to admit. If he'd been thinking straight, he would not have begun Russian III by saying Russian gerunds were different from English ones. He knew better. No one in the class (and quite possibly the English department) had the faintest idea what a gerund was. The whole thing had been a train wreck. The kids, thank God, had been good-natured and forgiving. They spared him the harassment they might have meted out to someone less popular.

Of course, when it came to the good will of his students, being warm had probably helped. Greg's classroom wasn't very big, and Andrea Velasquez's little radiator had pumped out more than enough heat to beat back the wintry air. Protected from the cold, the kids had ground through their exercises with stoic fortitude, his stumbling disquisitions on present participles and verbs as nouns already forgotten. The class had passed without further incident, and now his students were filing out the door a little more slowly than normal, no doubt aware that the rest of their day was going to be considerably less comfortable.

Greg, meanwhile, turned to the neat pile of Russian I notebooks stacked on his desk. He took the topmost one and opened it, intent on making a serious dent in the marking.

In doing so, however, he found himself suppressing a small sigh. It had been a pleasant surprise to discover that, like his mother, he had a knack for teaching. But it wasn't exactly exciting.

He ground the thought out of existence.

'Sir?'

Greg looked up to see Vicki Delcade hovering at the edge of his desk, notebook in hand. Physically, Vicki Delcade bore a striking resemblance to her mother. She had the same tumbling mane of bright red hair, albeit with dyed-blonde tips; the same tall, willowy build; the same porcelain-pale skin. But where Lindsay Delcade was wound tight and angry, Vicki flowed like water, her face gentle and open. Born into another time and place, it would be easy to imagine her as a hippy dancing in the San Francisco sun, her red hair swathed in daisies, legs obscured by the absurd flare of bell-bottom jeans.

'Can I help you with something?' he asked her.

In response, Vicki opened her notebook and thrust it toward him.

'I'd like you to tell me if I've got this right,' she said, her finger pointing to a line of untidy looking Cyrillic at the top of the page. 'Before I go mess it up at home.'

Greg threw her a quick smile.

'You won't mess it up,' he assured her, though he wasn't sure he was telling the truth. 'Let's have a look.'

'This is pretty good,' he said, after a moment. 'Except for this. It's *tantsuya,* not *tantsuyet*: "while dancing," not "dances".'

Vicki looked crestfallen.

'I'm never going to get this gerund thing.'

'Of course you are. It's just practice. That's why you do homework: to help you learn.'

'Yeah, well I'm never going to learn quick enough for my mom.'

'Just learn quick enough for *you*, Vicki. You'll get there in the end. And you know what?' He threw her an impish grin. 'When you do, you'll be one of the few Americans on the planet who understand Russian.'

Vicki smiled at that. Briefly.

'But I won't be understanding it at Stayard, will I, sir? Not the way I'm going.'

Not for the first time, Greg wished he were a trained teacher instead of a mildly talented fake. He didn't know what to say. If he agreed with her, Ellis would be all over him for not being sufficiently supportive. If he *disagreed* with her, he'd be telling an outright lie to someone bright enough to see it for what it was. So he said nothing, concentrating instead on looking as sympathetic as possible.

'I don't even *want* to go to stupid Stayard,' Vicki continued, her voice tight. 'It's Mom. *She* should go if she thinks it's so great. And she could, too. Mom's like, super, super intelligent. Me? I don't even want to go to college!'

'You don't?' Greg didn't try to keep the surprise out of his voice.

'No, sir. I want to sing and dance and be an actor. I'm good at it, too. I've been in two downtown shows this year, and I've got my Equity card and everything. I want to go to New York and try out for off-Broadway stuff. Build a résumé, you know?' Her expression glowed with the incandescent possibilities of youth, only to darken again. 'But Mom won't let me. Says I have to make something of myself so as not to be beholden to some *guy*. As if!'

Greg scratched distractedly at the underside of his eye patch.

'Lots of actors go to college, Vicki. I'm sure you could major in theater or something like that.'

Vicki gave a derisive snort.

'Yeah, I *could*. But not at stupid *Stayard*. There's a hundred colleges that are *way* better for performing arts. *Way* better. Stayard is for judges and politicians and guys who want to work in banks.'

Greg had a sudden image of Vicki Delcade manning a picket line.

'They turn out doctors, too,' he said, smiling. He vaguely remembered hearing that somewhere. 'I'm sure there's more to Stayard than corporate sell-outs.'

'I guess,' Vicki conceded. 'But for the performing arts it's just wack.' She executed a graceful pirouette. 'I think I was *born* for the stage.' Somehow, the joyful, matter-of-fact way she said it deprived the statement of any hint of pretentiousness. 'It's my one good thing.'

Greg, thinking of Lindsay Delcade's attempts to jam her square daughter into a round hole, felt profoundly sad.

'I had a friend like you when I was in high school,' he said, quietly. 'Well, not *quite* like you. One: he was a boy; and two: he had no interest in acting.' Vicki giggled at that. 'But he did *not* want to go to college. *Any* college, and his parents wanted him to become an engineer. He was bright enough, too. But he stymied them with the perfect solution.'

'What did he do?'

'He flunked his classes.'

'I couldn't possibly do that!' Vicki said, visibly shocked.

'Well, I'm not suggesting you go *that* far. But if it's really bothering you, you do have *some* control over the situation, you know. I'm pretty sure Stayard isn't interested in students who don't want to be there.'

Vicki was silent for a moment, her gaze unfocused; endless possibilities entering stage right in her teenage mind, feet soundless on the boards. Eventually, though, her eyes reconnected with the world around them. She shook her head sadly.

'I have to do my very best to get in,' she said, quietly. And then, seeing the puzzled look on Greg's face, added, 'If I don't at least try, it'll break Mom's heart.'

11:58 A.M. EST

'Sir? What are these? Are they pirate ships?'

A giggle ran around the class. Many of the lower and middle school kids genuinely believed Greg Abimbola was a pirate. Why else would he have an eye patch?

One of the seventh-grade refugees – Landon Worthington, if Greg had got their names straight – was pointing curiously at two ornate models of wooden sailing ships. Tiny brass cannon poked out from immaculately painted gun ports, miniature crosses of St Andrew flew proudly from gold-filigree sterns, streaming in an imaginary wind.

'They're the *Mirny* and the *Vostok*,' Greg explained. 'Ships of the imperial Russian navy. Among other things, they were the first ships to discover Antarctica.'

Across the room, another teenage hand shot up.

'I thought the English discovered Antarctica, like Captain Scott, or somebody?'

'Captain Scott made it all the way to the South Pole, slap bang in the middle of Antarctica,' Greg said, smiling. 'But that was almost a hundred years later. And even then, he wasn't the first to get there. The Norwegians beat him to it – by about a month, I think. Their leader was a man named Roald Amundsen. Who was also the first man to fly over the North Pole – in an airship, no less. Interesting guy.'

The bell rang. Lunchtime. Kids started to head out of Greg's classroom, though, like the students before them, far more slowly than usual. The corridor was still freezing. And Andrea's little radiator was still fighting the good fight. A small group of kids lingered around the model ships, apparently intrigued.

'God! I wish my lab was as warm as this.'

Demetrius Freedman, the school's chemistry teacher, waded upstream against the current of hungry children, and crossed over to Greg's desk. He was wearing a puffy, quilted coat, but no hat or gloves. He looked absolutely miserable. Demetrius had that tall, rangy, African American build that most Americans associated with basketball. To Greg, who was not American, he looked like a Maasai warrior. A cold one. One who'd swapped the East African savannah for the foothills of Western Pennsylvania and only just realized he'd got the shitty end of the deal.

'By all means come in and warm up.' Greg waved vaguely in the direction of the children. 'It's not like you'd be the first.'

'Not your regular class, then?'

'Nope. Kids are basically camping out here because it's warm. There are maybe half a dozen classrooms with some sort of heating, so the kids are being sent through on extended study. I've got Russian II straight after lunch, and then I think Emily told me to expect some freshmen for the rest of the afternoon.'

Demetrius nodded.

'Yeah. Emily's been sending kids my way, too. I've been running the Bunsen burners all morning, but it's not been having much of an effect.' He looked enviously in the direction of Andrea's radiator. 'Where'd you get that heater?'

'I threatened a custodian with torture and death.'

Demetrius chuckled.

'I hope you did. Vernon Szymanski's an old-school, racist bastard.'

'Aren't they all?' Greg said, mildly. He was not in the mood for one of Freedman's diatribes.

'I'm serious. He's—'

'There are kids here, Demetrius.'

'Yeah. *White* kids. Let's not hurt their feelings.'

The last of the children left the classroom. Greg braced himself for another onslaught and was pleasantly surprised when it didn't come.

'I hear you've been crossing swords with Lindsay Delcade,' Demetrius ventured. He was looking at Greg curiously, head cocked to one side.

'You could say that.'

'Well, you have my sympathies, brother. That woman is an A-grade bitch. God help anyone who says or does anything to "undermine my daughter's aspirations".' Demetrius's hands might be cold, but that didn't stop him from curling his fingers into air quotes.

'I take it I'm not alone, then.'

'No. But she has a special place in hell for the black folks who get in her way.'

'Demetrius, please. I'm too cold for this.'

'Yeah, well, just because you're English doesn't mean it don't apply to you. This whole country's a white supremacist shithole.'

'I'm sure it is. But there are far worse places in the world.'

'Do you think so? You might want to change your mind about that.' Demetrius glanced meaningfully across the classroom. Greg followed his gaze, landing on the *Mirny* and the *Vostok*. They were still sitting on their shelf, still sailing across invisible, iceberg-laden seas.

And yet.

Greg's long stride took him across the room in a handful of steps. The dark, varnished wood of the ships' hulls had been scratched over with jagged, clumsy letters.

Captain Bimbo, one said. Greg turned to the other. Took a slow, calming breath. Read it over. Reminded himself there were worse things in the world. Only then did he allow a wave of sadness to wash over him.

Nigger. The words stretched raggedly along the port side of the *Vostok*.

Nigger Go Home.

01:30 P.M. EST

Greg Abimbola's Russian II class, like all his classes, was small, just half-a-dozen students, all of them good kids, and a couple of them with real talent. Heads bent low over desks as they struggled to translate a simplified piece from Pushkin's *Metel*. It wasn't in the textbook, but as Russian without Pushkin was like breathing without air, Greg had assigned it anyway.

Besides, he didn't have the mental energy to do actual teaching and it would keep them out of trouble for the rest of the period. He needed time to think. He stared absently out the classroom window, thoughts floating across his mind like night snow passing a streetlight. Long, brown fingers tapped out a rhythmic tattoo against the edge of his desk.

It was several minutes before his eye regained its focus.

'Can I have your attention for a moment?'

Six heads raised themselves gratefully from the assigned toil.

'I have to step out for a few minutes. Needless to say, I trust you not to misbehave *too* badly while I'm gone.' He was rewarded with a couple of smiles. 'As an incentive, this week's homework will be finishing the passage, so if you get it done this afternoon, you're free and clear. Deal?'

Various flavors of 'yes, sir' came back at him. He rose from his chair and headed out, careful not to step on the *Mirny* and *Vostok* as he did so. He'd stashed the two ships out of sight beneath his desk. It was the only place he could think to hide them.

He marched down the corridor in long strides, headed to the admin suite next to the principal's office. Glancing briefly at the stenciled glass door that led to Ms Ellis's domain, he wondered if he'd be seeing her yet again over this latest dereliction of duty. He dismissed the thought out of hand. The elevated chatter of six kids behind a closed door was unlikely to attract attention, so his absence would almost certainly go unnoticed. And as for Russian

II, they would either work, or not. So long as they didn't burn down the building, Greg didn't much care.

None of them were likely to vandalize his classroom with racial epithets.

He slipped into the admin suite and leaned over the top of Emily Pasquarelli's cubicle.

'You got a minute, Emily?'

'For you? Always.'

She beamed up at him from a pile of polite letters reminding certain parents that fees were still due. Warmed by a space heater under her desk, the morning's red coat had been removed and was now hanging up on a nearby stand, her brown gloves placed neatly to one side of her work area.

'I need you to get hold of a few kids for me,' Greg said. 'I'd like them back in my classroom immediately after school.'

'Why?' A small frown had creased Emily's forehead.

'Discipline stuff. Nothing too serious, but I want it nipped in the bud.' He banished a sudden image of Demetrius Freedman, tight-lipped and disapproving.

'OK, sure.' Emily picked up a pen. 'Who am I looking for?'

Greg's mind flashed back to the group of kids who'd been lingering by the ships at the end of class.

'Landon Worthington, Chandler Delcade, Pamela Mercurio, Alexa James, and Corbyn McConnell.'

'Seventh grade? They'll all be in the same place, then. Should be easy enough. I'll check their schedules.'

'Thanks, Emily. You're the best.'

'Yes,' Emily agreed, chuckling. 'Yes, I am.'

Greg waved at her over his shoulder. Taking the stairs two at a time, he headed down to the first floor and the science department. The science labs and their associated classrooms were just off the main lobby, directly beneath admin and the principal's office one floor above. His progress was blocked, however, by glass security doors that had swung shut across the corridor, presumably in an attempt to keep the cold out. Normally, they were held open by magnetic latches when school was in session. But not today.

Greg swore under his breath. The doors locked automatically and wouldn't open without a keycard, which he hadn't thought to bring with him. He rapped impatiently on the glass. No one responded. All the classroom doors in the science department were closed. It was unlikely anyone could hear him.

'Need a hand, Mr Abimbola?'

It was Stacey, the security lady. She must have seen his predicament from her station at the front entrance. She waved her keycard over the reader. The lock to the doors clicked open. Greg smiled at her gratefully.

'Stacey, you're an angel. I owe you one.'

'No problem. You take care, now.'

Greg had no further trouble reaching Demetrius Freedman's classroom. The long, narrow laboratory was full of sophomores heating things up in glass tubes. Greg knew enough about chemistry to recognize the various set-ups as an experiment involving distillation, but that was about it. And whether the experiment was actually part of the curriculum, or simply Demetrius's way of putting the lab's only source of heat to good use, Greg had no idea.

Seeing him enter, Demetrius intercepted Greg at the doorway, his face reignited with righteous anger. Greg swallowed back a sigh.

'You can't just let this go,' Demetrius said, reiterating what he'd been saying from the moment they'd discovered the vandalized ships. Then, Greg had hustled him out of his classroom, unwilling to have a discussion right then and there. But now there was no avoiding it. He needed Demetrius. And the price of Demetrius was . . . this. The chemistry teacher kept his voice low to avoid being overheard, but it was insistent, nonetheless. 'You need to go to the principal and get the entire goddamned class disciplined. This is fucking outrageous. Someone has to pay. Whoever did this should be expelled.'

Greg shook his head.

'No one's getting expelled and you know it. It was one or more of five kids – I saw them hanging around the models. And not a one of those kids is on financial aid. They're all "good" students, whose parents pay full freight and have a ton of clout to match. I may not have been here long, Demetrius, but I know this: this is Pittsburgh. Everyone who's rich and powerful is connected to everyone else. So there's no way this school is going to bite itself in the arse by expelling someone.'

Somewhat to Greg's surprise, Demetrius nodded in slow agreement.

'But that doesn't mean we shouldn't raise hell over it,' he cautioned. 'We gotta lay down a marker. Show folks we're not going to be messed with.'

'And then what? After all the *sturm* and *drang* and concerned hand wringing, all that'll happen is a slap on the wrist, which is almost worse than doing nothing at all. Scratch that: it's *actually* worse. You make this a big deal that goes nowhere? Everyone will see how little you and I count for around here, and things will go downhill quicker than you can say "whitewash".'

'Principal Ellis ain't gonna look at this . . . this *shit* and do nothing!'

'She'll do *next* to nothing. And no matter how sorry Ellis is about what was done, some part of her will always resent the fact that I've just gone and caused her a whole load of trouble with the people who pay her bills.' He allowed himself an ironic smile. 'Thanks to our good friend, Lindsay Delcade, I'm on thin ice with her already.'

Demetrius shook his head.

'I think you're wrong, man. But even if you're right, leak it to the media. They'll be on top of this like a fat kid on candy. It'll be all over the news. Raise a real stink. Then she'll *have* to do something. And if she won't, the governors most surely will.'

'The media? *God,* no!' Greg could feel the blood draining from his face. 'The last thing I want is a bunch of effing journos sticking their noses into my business.'

'So you're just going to bow your head like some field hand, and thank the nice folks and the nice folks' kids for fucking you over?' Demetrius's long, thin body vibrated with anger. A couple of the closer students turned to see what was going on.

'I didn't say that,' Greg said, keeping his voice low. 'I'll deal with this myself.'

'How?'

'Do you have any activated carbon?'

'You . . . What now?'

'Activated carbon.'

'Uh . . . sure. But what do you need it for?'

'For repairing my ships. I need it to fix some of the pigments.'

Demetrius gave him a strange look before disappearing into the storeroom at the back of his classroom. He returned moments later with a large jar of black powder, his every step followed by curious, sophomoric eyes.

'Thank you.' Greg made to leave. Demetrius grabbed him by the elbow.

'You're welcome. But don't think this conversation is over. This is serious shit that just went down. You can't just let them get away with it.'

Greg made a non-committal gesture. Enough to get Demetrius off his back.

'Can you swipe me through the fire doors? I left my keycard upstairs.'

Freed from the confines of the science department, Greg found his way to the main lobby and clattered down the stairs to the basement.

'Twice in one day,' Andrea Velasquez said, archly. 'If only I was as popular with guys my own age.'

'I'm sure you are,' Greg said, smiling. 'But I *do* need a favor.'

'Another one?' Andrea's arms were folded across her chest in an imitation of annoyance.

'Another one. Where is *Señor* Sanchez?'

03:30 P.M. EST

Landon Worthington, Chandler Delcade, Pamela Mercurio, Alexa James, and Corbyn McConnell were lined up in front of Greg's desk in a shuffling approximation of stillness. Whether they were shuffling from guilt or the cold, time had yet to tell. Greg had turned off the borrowed heater and cracked open a window. Inside his classroom, it was close to freezing. Not that Greg cared. Contrary to the stereotype, he rather liked the cold. And he wanted the kids to be as uncomfortable as possible. In a different world, he'd have had them all attached to electrodes, their feet sopping with water.

He pushed the image away. Even Demetrius Freedman might draw the line at *that*.

The *Mirny* and *Vostok* were displayed prominently on his desk, their violated sides facing the students in a silent reproach. The kids' eyes repeatedly skittered away from what was written there, only to drift back moments later. A small torture. At least for the innocent ones.

Andrea Velasquez, too, was staring at the defaced vessels. Her eyes skittered not at all. They took everything in, her face a mask of disapproval. If she stole an occasional glance at the children, it was brief and less than friendly. She was rocking gently back and forth, cradling the black mass of Sanchez in her arms. The cat, at least, seemed entirely unperturbed by the situation. Its baleful green eyes were firmly closed, a soft purr brushing gently against the custodian's warmth.

Greg fought down the urge to sneeze. He scratched at the underside of his eye patch instead.

'You can all see why you're here, I assume?'

'It wasn't me, sir!' Landon Worthington protested, his eyes dangerously bright. 'I'd never do something like that.'

'Well, one of you did. Either alone or with the knowledge of the rest of you. So: who did this?'

The only response was a long, awkward silence.

'Last chance, ladies and gentlemen.'

'I don't know anything,' Chandler Delcade said, hotly. 'It wasn't like that when I left.' The other children nodded in earnest agreement.

Greg sighed.

'Do any of you know what's taught in this classroom?' he asked.

'Russian?' Pamela Mercurio ventured, beneath a raised hand. There was an eagerness to please in her expression, a desperate desire not to be associated with the words that were staring her in the face.

'Yes, Miss Mercurio. Russian.'

Greg, who had been leaning against the wall by his whiteboard, stood fully upright.

'Funny fellows, the Russians. Not many resources, not like we have here. But what they lack in stuff, they make up for in other ways.' He allowed the apparent good nature to leach from his face, replaced by a lazy, predatory smile. The sort of smile he'd used before, in abandoned basements, or broken-down huts with the rain pounding on a corrugated iron roof, uncaring insects buzzing against naked light bulbs. Landon, Corbyn, and Pamela looked absolutely terrified. He dialed it back a bit. These were kids, after all. Not his usual stock in trade.

'The Russian *politsiya* – the police – can't afford lie detectors. Did you know that?'

There was a puzzled shaking of heads.

'Do you know what they use instead?'

'No, sir,' Landon said.

'*Cats*, Mr Worthington. They use cats.'

Five worried pairs of eyes swiveled toward Sanchez, still asleep, still purring softly in Andrea's arms.

'Cats hate getting wet, they just hate it. So much so, that if your hand is even a little bit sweatier than normal, they react very badly. Lie detectors do exactly the same thing, actually. They detect elevated levels of sweat on the human body. Because liars sweat just a *tiny* bit more than someone telling the truth. A human being would never notice the difference. But a lie detector does. And so does a cat. If you're lying about something and you stroke a cat, he's ninety-nine percent certain to detect it the moment you touch his fur. So, unless you're one of the world's best liars, he's going to catch you. Understand?'

The children all nodded, mouths hanging open, eyes wide.

'Good. Because one after the other, you are going to stroke Sanchez here while uttering the words, "I did not vandalize Mr Abimbola's property". Got that?'

'Y-yes, sir.'

'Terrific. Let's begin, shall we?'

One after the other, with various degrees of hesitation, the children stepped forward and stroked Calderhill Academy's semi-feral cat. Sanchez took it all with surprising good humor. Only once, when petted by Alexa James, did he emit anything approaching a *meow*.

'I didn't do it, sir!' she protested. 'Honest to God, I didn't!'

'Let's leave God out of this,' Greg said, coldly. 'Next.'

Next and last was Chandler Delcade.

'I did not vandalize Mr Abimbola's property.'

Sanchez allowed the boy to pet him without any sort of reaction. Chandler grinned with the relief of the acquitted.

'See, sir,' he said. 'I *told* you I didn't do it. It must have been someone else.' He stole a quick glance at Alexa.

'Maybe so. But then again, I'd like to see your hands. All of you. Palms up, please.'

Expressions of bemusement were replaced by gasps as the children turned their palms up for inspection.

Pamela Mercurio ran a confused finger across the palm of her right hand. The palm was smeared black, stained like a coal miner's. The same black that now attached itself to the tip of her roving finger.

'It's charcoal,' Greg explained. 'Or, as Mr Freedman would no doubt describe it, activated carbon. I'm afraid I powdered the cat with it. Sanchez is already black, obviously, so he's the perfect place to hide it. You picked it up when you stroked him.' His eyes ran down the line of hands. 'Except for *you*, Mr Delcade. Your hands are completely clean, I see.' A red flush was spreading across the boy's cheeks. 'You, of course, only *pretended* to stroke the cat. Because you knew you were lying about the whole thing. Care to explain why?'

Chandler's face had gone completely red. He stared down at his shoes, unable to look Greg in the eye.

'I thought it would be funny,' he mumbled.

'I think you missed a word at the end of that sentence, son. Funny, what?'

'Funny . . . *sir.*'

'And your friends, here. Stood back and watched you do it, did they?'

'No, sir. No one saw me do it.'

Greg wasn't sure he believed him. But one confession would have to do.

'Right, then. Thanks to Mr Delcade, here, the rest of you are off the hook. You, Chandler, will see me after school tomorrow. And don't expect to be leaving any time soon. Understood?'

'Yes, sir.'

'Good. And Chandler?'

'Sir?'

'Why would you want to advertise to the world that you can't spell?'

'Sir?' Chandler wasn't the only one looking confused.

Greg tapped the side of the *Vostok*, his finger resting on the scratched racial slur.

'The word has one "g" not two. It's Latin: *niger.* It means "black". If you can't spell it, don't use it. All this does is mark you out as a knuckle-dragging illiterate. Now, get out of here.'

The children fled. As the door closed behind them, Andrea let out a low whistle.

'Wow. Never seen that before.'

'Nor will you again, I suspect.' Greg allowed himself a small smile. 'It's a one-shot trick. By this time tomorrow, it'll be all around the school. No one's going to fall for *Señor* Sanchez twice.'

'But what would you have done if they'd *all* stroked the cat?'

'Punished them all, I suppose.' He walked across the room to the open window and closed it. Sanchez, fully awake now, insisted on being released. Andrea bent down and deposited him gently on the floor. She stood up again, brushing flecks of charcoal from her chest.

'I'm sorry about your coat,' Greg said. 'I'll pay for the cleaning.'

'Nah, no worries. It'll brush off easy enough. Anyway, it was worth it to see the expression on the little prick's face.'

Sanchez was pawing at the classroom door, desperate to roam free. Greg was happy to accommodate him. The beast was no doubt shedding dander by the bucket load. Scratching absent-mindedly at his eye patch, he opened the door just as quickly as he could.

And found himself face to face with Vernon Szymanski. The custodian pushed past him without so much as an 'excuse me'.

'There you are,' he said to Andrea. 'Been looking all over for ya. School ain't paying ya to goof off.'

'She was helping me with something,' Greg said.

'Course she was. But whatever you people was up to ain't more important than the girl doing her job.'

It was difficult to know if Vernon Szymanski was sixty or six hundred. He looked old, but it was entirely possible (to use a phrase Greg had once heard at an American consulate) that he'd been rode hard and put up wet. His body was thin and slightly stooped, with a small but prominent gut. It bulged against the black-and-gold Penguins jacket he was wearing against the cold. A matching hat concealed a pink desert of scalp, and worn jeans hung loosely over legs that had withered away with age. Rheumy, slightly bulging eyes stared crossly at his assistant.

'I need you to get back down to the basement and fix the furnace.'

'That's not my job, Vern.'

'But can you fix it? I thought Mexicans could fix anything for a couple of bucks and a taco.'

'Vernon!' Greg interjected.

Szymanski's response was an unrepentant cackle.

'It's just friendly banter, Mr Abimboo. No harm in it. Girl knows I'm kidding, dontcha girl? But you *can* fix it, right?'

Andrea managed to both nod in agreement and roll her eyes at the same time.

'What happened to the contractors?'

'They can't make it, they say. Not till tomorrow, anyways, and maybe not even then. Lazy fucking bastards – 'scuse my French. If this ain't fixed by tomorrow morning, principal'll be writing us both pink slips. This needs doing, and it needs doing tonight.'

Andrea headed for the door, shaking her head.

'I can't, Vern. Fixing it's gonna take hours and I got class tonight.'

'There's overtime in it,' Vernon said, following her out.

'I just told you, I can't.'

'Aw, c'mon!'

'No, man. No means no.'

'No, it don't. It means maybe . . .'

11:21 P.M. EST

Greg knew he shouldn't be here. He knew it.

And yet.

It had been a more interesting day than usual. Almost fun, even. Shenanigans at school, rough justice for the Delcade boy, and then that rarest of things: a classic Russian movie in an American theater. No reason, he'd told himself, to think about anything else.

But here he was anyway, parked in a nondescript side street on the Southside Flats, neon light splintering against the windshield of his Mini Cooper. A muted bass wormed through his ears, the music becoming briefly distinct as the bar's worn wooden door opened and closed. Two young men stepped out, college students maybe, and unsteady on their feet. They headed past him in the direction of Carson Street. It was impossible to tell whether they were headed home, or merely en route toward trendier action. Greg watched them until they reached the intersection.

He remembered the first time the Devil had come to see him. At least, the first time he remembered that the Devil had come. Aged nineteen, the bedsheets damp against his skin, shocked awake by dreams. By what they said about him.

What his mother would say if she ever found out.

He'd told himself it would never happen again. He'd been drunk, after all; the *tsarskaya* too strong, hurling his sleeping mind into a pit of depravity.

And yet. The Devil kept returning. 'Where's the harm?' he would say, his voice a soft, honey-coated whisper. 'No one will care. You can be whole. You can be loved.'

'You can be free.'

His head would spin with the intoxication of it, the possibilities. But he would hold fast. Beat the Devil back.

Except the once. The once that ruined everything. Faltering

steps up narrow, creaking stairs. Whisky, not vodka, pounding in his veins . . .

He reached into the Mini Cooper's glove compartment, his hand seeking the worn, leather book that always lay there.

His mother's Bible. It was too dark to read the faded Cyrillic lettering, to open its tired pages and beat himself up over the contents. It was enough to hold it. To remember what it meant. Heavy in his palm, he picked it up and pressed it against his chest.

'*Otche nash, sushchiy na nebesakh,*' he murmured. '*Da svyatitsya imya Tvoye.*' The words were rhythmic. Soothing. He could hear the mellow delivery of the cantor, imagine himself swaying with the cadence, the sting of incense heavy in his nostrils.

It was enough. He found himself pressing the ignition button. The Mini's small engine purred to life, the newly wakened dash splashing his face with an orange glow. Relief and disappointment swirled through his head in equal measure as he joined the traffic on Carson Street. Even though it was Monday, its loud bars and noisy drunks were in full effect. Traffic lights turned to green in front of him, as if anxious to usher him home.

By the time he turned onto the Birmingham Bridge, the disappointment had faded away. The Devil, beaten back by prayer, had left him in peace. He sped across to the other side. The dark, rippled waters of the Monongahela rolled beneath him, silent and unseen.

TUESDAY, THE TENTH
05:17 A.M. EST

'Do not look so nervous,' Morosov said. 'It is wonderful day. The sun shines, the women are beautiful, and coffee is to die for. Even in Istanbul, you do not find coffee so good.'

'Maybe if you like Turkish coffee,' his companion snapped. 'Which I don't. Let's get this over with.'

For the moment, Mikhail Sergeevich Morosov chose to say nothing. He stared out of the café's broad, plate-glass window instead. Naked trees cast stark shadows across a narrow, cobbled street. Well-dressed Londoners, shocked, no doubt, to find themselves walking under a blue winter sky, slowed down a little and smiled at each other as they passed. Morosov took in the view with a sigh of contentment. The Paki, spineless weasel that he was, could wait.

Soho, he'd been told, had been more authentic in the past. Bohemian. Seedy, even. But Morosov didn't give a shit about any of that. He liked the modern-day version. The battered looking buildings hid expensive, well-appointed flats, and sleek, boutique businesses that spawned customers for the profusion of cafés, nightclubs and specialty shops that crowded its streets. It was trendy, and good looking, and reeked of money. More importantly, it didn't much care where the money came from or where it was going. Just so long as it got a piece of it along the way.

Morosov's eyes followed a Korean lady in a too-tight skirt. She skipped across the road in flawless make-up, and spiky, patent-leather heels. How much, he wondered, would it cost to buy her? Only when she vanished from sight behind a gaggle of early-rising tourists did he return, with some regret, to the slightly-built man on the other side of the table.

'Your bank make pages of *Financial Times*,' Morosov said. 'Record profit for three year in row. Good for you, yes?'

'If it was good for me, do you think I'd even *be* here?' Mohan Singh glared at him from beneath the blackness of his turban, immaculately folded in the fashion of the East African diaspora. The IT man was ill at ease, his fingers beating an irregular tattoo against the retro Formica of the tabletop.

The Russian let the man's irritation bounce off him. He was used to small manifestations of petulance. It was a way for people to live with themselves; to wake up in the morning and pretend they were something other than his property.

It was delusion, of course. Singh had a gambling problem – two, really. One: he liked to gamble. Two: he was no good at it. Morosov owned Singh's debts, and thus, Morosov owned Singh. Morosov sipped delicately at his coffee. He had told no lie. It really was good.

'It is problem of capitalism,' he observed sympathetically. 'Workers do all work; bosses take all profit. It is always way.'

'I've worked my arse off for that fucking bank for six years. You know how many pay rises I've had? *One!* For less than two percent. And their fucking profits are up by more than twenty! And yet without people like me keeping their fucking computers running, d'ya know where they'd be? Up shit creek without a paddle, that's where!'

'It is nature of bosses to be greedy. Steal always from workers.' Morosov leaned companionably across the table. 'I interrogate boss of big company, once. In Russia. Soft man. Easy to break. He say everything I tell him say without trouble, except one thing. The money he steal from workers? He thought he *earn* it! Truly!' Morosov gave a sharp bark of a laugh and sat back. 'Best always be own boss, like me.'

Singh waved a dismissive hand.

'We can't all be so lucky.'

'One day you try, no? Look at me. I work for government once. Hard work, low pay. Now I work for me. Less hard work, more better pay. Own boss. You IT guy. Easy for IT guy be own boss, too.'

'Not as easy as you think.' Singh took a sip of his coffee. Grimaced.

'I think what you think is good for me, no? You IT guy at big bank. No one except me pay what you worth, no one except me notice what you do. But IT guy everywhere. Every system, every account, password for everything, yes? And you find what I ask you look for?'

Singh nodded morosely. He fumbled with something in his trouser pocket, pulling out a small thumb drive. He pushed it across the table. Morosov put it in his own pocket without even looking at it.

'Inverclyde Institutional Pension Management Trust. They make and administer pension payments to retired workers,' Singh said. 'Tiny outfit. Don't understand why we even have it as a client. But that's a list of all the pension payments it's made in the last three years. Names, SWIFT codes, the lot.'

'I want new pension, yes? Pension opened in last three years, most likely last two.'

'It's all on the drive, bro. But the only one that looks like that went to an outfit called Berings LLP, in the Cayman Islands.'

Morosov frowned.

'A pension payment? To *company*, not person? Make no sense.'

'Probably a shell company. Money gets sent to the Caymans, then gets sent somewhere else.'

'Where?' The word came out more sharply than Morosov intended. Singh flinched.

'Can't say. Bank's involvement ends with the transfer.'

Morosov stared at him. A cold, forbidding probing of the eyes. A look Morosov had perfected in the dark, abandoned places where people give up their secrets. Singh, dark-skinned though he was, turned pale.

'Payments are in US dollars,' he mumbled. His Adam's apple was bobbing nervously up and down. 'Every month. Amounts aren't big enough to justify the cost of swapping currencies. So, I'm guessing America, or the Caribbean, or somewhere else that uses dollars as a local currency.'

Morosov beamed.

'I knew this to be so,' he said. 'Always, I am right.'

Singh stared at him in puzzlement. Morosov didn't explain. There was no need for the Paki to know, for instance, that Inverclyde Institutional Pension Management Trust was an MI5 slush fund.

Follow the money. For Pavel.

He clapped the IT guy on the shoulder, stood up, and exited the café without bothering to ask for the bill. The note he left behind, slippery and plastic to the touch, like all British money, would more than cover the damage.

07:35 A.M. EST

Pittsburgh is a city of brutally steep hills, so it was only when Greg crested the top of Joseph Avenue, the wipers of his Mini Cooper swishing against the sleet, that he realized something was wrong. The road plunged steeply in front of him before leveling out in front of the school. Down below, where teachers and the earliest of parents should be maneuvering for parking spaces, the road was blocked by a couple of police cruisers, hulking SUVs in the black and gold of the Pittsburgh PD, blue beacons spinning ominously in the fading dark.

He hung a quick left, going the wrong way down a one-way street barely wide enough for his tiny car, and turned right onto Dean Close, a two-block access road that ran along the back of the school, separating the redbrick majesty of the Calderhill Academy main building from the artificial turf of the sports ground.

Dean Close, too, was blocked. More police cruisers. But also luminous yellow tape and the huddled, hard-bitten figures of law enforcement. Greg swore softly, pulled up short of the closest police cruiser and parked against the edge of the playing field. He had barely unclipped his seatbelt when he was approached by a uniformed officer wielding a flashlight.

'You can't park here,' he said, brusque, but not unfriendly. 'You need to turn around.'

'Sure. What's going on here?'

'Can't say. Turn around.'

Greg tuned out a small upwelling of irritation and did what he was told. With Joseph blocked off, the nearest free parking was on a side street two hundred yards distant. Returning to Joseph as a pedestrian, no one stopped him walking past the road-blocking cruisers. He skipped hurriedly up the front steps and entered the building. Faculty were standing in the main lobby, talking together in tight, huddled knots. A police officer stood at the top of the stairs that led down to the basement, barring the way.

'Good morning, Mr Abimbola.'

It was Stacey, the security lady, eyes wide and anxious.

'Good morning. What in God's name is going on? Has some arsehole threatened to blow up the school?'

'They've found a body in the basement,' Stacey said. She was shaking, her hands clasped to her shoulders. 'Someone's been killed.'

Something like the old excitement stirred in his chest. His heart rate picked up, analysis kicked in: threats, escape routes . . . and the need for appropriate reactions. His face molded itself into a decent facsimile of shock.

'Who?' he asked, forcing his voice to rise.

'Ms Delcade. Vern Szymanksi found her. Says someone musta dragged her down there and stabbed her to death.'

07:37 A.M. EST

'Is that an accent I'm hearing? Australia, is it?'

'England.'

'Oh.'

The detective – he'd introduced himself as a Lieutenant Brendan Cassidy – seemed mildly surprised. Greg swallowed back his irritation. There was a certain type of American who found the idea of black men speaking with English accents wildly improbable. Unable to believe what they were hearing, they invariably plumped for Australia instead. And it was *always* Australia. Not South Africa, or New Zealand, or any other English-speaking country: Australia. One of life's more annoying little mysteries.

'My wife would love to go to England, one day. See Buckingham Palace and stuff. Maybe when we retire.'

Greg refused to be drawn. He was in the principal's office, sitting across her desk from the detective. Crammed into Ellis's chair, Cassidy seemed far too large for it. Ellis was slightly built. Cassidy, on the other hand, was big and powerful, though running to fat, with a distinct double chin, and close-cropped gray hair. Feeling the heat, he'd removed his overcoat and suit jacket, and was sitting in shirtsleeves, his tie loosely knotted beneath an unbuttoned collar. He was smiling – or trying to. It didn't quite reach his eyes.

The smile faded away.

'Can you tell me where you were last night between about seven p.m. and midnight?'

'Home. Then I went to the movies. And then home again.'

'And where's home for you?'

'Bloomfield. Two hundred and thirty-six Parkside Hill.'

'Uh-huh. And you were there at seven?'

'Yes.'

'And when did you leave?'

'About quarter past.'

'Quarter past seven?'

'Yes.'

'And you say you went to the movies?'

'Yes.'

'Which theater?'

'Row House Cinema, on Butler.'

'And how did you get there?'

'I drove.'

'When did you get there?'

'About half past.'

Cassidy raised an eyebrow.

'So that would be seven thirty, then?'

'It would.'

'And where did you park?'

'Forty-Fifth Street, between Butler and the railroad lines.'

'Uh-huh. And what did you go see at the movie theater?'

'*Solaris.*'

'Not familiar with that one. Who's in it?'

'Donatas Banionis and Natalya Bondarchuk.'

'*Who?*' Cassidy gave him a doubtful look.

'Donatas Banionis and Natalya Bondarchuk,' Greg repeated. 'It's Russian. From 1972. No reason for anyone sensible to have heard of it.'

'But you have?'

'I teach Russian.'

'Uh-huh. And you left, when?'

'As soon as it finished. I don't remember the precise time. I was home by around ten thirty, eleven.'

'And did you stop anywhere on the way home?'

'No.'

'Do you live with anyone, Greg? Someone who can confirm you were home when you say you were?'

'No.'

'Uh-huh. Did you know Lindsay Delcade?'

'I did.'

'And what did you think of her?'

'I thought she was a complete fucking cow.'

Cassidy paused a moment, then, swiveling the principal's chair from side to side. Something that might have been amusement crinkled his eyes.

'I understand she'd complained about you to Ms Ellis?'

'Yes.'

'Anything come of that?'

'Ms Ellis suggested that I be more diplomatic in my interactions.'

'Anything more than that?'

'No.'

'And did you see or interact with Ms Delcade after you spoke to Ms Ellis?'

'After?'

'That's right.'

'Then, no.'

'Uh-huh.' Cassidy stood up, handed over his card. 'In case you think of anything that might be helpful. Thank you for your time, Mr Ab . . . ah, Greg. We'll be in touch if we need anything more.'

Greg wandered out of the office. The school, understandably, had a very odd feel to it. Kids had been sent home wherever possible, the remainder warehoused wherever space and a supervising adult permitted. Most of the faculty were still penned up like cattle in the admin suite, waiting to be interviewed. The rest, he supposed, had gone either to their classrooms or the faculty lounge to await further instructions.

Greg didn't feel much like company. He headed to his classroom, which was, in fact, the closest one to the principal's office, being just down the corridor on the other side of the main stairs.

Its location was probably why it was occupied. He could hear voices coming through the not-quite-closed door. Curious, he walked past, stealing a glance through the door's glass window-pane. There was nothing to see. Whoever was in there had to be seated at his desk, which was out of sight from the corridor. He started to step away but then stopped. He recognized one of the voices.

'Between seven and midnight?' Andrea Velasquez asked. She sounded strangely tentative.

'Yes.' A woman's voice. Pittsburgh PD presumably.

'I finished up here at maybe, five? Then I went home. I was there till maybe, seven? Then I went to school. Was there till eleven. Then I come home again.'

'And where's home?'

'I live with my mom and dad on the North Shore, Oak Street.'

'And what school did you go to?'

'PCC.'

'Pittsburgh Community College?'

'Yeah. I'm taking my A.S. in Computer Information Science.'

'Good for you! Maybe you can help out with the department's computers when you're done. Just between you and me, they suck.'

Nervous laughter.

'And what classes did you take last night?'

'Just the one. Informatics with Professor Carbone.'

'For three hours?'

'It's night school. It's the only way to get in the credits.'

'Got it. I admire you for doing that. Me? I'd be *way* too tired. How many took the class last night?'

'Oh, about five or six.'

'Can you give me their names?'

'I don't really know them. Just faces I see.'

'Got it. But Professor Carbone taught the class? And he knows your name, I take it?'

'Sure.'

'And you left when, you said?'

'Eleven. I went straight home.'

'And how'd you travel to PCC?'

'I drove. I have an old beater Chevy, but it gets me where I need to go.'

'And did you park in the PCC parking lot?'

'I did.'

'So, I guess you used your student keycard to get in?'

'Uh . . . Sure.'

'And you didn't stop anywhere on the way home? For gas, or Twinkies, or anything?'

'Nope.'

'Do you know a Lindsay Delcade?'

'I know she was a parent and that she's dead. That's about it.'

'If you're the assistant custodian, you must use the custodian's room?'

'Is that where she died?' The shock in Andrea's voice was palpable.

'I can't talk about that right now. But you use the custodian's room?'

'Every day.'

'And when were you last in there yesterday?'

'At five. I stashed some equipment, mops and stuff, and headed out.'

'Anyone else there?'

'Just Vern.'

'I see. And did you notice anything unusual?'

'No way. Everything was, like, totally normal.'

'Understood. Well, that's about it. Just one last thing. We'll need your prints to eliminate them from anything we find at the crime scene. That OK by you?'

'Sure.'

'Awesome, thanks.' There was a sound of chairs being scraped back. 'Here's my card, in case you remember anything you think might be useful. Come down to the station after work for the fingerprint stuff – it won't take but a few minutes – and we'll be in touch if we have any further questions.'

Greg stepped away from the door just as Andrea stepped out, looking thoughtful.

'Oh! Hi there, Mr Bimbo. How are you today?' She plastered on a quick smile, but her voice was high and strained.

'Better than you, I suspect.'

Andrea shrugged, glancing back at the classroom door.

'Yeah, well. It's over now.'

Greg placed a gentle hand on her elbow, edging her out of earshot of whoever was in his room.

'Why'd you lie to them, Andrea? Do you think that was wise?'

Andrea wrenched her arm out of Greg's grip.

'I don't know what you're talking about.'

'Yes you do.' Greg smiled at her, sadly. 'The officer that interviewed you, what was she wearing?'

'Er . . . dark suit. What's it to you?'

'Mine was in shirt sleeves. Between you and me, I think he's a doughnut or six heavier than he should be.'

'So?' Andrea refused to smile.

'So . . . neither of them were wearing overcoats, were they? Because it's *warm* in here today, not freezing, like yesterday. Which means you fixed the furnace, just like Szymanski asked you to. Which means you were here half the night. Which means you did not go to PCC like you just told the police.'

'You were *listening*?'

'Couldn't help it. Your voice carries.'

'How *dare* you!' Andrea's dark eyes flashed with anger. 'That was a private conversation!'

'Andrea, I just . . .' He stepped forward, tried to lay a calming hand on her shoulder. The young woman moved sharply to avoid him.

'Leave me alone! Creep!'

Andrea stormed off, her gleaming Doc Martens raising tiny little squeaks from the polished hardwood floor.

Greg sighed. He spared Andrea's retreating figure a worried glance before turning back toward the stairs.

And almost ran into someone.

'So sorry,' he said, stopping abruptly. 'Should have been looking where I was going.'

It had to be the policewoman who'd questioned Andrea, he decided. She must have stepped out from his classroom while he'd been distracted. She was mid-to-late thirties and tall, maybe five-seven or eight, in sensible flats and a dark, slightly scuffed pantsuit. Thoughtful, intelligent eyes stared up at him from either side of a prominent, no-nonsense nose. How much had she seen, Greg wondered. Or, worse still, heard?

'No worries,' she said, sticking out her hand. 'I'm Sergeant Lev. Rachel Lev. Pleased to meet you, Mr . . .?'

'Abimbola. Greg Abimbola. I teach Russian.' He shook her hand, forced himself to smile. 'In that room, actually.'

'Oh. Sorry about that, Mr Abimbola. I don't think you'll be able to use it for the rest of the morning. Interviews and all.' She allowed her hand to drop away. 'Trouble with Ms Velasquez?'

'I hope not,' Greg replied.

'So do I, sir. She's a bit young for you.'

She turned and headed to the admin suite without giving him a chance to reply. Greg swore under his breath.

He'd rather have been suspected of murder.

05:00 P.M. EST

Morosov jumped out of the rumbling black cab, ran across the pavement, and took the steps up to 22A Brooklands Street two at a time. He had spent too long at the Dorchester Hotel, wasting time with a Chinese princeling too stupid to understand that he needed Morosov's services. Some of the shorter West End shows had been getting out, adding a snarl to the night-time traffic that Morosov could have done without. Now he was running late. His tardiness did not stop a small moment of pride as he caught sight of the elegant brass plate beside the door: *Rowley Consultants.* Very English, he liked to think. Very anonymous. But all his. His days of slaving away for the fucking government were over. If they needed him, they could pay him what he was worth.

He headed up the stairs to the first floor, where he let himself in to the compact space he rented as an office. In one corner was a tiny cubby hole, as secure from outside interference as Morosov could make it. Slightly out of breath, he squeezed inside and parked himself in front of a computer. Practiced hands fired up a TOR search engine and plunged him into the dark web. There was a single message waiting. Reproachful Cyrillic characters glowed up at him through the gloom.

> TORquil: Where are you? I will sign off at 10 past the hour
> and you will need to make new arrangements.

Morosov breathed a sigh of relief. He still had time. He switched his keyboard from Roman to Cyrillic and typed back:

> Aslan230: I am here.

There was only the briefest of pauses.

TORquil: About time. What do you want?
Aslan230: Have you heard from Dialogos?

It was a full ninety seconds before the response came through.

TORquil: No.
Aslan230: Do I need to remind you that, unlike Dialogos, I
           know who you are? Don't make me come find
           you.
TORquil: Fuck you, Aslan. It's the truth.
Aslan230: OK, then. I paid you good money to tell me if
           and when he gets in touch. I expect value for it.
TORquil: And what value are you expecting? You know as
           well as I that Dialogos is dead.
Aslan230: I like you, TORquil. I prefer business to more
           painful measures. Another $5,000 (bitcoin, of
           course) to remind you of my goodwill.
TORquil: Money is always welcome. But you are throwing
           it away. He's dead.
Aslan230: It is mine to throw and yours to catch. If Dialogos
           gets in touch with you, you tell me, and you tell
           me what he wants. You do that, you get another
           $5,000.
TORquil: That's all?
Aslan230: That's all.
TORquil: Then goodnight. It is not my job to destroy your
           illusions.

TORquil vanished from the chatroom. Morosov sighed and leaned
back in his chair. The sodium glare of streetlights flooded through
the window. He could picture TORquil, in his grungy Crimean
apartment, raising an ironic glass of Stoli in his honor. And perhaps
he was right to do so. He had been waiting for the bastard monkey
to surface for three years without any sign. But the Paki's information had given him fresh hope.

He rubbed at a small scar on his left temple.

The *negr*, murderer that he was, would pay for what he did.

'Have you heard?' Demetrius Freedman asked, sliding into the worn sofa on the other side of the coffee table.

'Heard what?' Greg was sitting next to the bay window that dominated the faculty lounge. He was reading the local news page of the *Pittsburgh Post-Gazette* on his smartphone, though he wasn't sure why he'd bothered. Yesterday's murder barely rated a mention. And what there was seemed to be a regurgitated Pittsburgh PD press release. He pocketed the device and gave Demetrius his full attention.

'The police have arrested Maybelline Velasquez,' Demetrius announced.

Greg made a half-hearted attempt to look surprised.

'Is that so?'

'Yes! God, you English are so phlegmatic! I thought it rated a "wow!" at least. Or even a "by Jove!".'

Greg smiled at the jibe.

'I'll remember to crank open the emotional faucets next time around. So, what happened?'

'Stacey told me. That detective . . . Cassidy? And his female sidekick came through here last period and picked her up. They've got her down at some station right now answering questions.'

'I hope she's got the good sense to keep her mouth shut.'

'I doubt it. She's got sass, that one. I'm always telling my kids, if the police ever pick you up, you do what they tell you, but you tell them nothing. But it's hard to do when they have you alone in some cell, believe me.'

Greg raised an eyebrow.

'You have experience, then, I take it?'

'I'm a black man in America. Which of us doesn't?' When Greg said nothing, he went on: 'Campus protest in my MIT days. I was the only black kid there, so of course *I* get hauled in. No one else was. Thank God for my prof. He got me out before anything bad happened. It's *real* easy in these here United States to end up with some fat-ass cop kneeling on your neck.' He shuddered in reminiscence. 'Prof Neumann was every conservative's idea of a liberal academic. Today, we'd call him a white guy with a savior complex. But *boy,* did I need saving! Never been so scared in all my life.'

Greg stared briefly out the bay window. It was sleeting again. Another half-hearted attempt at winter. A couple of cars swished by along Joseph Avenue, their wheel arches stained black by the weather. He wondered if Andrea, wherever she was, could still hear the outside world. He doubted it. No good interrogator would allow the outside world to intrude on their questioning. The outside world – even a hint of it – was a lifeline. It made people harder to break.

'I hope she didn't do it,' he said, mildly.

'Well, *someone* did. And Lindsay Delcade was found dead in *her* custodian's room, after all. Who else goes down there?'

'Me, for one.'

'Really?' Demetrius was grinning now. 'Did you do it?'

'I'm taking the Fifth.'

The chemistry teacher burst out laughing.

'Well said, my man. I'm with you. I'm not even slightly sorry the entitled, vengeful little bitch is dead. I'd take the Fifth, too. In a heartbeat!'

Demetrius's smile took on a harder edge.

'On the subject of the Delcade family, I hear you caught your racist student. Sweet move, by the way. I'd never have thought to pull off something like that.'

'It's a one-shot trick,' Greg said, yet again. 'Young Chandler will make amends.'

'He should be fucking expelled! Even if his bitch mother *is* dead.'

'We've talked about this, Demetrius. Expulsion isn't on the cards. Besides, a dead mum is almost punishment enough, don't you think?'

'You're not thinking of letting the little shit off the hook?'

'No. But I'm not having him publicly humiliated either. He can make amends some other way.'

'How?'

'I haven't completely decided. Kid's off school until next week, anyway, given the situation with his mother. It'll keep till he gets back.'

'If you'd grown up here, you wouldn't be so soft on people like that. You need to come down on them early and *hard*. Knock some human decency into their racist white skulls.' Demetrius rapped on the coffee table to emphasize the point.

Greg demurred with a quiet smile.

'You're giving one word too much power, Demetrius. It's just a word. You react to it like it's the end of the world. Let them see how much it hurts, and the people who use it will own you. Brush it off. Treat it with the contempt it deserves.'

'No one *owns* anybody anymore,' Demetrius growled, his voice dangerous. 'And it's not just the word, it's everything behind it. The racism. The cruelty. The fact that the people who use it, use it with impunity. The way they glide into things they'd never get on a level playing field because of the color of their skin.' Demetrius was shaking now, barely able to speak. 'I'd like to line the lot of 'em against a wall, and just pull the fucking trigger.'

'Bit extreme, old boy,' Greg said, his voice arch and ridiculously English. 'Can't they just do chores?'

Demetrius, caught off guard, found himself laughing, the anger leaching from his body like showered-off dirt.

'You need to make sure the kid is punished,' he said. But the words lacked their previous intensity. 'That's all I'm saying.'

'I'll think about it,' Greg said. And then: 'You think the Steelers will go with a new quarterback, Sunday?'

Greg knew nothing about football. But he was an assiduous reader of the *Post-Gazette's* sports section – the only section of the paper that appeared to have a staff – for precisely that reason. It helped him fit in with his male colleagues. And if it occasionally allowed for a bit of deflection, so much the better.

Demetrius looked at him in surprise. It took a moment or two for his mind to switch tracks.

'It's a question of experience over potential,' he said, sagely. 'A game like Sunday's, you go with experience.' Chandler Delcade forgotten, the chemistry teacher settled in for a long and detailed argument in support of his thesis.

A couple more teachers, both white, both football afficionados, sat down around the coffee table and joined the conversation. Greg let the whole thing wash over him, nodding at the appropriate moments and asking the occasional open-ended question. If any of his companions were ever asked about it, they'd swear blind he'd taken an active part in the conversation.

03:30 P.M. EST

There was a knock on his classroom door. One so soft that Greg almost ignored it.

'Come in.'

The door eased open just a fraction. A black mane of ponytailed hair poked into the room, followed by an olive, anxious face.

Andrea Velasquez. Seeing that there was no one else in the classroom, she allowed the rest of her body to slide through the narrow gap.

'Good afternoon, Andrea.' He couldn't – or rather, wouldn't – stop himself. 'I thought you were helping the police with their, ah, *inquiries.*'

Andrea winced.

'They let me go. For now, anyway.' She stepped further into the room, her hands spinning one about the other in an anxious dance. 'Thing is, Mr Abimbola, you were right about me lying to the police. I never went to PCC like I said I did. And they found out just like *that.*' She snapped her fingers in time to the last word, the sound flashing across the room like a gunshot. 'And now I think I'm in trouble. Real trouble.'

The woman's eyes were brimming with tears. Greg retrieved a box of tissues from his desk.

'Here,' he said, gently. 'Take a seat.'

Andrea did so. She was sitting hunched over, hands clasped around her knees, the toes of a ratty pair of Converse sneakers pointing inwards. She looked angry, hurt, and, above all, frightened. Greg had the sudden and disturbing impression of a recently beaten puppy. He shoved the image to one side.

'Do you have a lawyer?'

Andrea shook her head.

'I think they appoint you one if you can't afford it.' Greg had only the vaguest idea as to how American law worked, mostly from prime-time TV.

Andrea's response was a cynical little laugh.

'That only happens if they charge me. And by then it'll be too late. People like me, we don't do so well in the justice system.'

'Does anybody? Except the super-rich, of course.'

Andrea smiled at that. Brief and brittle.

'I was kinda thinking you might help me.' Her eyes sparkled with a desperate sort of hope. The intensity of it was too much for Greg. He averted his gaze, seeking solace in the winter daylight that seeped through his window.

'I'm not a lawyer, Andrea. I'm not at all sure what I could do for you.'

'I don't need a lawyer. I need someone who can help me prove I didn't do it. Someone *clever*, like you.'

Greg was not immune to flattery. Nevertheless . . .

'This isn't my skillset. I teach Russian. And sometimes French – if Ms Ellis looks at me the wrong way. What you're talking about requires a private detective. Someone like that.'

'No,' Andrea insisted. 'Private detectives take pictures of people doing the nasty in motel rooms in Butler County. I need someone clever enough to prove I didn't do this. Like *you*. You caught that POS racist kid with a *cat*, for God's sake, and you knew I'd get in trouble with the police before *anybody*. Including me. You're the only person I know who can get me out of this.'

Greg tried to ignore the stirring of interest at the base of his brain. It uncoiled in his mind like a dragon, one eye lazily open, shifting and sleepy on its hoarded pile of gold. He pictured himself once again prying into people's lives, upending their secrets, edging them this way and that. Peeling back the onion layer by layer.

And finding himself front and center with the police, maybe even the media; his face all over the internet.

He clamped his mouth firmly shut. Shook his head instead.

'I'm sorry, Andrea,' he said, finally. 'I just can't.'

'But—'

'No, Andrea. Get yourself a lawyer or a private detective. I'm touched that you think I can help you, but I'm simply not qualified. You need a professional.'

'I needed a friend. I thought it would be you. My mistake.'

She rose from the chair with quiet dignity and walked out of the room, her head high, the thick tresses of her ponytail waving gently against her back.

But he could hear her sobbing in the corridor outside.

04:07 P.M. EST

Greg had intended to head home, but found himself lingering in the main lobby instead, a prisoner of conflicting impulses. After a moment's hesitation, he turned on his heel and descended the stairs to the basement. He half expected to be confronted by a barrier of luminous yellow tape, or some kind of 'Keep Out' sign, but there was nothing of the sort. He stepped into the custodian's room unimpeded.

'What do you want?' Vernon Szymanski asked. The custodian spared him a sour look over the top of a mop and freshly filled bucket. The room reeked of bleach – from the bucket, Greg guessed. Nothing seemed to have been wiped down yet.

'Just indulging my morbid curiosity,' he admitted. 'I came to look at the scene of the crime.'

'Yeah, well, take a look and then leave me in peace. I got work needs doing.' He stared sourly at the floor. 'Goddamn cops. They come in here with their questions and evidence bags and their fancy little gloves lugging away God knows what, but do they clean up after themselves? Do they fuck.'

The object of the custodian's ire was plain to see. A dark, nebulous stain had spilled across the concrete floor, as if from an oversized can of paint.

It was right in the middle of the room, not far from the now roaring furnace, between the scavenged coffee table and the dungeon-like metal door that led out to the loading bay. Someone must have stepped on it while it was still wet. Greg could make out the faint remains of a couple of bloody footprints headed toward the metal door. Dark streaks stained the door's large, clunky handle, where the killer had presumably made his escape. He bent down to have a closer look at the footprints. It was impossible to tell much. Each print was only a partial outline, and devoid of any markings. At a guess, they were from the same shoe, and both prints seemed to be pointing toward the metal door.

He was suddenly conscious of the custodian leaning over him. The whiff of bleach was strong in his nostrils.

'Seen enough?' Szymanski was glaring at him, making it clear that he had outstayed his welcome.

'Yes, thank you.'

Politeness did nothing to divert Szymanski's anger. Greg tried again.

'I'm sorry the police left you with this ungodly mess. The least they could have done is clean it up.'

'You'd think, wouldn'tcha? But it don't work like that apparently. Best they would do was leave me a list of so-called "contractors". Like I don't know how to clean my own damn school. Tramping all over here for a day and a half, keeping me away from their precious fucking crime scene while the blood dries so deep it'll take forever to get it off.'

'Life's a bitch and then you die,' Greg observed, sympathetically.

'Ain't that the god's damned truth.'

Greg stepped to one side while Szymanski set to work on the bloodstain. The custodian scrubbed furiously at the floor, carpet bombing it with bleach, his face twisted into an even deeper scowl than usual. But he was no longer insisting that Greg leave.

'Someone told me you found the body?'

'Damn right I did.' Szymanski paused for a moment to point at the bloodied expanse of floor. Pinkish water was running across the concrete and into a small metal drain. 'She was lying right there, all stiff and awkward, like. Was easy to tell she was dead. Blood everywhere. Jesus! What a mess!'

'She'd been stabbed?'

'And the rest. She had to have been stuck maybe a dozen times. Right through her coat with a goddamned screwdriver.'

'A *screwdriver*?'

'A screwdriver. Believe it. One of the big bastards, like this one.' Szymanski stepped across to a large bucket full of odds and ends and pulled out a fearsome looking tool, over a foot long, with a flat, metal tip. 'Whoever killed her must have really hated her.'

'What makes you say that?'

'You don't stab someone twelve times with a screwdriver 'cause you like 'em, do you? Stands to reason.'

'I guess so.'

'And through a coat. Big fancy wool thing that cost a year of my wages. Gotta be real determined to do that, I'm thinking.'

The custodian made repeated stabbing motions with the screwdriver. Greg had no difficulty imagining the tool as a weapon. It was big, comfortable to hold, and the flat-bladed tip was easily as good as a knife for stabbing someone. He wondered idly if, after the long, cold metal had slid into her for the first time, the Delcade woman had been aware of what was happening to her. Maybe shock had set in. Maybe she'd been totally out of it. Nature could be merciful that way.

Sometimes.

Szymanski, demonstration over, replaced the screwdriver in the bucket. He gave a small grunt of surprise and reached into the bucket one more time, retrieving a large metal key. Greg had no doubt what it was for. The custodian hung it with its identical twin on the nail by the metal door.

'Stupid Mexican, always losing stuff. I keep telling her tidiness is next to godliness, but will she listen? Like fuck.'

'Andrea's key, then?' Greg guessed.

Szymanski nodded.

'Not that little miss *señorita* will have much use for it now, seeing she's downtown on a murder charge.'

Greg saw no need to correct him.

'You think she did it?' he asked.

Szymanski shrugged.

'Probably. Mexicans have a temper, everyone knows that. It's in the genes. She was in here smoking dope, the dead lady comes down here for some reason, threatens to report her to the principal, and the *chica* stabs her to keep her quiet.'

'Did the police find any dope?'

'Sure did. Right there, still in the foil.' Szymanski was pointing beneath the room's beaten-up sofa. 'Police reckoned it must have rolled off the coffee table. The little beaner had been smoking it, too. There was an ashtray on the floor, right over there.' The custodian pointed again, this time to a spot not far from the big metal door. 'Big heavy thing it was, from Stayard College.' His face grew somber. 'It was all streaked with blood. Slick, too. The cops almost dropped it a couple of times.'

Greg made a sympathetic noise.

'And were there any cigarettes to go with the ashtray?'

Szymanski shook his head.

'Cops asked me if I'd cleaned 'em away and I told 'em I hadn't touched a thing. Whatever *was* there, police bagged it and took it with 'em when they left.'

'Is there always an ashtray in here? I don't remember seeing one.'

'Nah. In the old days we'd use an empty mug or an old tin or something. But no one smokes any more. Not me, anyway. Doctor says I'm on my last lung. Haven't had one in years.'

'And Andrea?'

'Well, I always thought *señorita* was a pot head. You could smell the stuff in the morning sometimes.' A quick frown. 'Never seen her with *los cigarillos,* though, or I'd 'a' said summat.'

'And you left here at five?'

'On the dot. It was *freezing.* Couldn't wait to get out of here.'

'I'll bet. And I suppose you headed home?'

'I never head home.' A brief sadness flitted across the custodian's face. 'It's just me now. I went to the VFW like I always do. Chatted to some folks, had a few beers, got to the house around midnight.'

'And when you left to go to the VFW, Andrea was here alone?'

'Sure was. The kid was stubborn as all hell, but she finally agreed to fix the goddamned furnace. I left her to it.'

He gave a sudden, sly smile.

'Glad she got it done before the murder. The principal would have had my ass.'

10:02 P.M. EST

Greg had avoided his Mini Cooper, knowing full well where he'd end up if he slid behind the wheel. Instead, he'd trudged up the steep hill from his apartment and ended up on the East Liberty part of Liberty Avenue, a three- or four-block stretch of gently sloping, rapidly gentrifying asphalt, lined with pioneering Gen-Z bars, locavore restaurants, and 'woke' bookshops. Among the garish forest of signs and hoardings screaming for attention, it would be easy to miss the small shingle of the Muscular Arms.

The bar was old-school, a relic of the age of steel, of a time when the small row houses that clung to the hillsides had been occupied by factory workers, the air laden with belched soot and the orange glow of smelters. Its customers were older for the most part. Back in the day, they'd have spilled brawling into the street on a Saturday night just for the fun of it. Now, they sat sedately beneath shocks of white hair, chatting quietly at the counter while the hurly burly of the twenty-first century hurried by on the sidewalk.

The Muscular Arms was not a place for sinning. Not anymore. It lacked the energy. A banged-up, muted TV was tuned to the local news on Channel Seven. The president of the sanitation workers' local was mouthing silently to camera, followed by a shot of the mayor. Strike news, no doubt. No one paid it the slightest attention.

Greg sat by himself in a dimly lit booth, nursing his third or fourth vodka, wanting desperately to be somewhere else. The vodka had done nothing to silence the Devil's tormenting song. It simply drained him of the energy to do anything about it. Once his liver had done its work, the vodka would be gone, but the Devil would still be there.

If only . . .

If only . . . what? If only he *hadn't* climbed those narrow, English stairs?

But he *had.* They'd creaked beneath his feet, single-malt scotch trailing expensive vapors across his nostrils. He'd entered the apartment of his own free will, allowed his eyes to travel over a wall of hardbound, educated books and old leather furniture.

The Devil had won. And losing to the Devil had eventually brought him here, to the vertiginous streets of the Steel City and the safe, predictable life of a foreign language teacher.

A burst of laughter from the sidewalk attracted his attention. There was a group of twenty-somethings on the other side of the bar's plate glass window, bundled up against the weather and headed for a night out. They looked like they hadn't a care in the world. Even if that was almost certainly untrue, Greg was willing to bet that those cares did not encompass a dead body at their place of work.

He allowed himself a wry smile. If he'd had even a modicum of self-discipline, he wouldn't give a rat's arse about Lindsay Delcade either. It wasn't the Devil who had lured him down to the custodian's room instead of going straight home; or who had persuaded him to crouch low over the woman's stained aftermath; or who had encouraged him to subject Vernon Szymanski to an underhanded interrogation. He'd done that all on his own.

Because he was bored.

He slugged back the vodka.

If he was going to be honest with himself – and vodka was made for honesty of the worst sort – there was more to it than that. He *liked* Andrea. She was sailing an ocean he knew well, one where her name and the color of her skin dragged like a half-raised anchor. Even so, until Monday night, with her books and her hopes, she looked like she might be getting somewhere.

But now the storm was blowing. And this was an ocean without lifeboats, where no one would come to her aid.

He, at least, had had his mother. Clever, highly educated, ferocious in his defense. When the system had threatened to grind him into paste, she'd made sure he'd at least had a chance.

But when the police had come for Andrea Velasquez and she'd turned to the one person in the world who could help, he'd told her to fuck off.

There, but for the grace of God, go I.

The waitress delivered another drink without him even asking.

He didn't give much for Andrea Velasquez's chances. She'd been smoking dope in the custodian's room. Lindsay Delcade, doubtless looking for someone to shout at, had, for whatever reason, found her way down there and caught her in the act. It was only too easy to imagine what happened next: *So this is what I pay my tuition for, is it? To let doped-up Hispanics deal drugs to my kids in the school basement? Don't lie to me! Personal use, my ass! You think I was born yesterday? You only work here so you can sell this shit to the students. Like shooting fish in a barrel to someone like you, isn't it? I'm not having my daughter exposed to a drug-dealing illegal. Stay right where you are. I'm calling Principal Ellis and then I'm calling the police – and ICE. You are* done. *And I'll see to it that you never work in this country again . . .*

He stared into the clear liquid, admiring the way the world warped and blurred when you looked through it. The world, Greg knew, could be easier that way. It was sometimes better not to see things too clearly: to not see Andrea, for instance, terrified for her future, panicking and grabbing the first thing that came to hand; to not see Lindsay Delcade, suddenly fearful, raising futile hands against a plunging metal shaft; to not see a dead body lying on the floor in a spreading pool of red; to not see Andrea Velasquez, appalled at what she'd just done, stumbling into the winter's cold of the loading bay, a trail of bloody footprints in her wake.

Footprints.

Greg Abimbola, struck by a sudden thought, downed his drink, settled up his tab, and departed.

He left a bigger than usual tip.

THURSDAY, THE TWELFTH
04:38 A.M. EST

'The world,' Morosov announced, 'always simpler after vodka.'

'Is that why you're late?' Dianna Aldis asked, archly. 'You have that call from Dodoma at ten, remember.'

'Tanzania? Plenty time. No worries, yes?' Morosov grinned at his assistant. He liked Dianna, even though she'd not been his first choice for office help. His first had been younger, and prettier, and had allowed Morosov to explore her body for the best part of two weeks without a word of complaint. Then she quit, leaving him with no support for an upcoming meeting with a well-connected Zambian.

Dianna, who'd been sent by a temp agency at short notice, was significantly older, though still attractive, in that English, lady-of-the-manor kind of way. It hadn't been long before he placed his first friendly hand on top of her breast.

'Let go of me,' she'd said, in an even Home Counties accent. She might just as easily have been asking for a cup of tea.

'Why? It's just bit of fun. Don't be boring. You need job, yes?'

'I need the job,' Dianna had agreed. 'I'm divorcing, my shit of a husband has run off with some bimbo, I've a teenage son who refuses to talk to me, and bills to pay. But I don't need this job half as much as you need your fingers.'

'My fingers?'

'Your fingers. Take them off me right now, or I'll break 'em.'

Laughing, he'd allowed his hand to drop away. He'd kept his fingers to himself after that. And it was worth the effort. Dianna Aldis had proved herself to be an exceptionally good assistant, and – for a woman, at least – highly intelligent.

'I drink vodka,' he explained, bringing himself back to the present. 'Then I get great idea, then I get woman, then I sleep. No vodka, no great idea, and woman not so much fun, no?'

Dianna sighed.

'At some point, I imagine, we will get to this great idea of yours?'

'*Da*. Woman not worth further discussion. But I thinking about, ah, *side* project. Not paying but possible very big profit if go well. Also, big personal happiness. Understand?'

'Not really, but do go on.' Dianna reached for a pen and paper.

'I need you find country where US dollar used as currency.'

'OK. And by "country" do you mean countries where the dollar is the only currency, or should I also look for countries where the dollar is commonly accepted?'

'Hah! Good thinking. Both, yes.'

'Is that it?'

'No. That is not great idea. Get country and then identify city with population one million more big.'

'And if the country has no city that size?'

'Then country third-world toilet. You forget this.'

'Understood. And for city size, do I just look at the city population or the suburbs as well?'

'Hmmm. Suburbs, also, I am thinking. *Da*. Suburbs also is good.' He grinned expansively. '*Now* come great idea. In each city with suburbs one million big, I want list all Eastern Orthodox church. Russian, Greek, Serbian, all church. But only Eastern Orthodox. No Catholic. And for sure no Protestant.'

Dianna's lips twitched with what might have been mild surprise.

'And why am I doing this?'

'Because person I look believe in God. Big time.'

12:05 p.m. EST

'Vern said you wanted to see me?'

Andrea Velasquez stepped into Greg's classroom, her expression sullen. The soles of her shoes squeaked slightly as she walked across the floor. She was wearing the same ratty pair of Converse sneakers as she'd had on the day before. They didn't seem suitable for the weather. It had snowed overnight. Outside his classroom window the city was shrouded in white. The steep hills and tightly packed houses gave it the appearance of a Christmas decoration. Certainly not the weather for schlepping about in canvas shoes with holes in them.

A truck rumbled by on Joseph Avenue, its tires swishing over unplowed snow.

'Thanks for coming, Andrea. I wasn't sure you'd be in today.'

'Yeah, well I am. I need the paycheck and I didn't do nothing wrong, so . . .' She stared at him defiantly. 'You want something?'

'I wanted to apologize,' Greg began. 'I thought about what you said yesterday, about needing a friend. I don't think I was a very good one, and I'm sorry. I'd like to help you. If I can, that is. And if you'll let me.'

He thought for a moment that Andrea was going to burst into tears. She held it together, though, her dark eyes wide and luminous under the classroom lights. She nodded a mute acceptance of his apology, not trusting herself to speak.

'Take a seat,' he offered. Andrea did as suggested, waving away the proffered box of tissues.

'I'm guessing the police gave you a hard time for lying to them?'

Andrea nodded again.

'They have anything else on you?'

'Nah. They already got my prints; then they asked if they could have my freakin' shoes. They asked a bunch of questions about

Lindsay Delcade.' She frowned then. 'And they asked if I smoked dope.'

'And what did you tell them? About the dope, I mean.'

'Nuthin. Smoking dope is still a crime in this here city, man. I know better than that.'

Greg spared her a wry smile.

'*Do* you smoke dope?'

'Who doesn't? But not at work, Mr Bimbo. Never. I need the job.'

'I can't help you if you lie to me.'

'I ain't lying!' Andrea said, hotly. 'It's the god's-honest truth.'

'So the dope they found in the custodian's room isn't yours?'

'No way, man. No way.'

'On Monday, did you *see* any dope in the custodian's room?'

'No.'

'Have you *ever* seen dope in the custodian's room?'

Andrea hesitated.

'No. But . . .'

'But what?'

'I smell it sometimes. When I get in for work. I figure Vern has a prescription for it or something. Man ain't exactly healthy, know what I'm saying?'

'You ever talk to him about it?'

'You kidding? Old coot's difficult enough to work with as is. Don't need more trouble prying into his business.'

Greg's gaze drifted down to Andrea's feet.

'The police kept your shoes?'

Andrea glanced at her moth-eaten sneakers and grimaced.

'They surely did. Only decent pair I got.'

'They say when you could have them back?'

'Uh-uh. I do got the receipt, though. But you can't wear a receipt through the freakin' snow, man. I been freezing all day. Vern keeps sending me outside every chance he gets. He thinks I killed that lady. Don't want me near him.'

Andrea looked suddenly and indescribably sad. She fidgeted absent-mindedly, banging the rubber edges of her sneakers against each other.

'Let's talk about Monday, eh? Vern persuaded you to fix the furnace?'

'Yeah. Worst decision of my freakin' life. Shoulda gone to school like I wanted to.'

'And when did you start working on the furnace?'

'Dunno. Maybe four forty-five? Vern knocked off pretty much at five and I'd already gotten started by then.'

'And when did you finish working on the furnace?'

'About eight? I'm not really sure.'

'And while you were down there did you hear or see anybody else?'

Andrea shook her head.

'No one. There was probably some teachers up here, but you can't hear them in the basement. Floors are too thick.'

'And when you left here, where did you go?'

'Home. I got there maybe ten till nine.'

'Anyone see you when you got there?'

Andrea giggled.

'Yeah. Mom, Dad, two sisters and a brother. Home is real crowded, Mr Bimbo.'

Greg had to smile at that. He let her enjoy the moment before pushing on.

'What I don't understand,' he said carefully, 'is why you lied to the police.'

Andrea's cheerful expression faded away.

'I'm trying to get my associate degree, you know?' Her voice was very soft. 'Computer Information Science. It's my ticket outta here. Job with prospects, place of my own. A *life*. You understand?'

Greg nodded.

'Yeah, well, it's tough to make the tuition without working overtime. But if I work overtime, I can't make it to class, see? And I've missed a lot of classes. So the school has me on what they call academic watch. I miss any more classes without a good reason, and they're going to flunk me out. Then I have to sit the semester again and pay *more* tuition, which means more overtime, which means missing more classes. I can't keep doing that, Mr Bimbo. I ain't got the money, and I'm already in debt up to my eyeballs with student loans. My mom and dad don't got the money neither. If I get flunked out now, I'm like totally screwed. Forever.' There were tears in her eyes. 'I don't want to grow old here, man. I don't want to be some fat Mexican cleaning lady that wipes up other people's shit for the rest of my life. But that's where I'm headed if the school flunks me.'

Greg looked away for a moment, touched by Andrea's predicament. He didn't turn back again until he was good and ready.

'But you *didn't* go to class on Monday, right? So wouldn't the school flunk you out anyway?'

'No, man. I told them my *abuela* was sick and I needed to see her before she passed. They let you miss class for that, see?'

Greg did see. Andrea had lied to Pittsburgh Community College so she could stay on track, and had then lied to the police, thinking, somehow, that if she told them the truth it would get back to the school and they'd flunk her out. Of course, the police had gone to PCC to check out her story, anyway. They'd discovered she'd lied to them, and no doubt let slip that, wherever Andrea Velasquez had been that Monday night, it hadn't been at the side of a terminally ill grandmother.

The door to his classroom burst open. Startled, Greg looked up to see Lieutenant Cassidy and Sergeant Lev striding across the threshold, followed by a uniformed officer. Flakes of snow were slowly melting on the officer's cap.

'Maybelline Velasquez?' Cassidy intoned, without preamble. 'You're under arrest for the murder of Lindsay Delcade. You do not have to say anything . . .'

The words flowed by in a blur, accompanied by the clicking of handcuffs.

'I didn't do nothing,' Andrea protested, her voice low and cracked.

Cassidy was having none of it.

'Sure you didn't, *chica*. That's why your prints are all over the murder weapon.'

'You're making a mistake,' Greg said.

'You keep out of this, boy, or I'll have you arrested for obstruction.'

Greg stepped back, arms wide.

'I'm not obstructing anything, officer.' He was careful to enunciate every word, the Englishness of his accent his best defense against an impulsive exercise of authority. 'I'm just trying to remind you that Ms Velasquez's shoes don't match the crime scene.'

'This is your last warning. Shut it. Or—'

'What do you mean?' Sergeant Lev interrupted. She withstood a withering stare from her boss with apparent equanimity.

'Ms Velasquez wears Doc Marten boots.' Greg looked pointedly at Andrea's poorly shod feet. 'They're the only decent pair she has, and you have them in your custody.'

'So?'

'So . . . Doc Martens have a tread. The footprints in your crime scene are smooth. Whoever stepped in Ms Delcade's blood on the way out had smooth-soled shoes.'

'How do you know that?' Cassidy asked, his voice dangerous. He stepped across the room and thrust his nose pugnaciously into the teacher's face. 'You been interfering with my crime scene?'

Greg fought to keep his voice calm, and reasonable, and English. The temptation to incapacitate the man was almost overwhelming.

'Not at all, officer. I was simply chatting with the school custodian while he cleaned up the mess. *After* you'd all finished, obviously.' A smile of studied insincerity. 'I just happened to notice.'

'Yeah, well, they're only partial footprints,' Cassidy said, goaded into what, by police standards, was a shocking indiscretion. 'And the fingerprints are solid.'

'Well of course they are. They're on a screwdriver. I daresay Ms Velasquez used it all the time. Doesn't mean she was the one holding it when Ms Delcade got stabbed.'

He hoped to God Andrea was switched on enough to take the hint. If she tried to get off by claiming she'd never touched the bloody thing, she was finished.

'Goddammit, who do you think you are?' Cassidy fumed. 'This is a police matter. For trained officers, with years of experience. Stick to teaching Swahili or whatever it is they pay you to do.' He pointed at the uniformed officer. 'Get her out of here.' He followed Andrea and the officer into the corridor. Sergeant Lev went too.

But she raked him with a thoughtful glance on the way out.

01:54 P.M. EST

'You'll catch your death, Mr Abimbola!' Stacey said. Sitting warm and comfortable at the front desk, she looked mildly scandalized.

'I was only out for a few minutes,' Greg said, by way of defense. It had stopped snowing a little earlier and, driven by an impulse he hadn't fully understood at the time, he'd stepped outside and circled the long oblong of Calderhill Academy's main building. He hadn't bothered to put on coat, hat, and gloves. He'd simply tramped through the wet snow in his plaid-patterned, open-neck shirt, wool-mix jacket, and gray pants – a look he hated, but which was well within the mainstream of faculty fashion. As a result, his shoes were soaked through and dripping on the lobby floor. But he'd found the bracing cold to be exhilarating. And informative.

There was no explaining this to Stacey, though.

'Well, don't blame me if you call in sick tomorrow,' she said. 'If I'd known you were going to be out for so long, I'd have said something.'

'You sound like my mother,' Greg laughed.

'It looks to me like you need one. Or maybe a slap upside the head. Knock some sense into you.'

'You may be right, Stacey. If I had any sense, I'd be tucked behind that nice warm desk of yours.' He peered over the top of it, looking down. 'This thing has more controls on it than the Starship *Enterprise*. What are they all for, anyway?'

'These,' Stacey said, pointing to a panel of dials, 'are for the PA system. So if we have a fire or some kind of emergency, I can make the announcement from here. But I can also have the PA sound out on a particular floor, or even a single classroom if we need a student to come down for any reason.'

Greg nodded, looking impressed.

'And all this?'

'Security cam stuff. This screen here, which is split three ways? Those are the views of the school entrances: main entrance, the loading bay, and the door from the gym out to the playing fields.' She toggled a switch. 'We can concentrate on just the view from one camera, or two, or back to all three.'

'Wow. It's like you're guarding a super-secret facility in the movies.'

Stacey giggled at that.

'And the cameras,' Greg asked. 'Can you make them move?'

'Sure, but we never do. They're set up fine just the way they are.'

'Cool. So, if this *were* a movie, and I was an action hero trying to break in here, you'd see me?'

'For sure.' She grinned widely. 'It'd be a very short movie.'

'And at night, when you're not here?' Greg grinned back and pointed to a large red bell above the main entrance. 'Assuming I could get in without tripping the alarm, how would you even know I'd been in? Of course, in this movie, I could disable an alarm like *that*!' He snapped his fingers to emphasize the point.

'Well,' Stacey said, still smiling, 'you'd better be good enough to disable the cameras first. The system records everything. I think it gets sent to some computer at the security company.' She pointed vaguely upwards. 'Or the cloud.'

'And if someone here wanted to see the feed, how'd they do that?'

Stacey looked slightly uncomfortable.

'I'm not sure I sh—'

'Aw c'mon now, it's not like I actually *want* to see it. But *how* you get to see it can't be that big of a secret, can it? I mean, what would you tell the police if they asked about it?'

'They did ask. I told them to go see Ms Pasquarelli. She's in charge of talking to the security company and stuff.'

'Makes sense. After all, Ms Pasquarelli is pretty much in charge of everything around here, isn't she?'

'She surely is, Mr Abimbola. Don't tell Principal Ellis, though.'

Greg tapped his nose conspiratorially.

'Your secret's safe with me.'

With much to think about, Greg Abimbola climbed the stairs toward his classroom, his steps slow and deliberate.

03:31 P.M. EST

'You're leaving?' Greg was unable to keep the disappointment out of his voice.

'Errands,' Emily Pasquarelli explained. 'I need to pick up my mother's meds and go grocery shopping.' She was standing at her cubicle, her beautiful red coat halfway buttoned, scarf stylishly wrapped around her neck. 'You need something?'

'It can wait.' Greg wasn't entirely sure that it could, but he wasn't going to get anywhere by pushing.

'No, no, it's OK. For you, anything.' She smiled at him coquettishly, eyes bright, flicking across his face with that incredibly focused look that women have when they like someone. The effect was distracting. Not for the first time, Greg thought about asking her out. She was pretty, bright, the right age, and someone even his mother might approve of, given the chance. It took him a moment to get back on track.

'I'm being a bit self-indulgent,' he confessed. 'It's this bloody murder. I can't get it out of my head.'

'Me, neither.' Emily looked incredibly sad. 'So . . . horrible. And such a waste.'

Greg smiled ironically.

'You know, "waste" is possibly the nicest thing I've ever heard anyone say about Lindsay Delcade.'

'Maybe because I'm the only one at this school who actually liked her.'

Greg looked at her, surprised.

'It's true. She could be a piece of work, but we were friends. Have been for years.' Emily was looking teary now. 'We were at high school together. She was Lindsay Harris, then. Very popular. Everyone wanted to be her. Or near her, at least. I was one of her little . . . clique, I guess. We lost touch after graduation, but reconnected when Lindsay came back to town and married Bryan.'

'I get the distinct impression,' Greg said, only half joking, 'that

Pittsburghers never come "back" to town. That would require them to leave in the first place – and they love it here.'

Emily smiled at that.

'Well, Lindsay definitely went away to college. Penn, actually: she was valedictorian of our high school class. Super bright. Then she was at Georgetown Law—'

'She was a lawyer?'

'Oh, yes. But not for long. Practiced at one of those big political law firms in DC for a couple of years, met Bryan, and came back here to start a family. The rest, as they say, is history. Or it was history until . . .' She was too choked up to go on. She sat back down and grabbed a box of tissues from a desk drawer.

Greg pulled up a chair next to her, reached out and held her by the hand.

'I'm so sorry, Emily. I didn't mean to drag this all up for you. I had no idea the two of you were so close.'

'It's OK.' Emily sniffled. And then, with an effort: 'You wanted a favor?'

'Yes. But only if it's not too much trouble. Really.' He gave her hand a sympathetic squeeze. 'Stacey, the security lady, tells me you're the one to talk to about looking at footage from the security cameras?'

Emily gave him a sharp look.

'Why?'

'Honestly? I can't think of a single good reason why Lindsay Delcade would have been all the way down in the custodian's room. I mean, it's not even a place the faculty go to, is it?'

'You do,' Emily said pointedly.

Greg grinned.

'Guilty. But then, I'm super nosy.'

'You are at that.' A little squeeze of his hand made sure the words lacked sting.

'And being super nosy, I was also wondering what she was doing here so late at night, after the school was closed.'

'How do you know she wasn't here earlier? God love her, she was always hanging around for one reason or other.'

Greg shook his head in rueful remembrance.

'And don't I know it. But the thing is, when I was interviewed by the police—'

'Wasn't that just *awful*? Keeping us cooped up here like that? It was like we were all under arrest. And the interview was even worse. That nasty-minded lieutenant asked me what I was doing that evening and then, when I told him, he acted like he didn't believe a word.'

'And what were you doing, Ms Pasquarelli? I do hope it was something scandalous.'

Emily giggled.

'I wish. The boring truth is that I was home with my mother. She was having one of her episodes. And now her doctor wants her to try a new prescription. Which is why I'm off to the pharmacist's.'

Greg made one of those wordless noises that exuded sympathy.

'I'm sorry to hear that. Your mother is lucky to have you.'

'Thank you.' Emily shrugged, as if to say any daughter would do the same.

'But here's the thing. Did the police ask you where you were *all* evening or only between seven p.m. and midnight?'

'Seven and midnight.'

'Which means that's when Lindsay was killed. Lindsay had *no* reason to be in the building at that time, never mind the custodian's room.'

Emily looked thoughtful.

'I guess. And is that why you want to see the video recordings?'

'Exactly. I'm hoping to see her entering the building. Maybe she came with someone, or around the same time as someone. It might help the police figure out who the killer is.'

'You don't think it's Maybelline?'

'Hand on heart? I don't know. It could be. She was certainly in the custodian's room on Monday night. But if it isn't, the answer might be on the tapes.'

Emily nodded sagely.

'That would explain why the police wanted the recordings.'

'You gave them to the police?'

'For sure. Monday through Tuesday morning. The woman detective asked to see them.'

'Great minds think alike.'

'Apparently. Though I'm told that fools seldom differ.' Emily shot him a regretful smile. 'I'm sorry, Greg. The file I sent the detective is on my computer, but I can't let you have it. It's super confidential. Privacy and all that good stuff.' The smile turned arch. 'Besides, I'm saving you from yourself. What if Ms Ellis found out? Or a parent? I think you've been in enough trouble for one week, don't you?'

Greg was careful to mask his disappointment.

'Thanks for looking out for me. Curiosity would undoubtedly get me killed otherwise.'

Emily chuckled at that.

'But while I'm here,' Greg went on, looking serious. 'Could you let me have Chandler Delcade's schedule for next week? I'm trying to figure out what to do with him.'

Emily's mouth tightened.

'That little . . . I am *so* sorry about what happened. You must be . . .'

'It's nothing. Well, it's not *nothing* obviously, but I'd rather not make too much of a fuss, if you don't mind. I just want to punish him and move on.'

'I don't understand how you're so *calm* about it. And merciful. Too merciful, if you ask me. That boy should be expelled.'

'Way too much paperwork. Besides, he's just a kid.'

'Like I said: too merciful. But if getting his schedule will help you stick it to him, even a little, I'm all for it. Just give me a moment here while this thing wakes up.' Emily's face glowed angelically in the light of the startup screen.

'Thanks, Emily. You really are the best.' Greg leaned a little closer in his chair, admiring Emily's hands as they swept across the keyboard. Delicate strands of strawberry blonde hair brushed against his cheek, accompanied by a faint hint of perfume.

'No problem. Like I said: for you, anything.' With a few deft clicks the office printer began to purr. Emily stood up once more. 'But I really should get on with those errands.'

'Of course,' Greg said. But he lingered a little, admiring Emily's slim, boyish figure as she buttoned up her coat and readjusted her scarf. She gave a mock shiver.

'What a miserable day,' she said. 'I can't stand having cold hands. I'll be lucky if I make it home alive.'

'If you don't make it, I, for one, will miss you.'

'Glad to hear it.'

Emily started to head out, so Greg offered to walk her to her car. She happily took him up on it.

05:45 P.M. EST

Beans of Steel, the coffee shop down the hill and around the corner from Greg's apartment, had three things Greg valued: a warm, roaring fireplace mocked up to look like a smelter; comfortable seating; and a Wi-Fi system powerful enough to cope with the couple of dozen students and young techies sucking up bandwidth. The coffee was very much secondary, although Greg, who knew nothing about coffee, had read somewhere that it was pretty good. He sipped at it in absent-minded ignorance, staring at the startup screen on his laptop and feeling vaguely disappointed. He'd hoped to feel at least a little guilty for logging on as Emily Pasquarelli.

Emily had nice hands. Manicured but not garish. He could remember every curve of every finger as she'd typed in her password.

Ba$ra01.

Finding the video footage on Emily's hard drive took only a couple of minutes. Jerky, monochrome images began to flit across his laptop. Every now and then he would freeze the picture, make a quick note on his cell, and move on.

The parade of images from the school's three entrances depicted a typical day in the life of Calderhill Academy. There was no hint of the horror to come.

Greg had watched various people arrive first thing Monday morning, including the Delcades. Lindsay, determined to pursue her various grievances at the earliest possible moment, had arrived at seven ten, far too soon for the scowling teenagers she had dragged in her wake. She had parked her silver minivan – in full view of the camera and quite illegally – right outside the main entrance and marched up the steps with Vicki and Chandler trailing behind. He himself, of course, had arrived at seven thirty, and Lindsay had stormed out of the building a little after seven thirty-five. She had jumped back in the minivan and driven out of frame.

Never to be spotted again. Which was a problem. How did a

woman, indisputably found dead in the basement, get back into Calderhill without being seen?

Andrea's movements, on the other hand, were easy enough to trace. She, like Vernon Szymanski, didn't bother with the main entrance. The cameras picked up her ghostly image in the loading bay at six forty-three a.m., dressed as he'd seen her slightly later in the day, in a woolen Steelers cap, heavy coat, and Doc Martens. She'd entered the bay as a truck would, walking in off Dean Close, then turned to her left and climbed a set of steps to the wide, four-foot-high concrete ledge that bounded the bay on three sides. She'd then disappeared off camera and had no doubt let herself in through the metal door that led directly to the custodian's room.

She'd left the same way at eight nineteen p.m., appearing suddenly at the right of the frame and descending the steps to the bottom of the bay. She'd then headed off in the direction of Dean Close before vanishing from sight. So far as Greg could tell, there was nothing unusual about either her appearance or behavior. She wasn't obviously disheveled, and she wasn't running or doing anything else to indicate she was fleeing the scene of a murder.

But then again, outward appearance didn't always provide a window to inner turmoil. Even if it did, the camera image wasn't good enough to pick out the nuances of Andrea's expression. And besides, she would have had plenty of time to compose herself before opening that big metal door and letting herself out.

He consulted the notes on his phone. He had painstakingly tracked every member of staff into the building that morning and crossed them off his list when they departed at the end of the day. By seven p.m., the earliest Lindsay Delcade could have been murdered, there were, by Greg's reckoning, only three people left in the building: Andrea; Frank, the second-shift security man at the front desk; and one member of the faculty. Unless, of course, he'd missed that person in the general scramble at the end of the school day. Greg frowned, pushing the timeframe forward minute by minute.

Turned out he hadn't missed them at all.

At eight fifty-four, shortly before security would have shut up the school for the night, a tall, thin figure trotted down the front steps, shoulders hunched against the cold.

Demetrius Freedman, the chemistry teacher.

11:11 P.M. EST

Greg was still pretending that he was ready to fall asleep. He lay in bed, hands tucked behind his head, reciting the psalms his mother had pounded into him to settle an unquiet mind. Somewhere above him was the slanted wall/ceiling, invisible in the thick darkness, except for an errant streak of light that had somehow made its way through the thick drapes covering the window. A freight train's plaintive whistle keened distantly into the night.

'*Gospod – pastyr moi,*' he whispered to himself. '*Ya ni . . .*'

Psalm Twenty-Three vanished in an image of pooled blood, followed by that of a tall, hunched man moving quickly past a camera lens. He gave up. A sigh of defeat exploded into the darkness.

Was Demetrius Freedman really nursing a strong enough grudge to plunge a screwdriver into Lindsay Delcade not once, but at least a dozen times? And if he was, why hadn't the police dragged him in for questioning? Why were they so fixated on Andrea Velasquez?

Greg scratched at the invisible ruin of his left eye.

The crime scene mattered, obviously. Andrea had been in the custodian's room. Her prints were on the murder weapon. She'd lied to the police. But Demetrius was at least in the building, so he had the opportunity. Not only that, he disliked Delcade intensely, which, people being people, was motive enough for murder.

There were a couple of reasons Greg could think of that would spare Demetrius the jaundiced eye of law enforcement. One: the police were simply unaware that Demetrius was in the building. If a person didn't know him well, they might not recognize his blurry image on the video. And besides, if they stopped watching the moment Andrea Velasquez stepped out of the custodian's room, they might not have watched for long enough to see him in the first place. Second: perhaps he'd been up front with the police from the get-go and the detectives were inclined to believe him.

Still, if *he'd* been Cassidy, he'd have given Demetrius a hard time anyway, just to see if something broke loose.

Which is probably why he wasn't a police officer. They had procedures and experience. He, on the other hand, was little more than a bumbling amateur. He was already in way over his head.

Another sigh heaved itself into the night air.

And regardless of who'd actually killed Lindsay Delcade, there remained the most exasperating question of all: how, in God's name, had the bloody woman sneaked into school? And why? What the hell was she doing there?

In a nutshell, what was going on in Lindsay Delcade's life that made wandering around Calderhill Academy between seven p.m. and midnight a rational thing to do?

The question rattled about his skull like a pinball, striking alarm bells wherever it went, refusing to go away.

And then it occurred to him: there might be a way to find out.

He sat up in bed, weighing the pros and cons.

There were a lot of cons.

A lot.

But the pro was overwhelming. He needed to know what Lindsay Delcade was thinking in the last hours of her life. And this – for him, at least – was the only way. He padded into the living room and retrieved his laptop. He didn't bother with the lights. Face illuminated by the soft glowing of the screen, he dropped into the dark web, tapped a few keys, and entered a chatroom.

Dialogos: I'd like an appointment. Hours not days.

FRIDAY, THE THIRTEENTH
12:00 P.M. EST

The lunch bell rang just as Greg reached the science department. Within seconds, the corridor was filled with students heading anywhere but here, dragging along with them the slightly pungent aroma of freshly scrubbed laboratory. They slid by him on either side, almost but not quite touching. One or two smiled at him in passing; a few more stared openly at his eye patch; the vast majority ignored him.

'You got a minute?' he asked, sticking his head around the door of Demetrius Freedman's classroom.

'Sure, my brother,' Demetrius said, smiling broadly. 'I was hoping to catch up with you, anyway. Steelers this Sunday. My house. I'm having a bunch of people around. I'd love for you to come meet some folks.'

'Then I'd love to be there.'

'Great! I'll email you the address.' Desk behind him, Demetrius leaned backwards against it, bracing himself with long arms. 'So, what brings you down here? More activated carbon?'

Greg chuckled before assuming a more serious demeanor.

'I'm worried about Andrea Velasquez,' he said. 'I think she's being fitted up.'

'Fitted up?' Demetrius looked puzzled.

'Framed,' Greg translated. 'Because she's Hispanic.'

Demetrius nodded slowly.

'Always possible with Pittsburgh's finest. Though word is they have a ton of evidence against her.'

'I know, but I got a really bad vibe off that chunky thug of a police lieutenant, if you know what I mean. I'm not sure he isn't above making the evidence fit the crime, and I just thought I'd check in with you, because you understand what goes on here so much better than I do. What I'm getting at is: did you sense any . . . *animus* when they interviewed you? After all, you were the last person out of the building Monday night. I thought maybe they gave you a hard time about it.'

Demetrius threw him a sharp glance.

'Who told you that?'

'Word gets around. But I was thinking they might have tried pinning it on you before they settled on Andrea. If they did, then I was thinking we might try and get a civil rights lawyer involved.'

Demetrius looked both surprised and impressed.

'And here was me thinking you don't listen to a word I say. Those crackers got it in for anybody that don't look like them. And the closer we get to *real* power in this country, the angrier they gonna get.'

Greg nodded in what he hoped was solemn agreement.

'Dealing with the police up close and personal was a real eye opener, Demetrius. That lieutenant fellow was *harsh*. Unnecessarily so. I can't help thinking the whole experience would have been a lot different if my last name had been Cholmondley-Smythe instead of Abimbola.'

'I hear ya, man.' Demetrius stared down at the floor, as if collecting his thoughts. 'I had the woman, so it may have gone a little different for me. She seemed alright: very respectful, very polite. But you still gots to watch every goddamned fucking word. Police is still police. Can't trust 'em further than you can throw one of their frigging cruisers.'

'So what did she ask you?'

'She mostly wanted to know where I'd been all Monday night. So I told her. Here until just before nine and then home. Then she asked me if I'd seen or heard anything unusual and I said I hadn't.' He shuddered involuntarily. 'Jee-sus fucking Christ! That woman might have been murdered while I was right here in this lab, and I had no goddamned idea! Life is just . . . strange, man. Fucking strange.'

'If anyone's strange,' Greg said, laughing, 'it's you. What were you *doing* here till nine at night? You must have been *freezing*. Couldn't it have waited till Tuesday? Or better yet, been done in the warmth of your own home?'

'Hah! Spoken like a true student of the arts. Science, my man, requires actual work. I was in here freezing my ass off prepping an experiment. Quite literally something you should never do at home.'

'You prep experiments?' Greg was genuinely surprised.

'Of course I prep experiments.' Demetrius threw him a good-natured glance. 'Think of it like . . . like a dress rehearsal for a play. Or maybe you've got people coming around, and you're cooking something you've never cooked before. So you test it out on the kids a week ahead of time, just to make sure everything goes right.'

'And that's what you were doing Monday night?'

'I surely was. I was working through the steps for a class experiment using sulfur hexafluoride.'

'What the hell is that when it's at home?'

'Sulfur hexafluoride, Arts-man, is an odorless and colorless gas. All you need to know about it is that it's invisible and incredibly dense, way denser than air. So . . . if you pour sulfur hexafluoride into a container, you can float things on it – light things, for sure – but get it right and they'll float just like a boat on the ocean, except this is an ocean of gas and completely invisible. Total showstopper.'

'I'll bet!'

'But you've got to get everything just right, otherwise you're looking at complete – and I mean utterly humiliating – catastrophe. So I was here running the damn thing again and again until I was certain I could pull it off. Finished around eight twenty, tidied up and left. Never left the department the entire evening. Cause, unlike you, I have a real job.'

'More fool you, then.'

Greg took his leave, still smiling at the exchange. He made his way back down the corridor toward the lobby. With a sudden jab of memory, he recalled that he had yet again left his keycard upstairs. He didn't need it, of course. The security doors – doors that on Monday had been shut tight against the freezing cold – were latched tamely against the walls.

Greg stared at them thoughtfully. He wandered across the lobby and loitered by the front desk.

'Stacey?'

'Yes, Mr Abimbola?'

'Our keycards: does the system log them in and out?'

'Oh yes. Every time you use it, there's a record.'

'And where would that record be kept?'

Stacey grinned at him.

'You get one guess.'

'Ms Pasquarelli?' Greg grinned back.

'Yay! Give the man a prize!'

'Thanks, Stacey.'

Greg headed up the stairs to the second floor, turned left instead of right and found himself in the admin suite.

Emily's cubicle was empty. She couldn't be far, though. Her coat and scarf were hung neatly on the coat rack. She was probably in the cafeteria or attending some lunchtime meeting – often the only time you could get a bunch of faculty to sit around the same table.

Greg sat down at her desk. The seat was far too low for him and smelt vaguely of Emily's perfume. His head swam a little at the scent. He tapped her keyboard. The screen came up, demanding her now-compromised password. Greg entered it.

This way he didn't have to come up with some cock-a-mamie reason for wanting something as esoteric as keycard logs.

The keycard security software required a different password – in theory. Greg knew, however, that there was a better than even chance that Emily used the same password for everything. He pecked it out again: *Ba$ra01*, and he was in. Ignoring a complicated looking budget spreadsheet, he found the icon he was looking for with a quick sweep of the mouse. The contents made for absorbing reading.

So absorbing, he didn't hear Emily Pasquarelli re-enter the admin suite.

'What do you think you're doing?' Her face was a mask of suspicion.

'Waiting for you, actually,' Greg drawled, even though his heart was hammering. 'I just wanted to see what it felt like to sit in the seat of power.' He made to get up, casually dislodging a ruler and two neatly aligned pens onto the floor.

'Let me get that.'

'Don't bother.' Emily, still irritated, bent down to pick them up. Greg took the opportunity to shut down her computer – and to keep her distracted.

'Faculty meeting?'

'What?'

'I was wondering if you'd been at a faculty meeting.'

'Oh. Yes. Art department. They're spending way too much on materials.' A quick sigh. 'Science is next. We need to talk to them about their lab costs. They seem to have increased without rhyme or reason.' She moved past him, sat down at her desk and primly placed the pens and ruler in their customary position. 'You said you wanted something?'

'I did. But I also really didn't mean to annoy you. I'm sorry about sitting at your desk. I'll swing by another time.'

'No, no. It's just me being silly.' Now it was Emily's turn to look apologetic. 'It's just that I handle all the school's finances, so pretty much everything on my computer is super confidential. I get really paranoid about it. Sorry. You want something, I'm here to help. What can I do for you?'

Which turned out to be the most difficult question Greg Abimbola had faced in some time. He'd been so busy covering up his tracks he hadn't had time to come up with a plausible reason for being there. His mouth came to the rescue before his brain had a chance to intervene.

'I was wondering,' he said, not quite believing his ears, 'if you might be interested in going out to dinner?'

03:30 P.M. EST

The rap at his door didn't sound like a student – or even a teacher. It was too insistent: demanding, even.

'Come in.'

The first thing that struck Greg about the man who entered was that he was shockingly good looking. A well-toned mid-forties, tall, with an immaculately tailored dark-blue suit underneath an unbuttoned cashmere coat, precisely combed sandy-blond hair, and trendy, steel-rimmed glasses that served only to accentuate a pair of limpid, blue-gray eyes.

The second, was that he looked vaguely familiar. Greg could not, however, place him.

'Bryan Delcade,' the man said, putting the puzzle to rest. 'Chandler's father.' He was wearing a slightly forced smile.

'I'm sorry for your loss,' Greg said, sympathetically.

Delcade nodded, keen to push past pro forma expressions of condolence.

'I'm here about my son,' he said.

'I see.'

The silence stretched out between them, filling the room with tension.

'I understand Chandler's done something stupid,' Delcade said at last.

'That would be one way to describe it.'

'He tells me he scratched a couple of toy boats.' Delcade glanced around the classroom, looking in vain for the objects in question, which were still tucked underneath Greg's desk. 'I'm happy to pay for the replacement.'

'That's very generous.'

'Thing is, Chandler tells me you're giving him detention.'

'Yes.'

'Which I'd rather you didn't do.'

'And why is that?'

'He shouldn't have to be putting up with some BS punishment while he's mourning the death of his mother.'

Greg raised an eyebrow.

'Not a problem. He can do it after he's finished mourning.'

'What? No.' Delcade looked momentarily confused. 'I said I'd pay for the damage.'

'Which is, as I've already said, very generous. But your son's actions have consequences. What he did can't go unpunished.'

'Oh, come on . . . Greg, is it?' Greg nodded. 'Come on, Greg. It was just boys being boys. No need to make a big deal of it.'

'I don't think writing "nigger" in a school classroom is just boys being boys, Mr Delcade.'

'Of course it is. Boys do dumb things sometimes. It's just banter, nothing more. He'll grow out of it. I've already had a word. It won't happen again. I promise. And . . . we will, of course, make a generous donation to the school. *Very* generous. Perhaps in Lindsay's name?'

Delcade stuck out a beautifully manicured hand.

'Do we have a deal?'

'No, we do not. Your son did something wrong. He will be punished. Everyone will move on. If you want a delay for a certain period of time, I'm happy to accommodate you. But there *will* be consequences for what your son did here.'

'I'm trying to be the good guy here, Greg. I'll pay for the damage and I'll make a five-figure donation to the school. All I'm asking in return is that you drop this whole silly business.'

'I'm not prepared to do that.'

Delcade took a step forward, fists clenched. So did Greg. There must have been something about Greg's bearing that stopped the other man in his tracks. He kept a discreet distance. His expression, however, remained menacing.

'You haven't been here long, Greg. And I can tell by your accent that you probably don't understand how things work around here. Let me assure you, it will not go well for your career if you insist on blowing a minor infraction out of all proportion.'

Greg smiled sardonically.

'*Pedicabo ego vos et irrumabo.*'

'What?'

'It's Latin for what you just said. Which I fully appreciate. Nonetheless, my mind is made up. Sorry.'

What little was left of Bryan Delcade's polite veneer slid away entirely.

'Oh, don't you worry,' he snarled. 'You will be. Sorry, that is. You think what happened to your Dr Freedman was bad? Just you wait.' He jammed a hand into the pocket of his cashmere coat and yanked out his gloves, angrily pulling them on. Pieces of paper came out of the pocket too, raining chaotically onto the floor. Delcade didn't bother to pick them up. 'Uppity n . . . limey bastard.' He turned on his heel and stormed out. The door slammed shut behind him.

Greg stared at the door for several seconds, heart thumping as if he'd been in an actual fight. Then, with a world-weary sigh, he bent down and picked up the litter that Delcade had left behind for him.

Among which was something that looked like a receipt. It was an innocuous looking strip of paper, bounded by a faint magenta band at top and bottom. Regardless of Delcade's views, Greg had been in Pittsburgh long enough to recognize it for what it was.

A parking ticket.

Greg grinned. If there was any justice in the world, Delcade would forget to pay on time and then get stuck with the increased fine. Better yet, he'd get booted. Mildly curious as to how old the ticket actually was, he took a look at the date.

The grin faded from his face.

The ticket was from Monday night, at eight eleven p.m.

At the time of his wife's death, Bryan Delcade had been illegally parked in front of a fire hydrant on Joseph Avenue, Pittsburgh.

Less than a block from the school.

03:54 P.M. EST

'**M**r Abimbola, could I have a word?'

Greg looked up from the door handle of his Mini Cooper to see Detective Lev walking along the slushy sidewalk toward him. Her manner was open and casual, a chance meeting of acquaintances. Which was nonsense, of course. She must have been waiting for him.

Greg glanced around. She seemed to be on her own. There was no sign of Cassidy, or anyone else for that matter. The FSB, when they stopped you on the street, always came for you in pairs. Pittsburgh PD operated more leanly, apparently.

'Of course, Sergeant. What can I do for you?' Greg, who had been standing in the street as a prelude to getting into his vehicle, drifted back to the sidewalk.

'A couple of things, if you don't mind. First, what's a person of extraordinary ability like yourself doing in Pittsburgh?'

'I wouldn't describe myself that way.'

'Maybe not, Mr Abimbola, but the US government does. You're here on an O-1 Visa. For, and I quote, "persons of extraordinary ability". So, why are you here?' Lev allowed herself a dangerously amused smile. 'And what makes you so special?'

Greg was careful to keep his expression bland.

'I'm here to teach,' he said, gesturing toward Calderhill's high, brick façade. 'As for the visa, I have a knack for languages.'

'Really?' Lev looked skeptical. 'How many?'

'Five. Russian, French, Arabic, Latin . . . and English, of course.'

The sergeant, Greg noticed, was trying not to appear impressed.

'And why Pittsburgh? Why not New York, or Chicago, or LA?'

'Too big. Pittsburgh is the perfect size. It has all the advantages of a major city without any of the hassles.'

For Pittsburghers, it was almost an article of faith.

Rachel Lev nodded.

'OK. Second thing. I was wondering if you could maybe explain to me your relationship with Maybelline Velasquez.'

'I don't really have one. We both work at the school, we chat from time to time, that's about it.'

'You seemed kinda intimate when I saw the two of you in the corridor on Monday. And you went to a lot of trouble – and detail – to tell my lieutenant that we were making a mistake arresting her. So it seems to me that you have a more than casual relationship.'

'It's a free country, Sergeant. You can think whatever you want.'

'Then explain to me why you've tried so much to help her.'

Greg shrugged his shoulders.

'She asked.'

'She *asked*?' Lev sounded incredulous.

'Wouldn't you?' Greg responded. 'Love your neighbor and all that.'

'So you love her, then, is that it?'

'Only in the Christian sense.'

'And not the biblical?'

Greg had to smile at that. The woman was quick.

'No, Sergeant, not the biblical. I'm sure Ms Velasquez would tell you the same thing.'

'This "Christian" love of yours didn't extend to Ms Delcade, did it?'

'A failing for which I should berate myself every day,' Greg said, ironically. 'I didn't like her. But then, almost nobody did.'

'But you're the only one that got hauled into the principal's office on Monday morning, sir. Because Lindsay Delcade complained about you. That's true, isn't it?'

'Yes.'

'So you admit you had a motive to kill her?'

'I admit that I didn't like her. I had no desire to kill her.'

'And I understand there was some trouble with the son? What was that about?'

'I'm afraid that's confidential.'

'This is a murder investigation, Mr Abimbola.'

'It's still confidential.'

Lev sighed.

'So, a woman you don't like, plus trouble with the woman's son on the same day. You can see why I have to ask you about this?'

'Not really. I know you've looked at the security footage. You know I left the school well before seven p.m., and you know I didn't come back until the following day. So I couldn't have killed her, could I?'

'Any other murder, I might agree with you, sir. But not this one.'

'And why's that?'

'The footage doesn't show Ms Delcade coming back to the school, either. Yet that's where we found her, inside *your* school, large as life and deader than roadkill. Odd that, don't you think?'

And with that, the detective turned on her heel and headed back up the street, her tall frame unbowed by the weather, slush ground to paste in the deep tread of her winter boots.

Greg watched her go, absent-mindedly scratching his eye patch as he did so.

05:00 P.M. EST

> Dialogos: Ready when you are.
> TORquil: Glad to hear it. And how is Aunt Ludmilla?

The noise and chatter of Beans of Steel faded into the background. Greg stared at the suspicious Cyrillic characters populating his laptop. TORquil, whoever he or she was, did not believe they were talking to the real Dialogos. Hardly surprising in the circumstances. He took a quick sip of coffee before typing.

> Dialogos: Aunt Ludmilla is as she always is. Drunk on sake
>   in a Vladivostok whorehouse.
> TORquil: It's been years, D! Thought you were dead!
> Dialogos: Just taking it easy.
> TORquil: What can I do for you? Have you brought me a
>   voting machine to play with?

A couple of students, one Asian, the other Asian-American, sat at the table next to Greg, chatting animatedly about some project. Seeing his eyepatch, they both gave him a curious look before returning to their conversation. Greg watched them back until he was satisfied they were exactly what they appeared to be. Only then did he return to his screen.

> Dialogos: Something less interesting, I'm afraid. I want you
>   to hack a mobile phone. The number is . . .

Cursing himself for growing old, he switched screens and rechecked the school's parent directory. It was, in fact, as he remembered it.

> Dialogos: +1 412-555-4769.

TORquil: Is there anything I need to know about this phone?
           Anything unusual?

Greg hesitated.

Dialogos: I have reason to believe it might be in the hands
           of the police.
TORquil: Local or something more high-powered?
Dialogos: I don't know. I'm too far from the situation to
           tell.
TORquil: OK. I will be more careful. Understand: if the
           phone is unpowered or inside a Faraday cage, I
           won't be able to get to it. No refunds, remember?
Dialogos: I remember. Your usual fee?
TORquil: It's been three years, D. Add thirty percent.

Greg winced. His 'pension' wasn't really big enough for this.

Dialogos: Done. Let me know ASAP.

07:30 P.M. EST

Aslan230: I am here. I hope this is worth my time. I left a warm bed and a warmer woman for this.

TORquil: Of course it is. You paid me to do this, remember?

Aslan230: So do what I pay you to do. Talk.

TORquil: You were right. Dialogos has been in touch. Two-and-a-half hours ago.

Morosov, bleary-eyed in the security of his office, rocked back in his chair. He forced himself to remain calm. Powerful fingers thumped the keyboard of his computer.

Aslan230: You're sure it was Dialogos, not an impostor?

TORquil: Reasonably sure, though nothing is certain in this life. This Dialogos knows the back-up safe words.

Aslan230: What did he want?

TORquil: He wants me to hack a mobile phone. In America.

Goosebumps prickled on the back of Morosov's neck.

Aslan230: Where in America?

TORquil: The phone has an area code associated with a town called Pittsburgh. According to GPS, that's where the phone is right now.

Aslan230: You've hacked it?

TORquil: Almost. Reception there is very bad. I suspect it's in a basement or something. But it will not be long. It is only the reception that is slowing me down, not the phone itself.

Aslan230: Understood. Whatever you give to Dialogos, you give to me also, you understand?

TORquil: And my fee?

Aslan230: As agreed. Do what you do. I'm going back to
           bed. Goodnight.

Morosov vanished from the chatroom but made no move to
return home. He couldn't sleep. Not now. The *negr* was alive. And
interested in a mobile phone in Pittsburgh, America. Was the
mongrel shit in this Pittsburgh, too, or somewhere else entirely?
What was he up to over there that needed TORquil's very special
sort of assistance? And for whom?

Morosov paced the bounds of his office like a caged animal,
thinking.

SATURDAY, THE FOURTEENTH
05:16 A.M. EST

Dianna Aldis, dressed casually in jeans and, to Morosov's eye, a deliberately baggy and unattractive sweater, swiveled in her chair as her boss entered the office.

'I know,' he said, grumpily, before she could say anything. 'Late again. Call in on Saturday, tell you urgent so urgent, no courtesy to be on time. Yes?'

The ghost of a smile crossed his assistant's lips.

'Something like that.' She pointed to his desk. 'I made you tea.'

Sure enough, a mug of tea, hot and milky in the English fashion, was waiting for him. He grabbed it gratefully, its temperature telling him he was not as late as he'd feared.

'You make list of Orthodox church I ask, yes?'

'Yes.'

'Do you have on this list town call Pittsburgh?'

Dianna swiveled back to her computer screen, scanning the spreadsheet she'd been working on for the last couple of days.

'Yes. Pittsburgh, Pennsylvania, United States of America. The population of the city and suburbs is just under three million. There are several Eastern Orthodox churches in the area. Saint—'

'*Da.* Is good. All church in this Pittsburgh, have website, no?'

'I'm not sure. I haven't—'

'*Ach.* Is America. Website for everything. You want society for protection American house mice? Website. Models of American coat button? Website. Is America. Church have website.'

'OK. Let's agree that an American church is likely to have a website. What would you like me to do?'

'Every church Pittsburgh, go website, download picture. News . . . *letter,* yes? Baptism. Funeral. Good workings. Anything with picture of congregation. Then we look pictures.'

'I see. And when we get these pictures, what, exactly, are we looking for?'

'Black people.'

08:17 A.M. EST

S till breathing hard from his recently completed run, Greg pushed open the door to his apartment. He had left the radio on. WESA, the local NPR station, was devoting its tiny allowance of local morning news to the prospects of a settlement in the sanitation strike. Entirely uninterested, Greg switched it off, turned on the TV, and tuned into a DVR of the previous evening's Penguins–Flyers game. Showering as quickly as possible, he settled in to watch the match: fast moving skates slicing across manicured ice, black and gold smashing into white and orange, the crowd roaring through the TV screen.

Let's go Pens! Let's go Pens!

He failed to notice until well into the third period that someone had texted him. He didn't recognize the number. Mildly curious, he opened up the message.

Can we meet?

To which Greg replied:

Maybe. But I don't know who you are.

It's Andrea Velasquez.

Greg found himself raising an eyebrow.

Sure. Do you know the Beans of Steel coffee shop?

Just as he hit send, a roar erupted from the TV set. Greg turned just in time to see a triumphant pile of Penguins swarming behind the Flyers' goal.

The only score of the game and he'd managed to miss it. But then again, that was the joy of DVR. He hit the rewind button, tingling with anticipation.

Andrea got to the coffee shop about an hour later. Her weekend gear, Greg noticed, was little different from what she wore to work. Steelers hat, dark sweater under a quilted coat, jeans, and, in the absence of her Doc Martens, the same ratty pair of Converse sneakers she'd worn previously. The soles were caked with black street slush, which she stamped off as she came in through the door.

Greg bought her a chai tea latte and ushered her to his table, right next to the fireplace that looked like a smelter. Andrea seemed grateful for the heat.

'I'm glad to see you're out of police custody,' he said. 'Does this mean you're off the hook?'

'Nah,' Andrea replied, scowling. 'I'm guessing someone told the detectives they don't have enough evidence, so they sprang me. They weren't happy about it, though. That Cassidy guy definitely wants to nail my ass – and not in a good way.' Andrea shuddered at the thought, though Greg couldn't tell whether the thought involved jail, or relations with Cassidy, or both.

He hid an amused smile behind a quiet sip of coffee.

'And the woman? The police sergeant?'

'Not so much, I think. Or maybe she's just playing the "good" cop. She seemed like she might believe me when I told her I used their murder weapon every day, so of course my freakin' prints were all over it.'

'They ask you anything else?'

'Just more like before. Why did I lie to them, that kinda crap.'

'And did you tell them the truth this time about why you lied?'

Andrea had the decency to blush.

'Yeah. They sprang me not long after.'

'Then maybe you don't have anything to worry about. If they thought they had a case, you'd still be in the slammer.'

'Yeah, well, tell that to Ms Emily frickin' Pasquarelli.'

'I'm sorry?'

'She's only gone done and suspended me. Sent me an email saying that "in the interests of all concerned" it would be "better if I didn't come to school for the time being". "Interests of all concerned", my ass. Biatch is going to fire me.'

'Is that why you wanted to see me?'

'Yeah.' Andrea looked at him pleadingly. 'I was kinda hoping you could put in a good word.'

'With Emily?'

'Who else? She's totally into you, dude. So I thought you might . . .' Andrea lapsed into silence, suddenly embarrassed.

Greg smiled at her gently.

'I'm sure Ms Pasquarelli is just being careful. It's probably nowhere near as bad as you think it is.'

'But . . .'

'But I'll put in a word anyway.'

Andrea beamed with gratitude.

'Thanks, man. I owe you.'

'Then you can pay me back by giving me a ride. Do you mind dropping me off at the school?'

'Sure thing. You working the weekend?'

'Not exactly. I got stopped on the street by that woman detective yesterday. She said something that got me thinking. Thought I'd check it out. You can come along if you like.'

Andrea looked hesitant.

'I'll cover for you with Ms Pasquarelli.'

'Then, sure. Why not?'

Andrea Velasquez's beaten-up Chevy was almost certainly older than she was. A worn-out orange that might once have been red, it climbed its way out of Bloomfield and then plunged down into Oakland, accompanied by the steady roar of a cracked muffler. From Oakland they crossed into the genteel avenues of Shadyside, vast houses peering down at them across vaster lawns. The Chevy and its unhinged engine stood horribly out of place among the expensive foreign imports lined up at the intersections. Andrea, ignoring disapproving stares from dog-walking pedestrians, gunned the vehicle at each and every stop sign until they reached Joseph Avenue. With a final, defiant roar, the Chevy's motor shut off just across from Calderhill's main entrance. It was exactly where Lindsay Delcade had parked the morning of her murder.

'Won't you get a ticket?'

'On a Saturday? Nah. They only ticket you here during the week.'

'Hmmm.' Greg was thinking about Bryan Delcade.

Stacey, the security lady, buzzed them in.

'Morning, Mr Abimbola. Wasn't expecting to see you here today.' Stacey gave Andrea a slightly disapproving glance but said nothing otherwise.

'Good morning, Stacey. Don't you ever take a day off? It *is* Saturday.'

Stacey sighed theatrically.

'Mouths to feed,' she said. 'Bills to pay. You know how it is.'

'Seldom has a truer word been spoken,' Greg agreed, smiling.

He leaned companionably against the front desk. 'Actually, seeing as you're here, can you do me a favor?'

'Sure thing. What do you need?'

Greg tapped the monitor showing the security cam feeds.

'Can you keep your eyes peeled on the loading bay for the next few minutes? Tell me if you see anything unusual?'

'Yeah. I can do that.'

'Brilliant,' Greg said. And then, to Andrea: 'Come with me.'

He led the way down to the basement and, from there, to the custodian's room.

'So, what are we doing?' Andrea asked. 'Revisiting the scene of the crime?'

'Kind of.' Greg pointed to the hook by the battered metal door. As on his previous visit, there were two large keys hanging from it. 'Can you unlock the door and let us out onto the loading bay?'

Giving him a quizzical look, Andrea did as asked. The door unlocked with an audible *click*. The hinges, though, were well oiled. Despite its slightly rusted appearance, the gray metal swung open smoothly and without a sound. Biting cold air flooded the room. Andrea shivered, winter picking at the holes in her canvas sneakers.

'Right,' Greg said, all business. 'All I want you to do is go out the door, head back to Joseph Avenue and wait for me by the front entrance. OK?'

'Course. I can do that.'

Andrea stepped through the door and onto the broad ledge that ran around three sides of the loading bay. Then she skipped down the steps to road level and turned right, disappearing from sight.

Greg followed more slowly, taking care to shut the door behind him. Eschewing the steps, he walked along the ledge instead, his right shoulder brushing against the red brickwork of the building. The ledge ended abruptly, leaving what would have been a four-foot drop but for a fortuitously abandoned packing crate that took the edge off the descent. Greg stepped down and wandered past a couple of dumpsters. Thanks to the sanitation strike, they were filled to overflowing with almost two weeks' worth of uncollected garbage. He made his way to the front entrance, patches of still-white snow crunching under his boots.

'You took your time,' Andrea said, stamping her feet against the cold.

'I'm old. I believe in stately progress.' Greg pointed to the wide steps in front of them. 'Shall we?'

Stacey buzzed them in.

'So,' Greg asked the security lady, 'did you see Andrea leave the loading bay?'

'Sure did.'

'Did you see me?'

'No.' Stacey frowned. 'That can't be right. How'd you gone done that?'

Greg leaned against her desk, peering down at the video monitors.

'The camera in the loading bay is focused – shock, horror – on the loading bay,' he explained. 'You can see the delivery trucks, garbage collection and whatnot just fine. What you *can't* see, at least, not properly, is the raised ledge that runs around the edge of the bay. If you come out of the custodian's room and walk along the *ledge,* rather than take the steps down to the asphalt, the camera won't pick you up. So, *ta-da*! Here I am, sight unseen.'

Stacey nodded, impressed despite herself.

'Well, who'd a thunk it? You should have been a policeman, Mr Abimbola.'

'What? And actually work for a living? Not on your life.' He flashed Stacey a quick grin before turning to Andrea. 'Come on, Ms Velasquez. We need to lock up the custodian's room before we leave.'

Heading down to the basement, Andrea asked, 'How'd you know you could get out of the custodian's room without anyone seeing you?'

Greg looked chagrined.

'Honestly? I should have seen it earlier. It was staring me in the face. While you were otherwise engaged with Pittsburgh's finest, I went through last Monday's security footage. It showed you coming into the loading bay and going up the steps toward the custodian room. Thing is, it didn't show you *entering* the custodian's room. It didn't even show the door opening. You just disappeared from the shot.

'It was the woman police detective who got me thinking about it. She "stopped by" to ask me some rather pointed questions about

my possibly killing Ms Delcade. When I told her that the security
footage showed I left the school Monday night and didn't come
back, she reminded me that the security footage had never shown
Lindsay coming back to school either. Yet there she was.

'Lindsay Delcade was many things, Andrea. But I'm pretty sure
cat burglar wasn't one of them. She had to have *walked* into the
building somehow. That's when I got to remembering about how
you disappeared from the camera shot.'

'So you think she got into school through the loading bay?'

'Absolutely. Through the custodian's room.'

Andrea laughed bitterly.

'Biatch didn't get far, did she?'

They had reached the custodian's room. With a noticeable effort,
Andrea relocked the big metal door and hung the spare key on
top of its partner. When she turned back to face Greg, the expression beneath the Steelers hat had morphed into a frown.

'Yeah, OK. She climbs up onto the frickin' ledge – which would
be a pain in the ass by the way – and gets to the door like you
say, like, totally unseen. But how the fuck does she get in? Dude,
door's freakin' *locked.* There's no way.'

'Unless someone opened it for her.'

'Oh. Well, *duh.*' Andrea smacked her own forehead sarcastically.
'But who, then? Cause I'm telling you, Mr Bimbo, on my family's
life, it wasn't me.'

'It would have to be someone who was already in the building,
which, accepting it's not you, of course, is a very small pool of
people.'

'Who?'

Greg, thinking of Demetrius Freedman, did not answer. Not
directly, anyway.

'Maybe whoever let Lindsay in wasn't *in* the building. Maybe
whoever let Lindsay Delcade into the building came into the school
the same way.'

'But you still got the problem of how did they get in? They'd
need a key.'

'Right,' Greg agreed, morosely. 'And if they came in after hours,
they'd set off the alarm.'

Andrea laughed.

'Did I say something funny?'

'There's no alarm, dude.' She pointed at the battered rectangle of gray metal. 'That thing's for the dinosaurs. Ain't nobody ever bothered to wire it up. Too much of a pain in the ass. Alarm is armed and disarmed at the front desk. We're always getting deliveries out of hours, especially in the morning, first thing. Vernon and me are often here before security to let them in. Can't be doing that if we have to wait for the front desk to crawl outta bed and disarm the system.'

'So, if I want to get into the school without tripping the alarm, all I have to do is come down to the loading bay?' Greg tried not to sound disapproving.

'If you have a key, yeah.'

'So who has the keys?'

Andrea pursed her lips, thinking.

'Vern and me, obviously. Then Principal Ellis and Ms Pasquarelli – biatch has keys to everything.'

'What about security? Do they have keys?'

'Nah. They work the front entrance and the back door to the gym, no need for them to be down here.'

'Do you ever see Principal Ellis or Ms Pasquarelli down here?'

'Occasionally, but only if something's gone wrong.'

'And when was the last time?'

'Monday, when they both came to look at the furnace. Faces so sour, Sanchez took one look at 'em and ran like hell.' Andrea smiled at the memory.

'And have either of them ever used their keys?'

'Ms Ellis did last year. There was some screw up with the sets for the school play. Vern and I were somewhere else at the time. She, like, paged us, but by the time I got down here she'd already let in some carpenter dudes. They had maybe two hundred feet of lumber and enough paint to cover the entire damn building.'

Greg wasn't quite sure what two hundred feet of lumber would look like, but he was having trouble imagining someone tramping through the custodian's room with it. The place was crowded with furniture and shelving, and you'd have to work your way around the metal bulk of the furnace.

'Why didn't she use the roller door?' Greg asked. 'That's what it's for, isn't it? The big deliveries?'

Andrea snorted.

'Yeah, if the drive chain doesn't come off the cogs. Principal's no fool. She wasn't about to operate it without me or Vern being there. By the time I arrived, dudes were already coming in and out through here with this stuff. They didn't seem to mind, so I left them to it.'

Greg stared at the door, lost in thought.

'Does this help me, Mr Bimbo?' Andrea's voice was high and tentative, like a child who thinks she's done something wrong.

Greg forced his mind back into the here and now.

'Maybe a little. It widens the pool of suspects. The video shows you left the building at eight nineteen on Monday night.'

'And everything was normal.'

'Right. So, either someone already in the building let Lindsay Delcade in using one of the spare keys; or one of the actual keyholders – Vernon, Emily, or Principal Ellis – opened the door from the outside.'

Andrea looked unhappy.

'None of them looks more like a killer than me, though, do they? Vern's totally sexist and a little bit racist, but he's an old man. He couldn't hurt a fly, even if he wanted to. And the principal and Ms Pasquarelli are good, upstanding, middle-aged, white women. Police aren't gonna believe it was any one of them over me.' A sudden spark of hope flashed across her face. 'What about whoever was in the building?'

'Maybe,' Greg agreed. He still didn't want to tell her about Demetrius Freedman. Not yet, anyway. He sighed heavily.

'What?' Andrea demanded.

'Oh, nothing. It's just a lot of tricky problems.'

Not the least of which was what to make of the person statistically most likely to have killed Lindsay Delcade: her husband. Bryan Delcade had been parked less than a block away around the time his wife was murdered.

But of all the possible suspects, he was the only one who *couldn't* have got into the building.

Shit.

He was sitting on actual evidence in a murder investigation: Bryan Delcade's magenta-topped parking ticket. He should call the police detective, Cassidy. The man's contact information was sitting in his desk somewhere.

An image of Brendan Cassidy's flushed, angry face flashed across his mind, furious at being told he was arresting the wrong woman.

Stick to teaching Swahili or whatever it is they pay you to do.
'Say, Andrea?'
'Yeah?'
'You still got that woman detective's business card?'

09:51 A.M. EST

'Your Eastern Orthodox churches don't appear to be very BAME friendly,' Dianna said, sipping gently at the day's third mug of tea. Her slim fingers were curled inside the mug's handle. A weakening afternoon sun picked out small gleams in dark, immaculately applied nail polish.

Morosov looked up from his computer, frowning.

'"Bame"? What is this bame?'

'Black, Asian and Minority Ethnic,' Dianna explained, crisply. 'As far as I can tell, there are almost no BAMEs in any of the churches you've been having me look at.'

'Not interested in BAMEs. No Asian, no minority ethnic. Only blacks. Thick lips, fat noses, hair like – what you say? – brillo pad.' He ignored Dianna's disapproving stare. 'Target is black, like monkey. Belong to Eastern Orthodox. Very rare, like you say. Should be very easy to see, like lump of coal in iceberg.' He laughed at his own joke. When Dianna didn't respond, he assumed a more businesslike demeanor. 'You say "almost". You find some black people for me?' He wandered across to Dianna's desk and peered over her shoulder, his attempt to enjoy her breasts in the process defeated by the annoyingly baggy sweater. 'What have you got?'

'Just these three – well two-and-a-half, really.' A large image suddenly filled her computer screen. 'There's this one.'

'*Nyet*. This is black family receiving charity because they too lazy to work. Not member of church.'

'And this. But I think he's just a passerby.'

'*Da*. Not of use.'

'And then there's this one,' Dianna said, hesitantly. 'I can't be sure, but . . .'

'But what? Is just picture of church fete. Normal white people. Almost white people. They are Greek-American, yes?' He tapped the picture's caption, which identified the bearded, black-robed priest in the center of it all as a Father Kyriakos.

'Yes. But look here . . .' Dianna blew the picture up. Father Kyriakos disappeared out of shot. She directed Morosov's attention to a figure in the background. The slim silhouette was not part of the group. He – if it was a he – was standing apart, hands in pockets, caught in the shadow of an ornate, overhanging balcony. 'I can't tell if it's just the shadow, but his hair is *very* short, don't you think? And the skin tone—'

'Is maybe black, maybe not,' Morosov finished for her. The picture was too indistinct to manipulate the silhouette into something more substantial. He pulled his lips against his teeth, making an absent-minded sucking noise.

It had been three years. The figure *looked* familiar.

But it could just as easily be a trick of the light.

'Send me copy,' he ordered. 'Then make tea.' He tapped Dianna's screen. 'This . . . this I need think about.'

Dianna's jeans were considerably tighter than her sweater, so he enjoyed watching her bending over the kettle. The distraction was all too short, however. His gaze returned to the indistinct outline in the shadows of St Andrew's Orthodox Church, Pittsburgh, Pennsylvania. Morosov continued to stare at it, face impassive, his mind traveling back in time and halfway across the world. He seemed not to notice as the first hints of night placed twilit fingers on the windowsill.

11:01 A.M. EST

G reg's phone emitted a discreet chime: notification that there was a new addition to a comments section he had flagged a few hours earlier. The section was attached to an obscure column in an obscurer German newspaper. Greg was stretched out on his couch with a Russian-language edition of Agatha Christie's *And Then There Were None*. The Russian title, *Desyat Negrityat,* did not match the English even remotely. Greg had no trouble picturing the scandalized reaction in the faculty lounge if he were to translate it back into English. And maybe one day he would: just for the entertainment value. He put the book down with a certain reluctance.

The comment, Greg guessed, would have nothing to do with the subject matter of the column, looking instead like the interjection of some random troll.

'Stimme für Veränderung,' it said. 'Stimmen Sie für die Dialogos-Party.'

Greg, who neither read nor spoke German, had no idea what the message said. But he didn't need to. It contained the one word he was looking for: 'Dialogos'.

TORquil was ready for him.

Desyat Negrityat forgotten, Greg seized his laptop and plunged into the dark web. Knowing full well that TORquil wouldn't be in his chatroom, Greg didn't bother with it, heading instead to a virtual drop box. He entered the required password and opened it up.

It was loaded with gigabytes of data. An almost random mess of documentary files, executable programs, and cookies – emails, texts, and social media posts. The data went on and on, pouring across Greg's screen in a torrent of mostly meaningless file names.

The contents of Lindsay Delcade's phone.

With a sigh, Greg downloaded the contents. This was work for nerds, not one-eyed, middle-aged has-beens. It would take months

to read through everything on the woman's phone. Months he
didn't have. He scrolled through page after page of file titles,
looking for something he could recognize – and that could be
opened with accessible software. A few things caught his eye. But
even then, it still took him the best part of an hour to track down
the various apps he needed to read them.

Lindsay Delcade, it turned out, was an inveterate poster on
social media. Much of it was political and to the right of the
spectrum: a lot of stuff about the evils of unrestricted immigra-
tion; the threat to civil liberty posed by gun control; and, on the
morning of her death, a long post about defeating the gay agenda.
What wasn't political was mostly about her family. Or rather,
about her daughter. The male Delcades featured hardly at all.
Vicki Delcade, on the other hand, was everywhere. Onstage at
a downtown theater, helping out at Habitat for Humanity, standing
with her mother on the imposing steps of the Stayard College
library. This last picture provoked a raised eyebrow from Greg
Abimbola. There was Vicki, with her mother's arm draped over
her shoulder, the two of them smiling at the camera, the redbrick
temple of the Stayard Library as stately background. Mother and
daughter on a college tour.

But if you looked closely at Vicki's waist, you could just about
make out a hand that belonged to neither mother nor daughter.
The hand of a man who must have been standing on Vicki's other
side, embracing her with equal affection.

Lindsay Delcade had made the conscious effort to crop her
husband out of the shot.

Filing the observation away, Greg moved on to Lindsay
Delcade's texts, of which there were literally thousands. Greg
scanned only those from the previous Monday. Swamped
in garbage characters, they were difficult to figure out. And even
when he did, the texts turned out to be mostly short and often
incomprehensible: continuations of conversations being conducted
by other means. The last one, a text to her daughter about tutoring,
took place at seven thirty-seven p.m. A time frame that didn't help
Andrea Velasquez at all. It had been sent forty-two minutes before
the assistant custodian had been filmed leaving the building.
More than enough time to stab Lindsay Delcade to death with an
oversized screwdriver.

Tiring from the effort of plowing through so much electronic data, Greg skipped what looked to be a mountain of emails and dipped into Lindsay Delcade's rideshare accounts instead.

'Gotcha.' He said the word aloud and in English.

Lindsay Delcade's phone contained a last rideshare receipt. 'Jamal', the proud owner of a 2021 Ford Escape SUV, license number KGB 91076, had picked Lindsay Delcade up from her home in Fox Chapel at seven fifty-six on Monday evening. He had dropped her off at the back of the school, in Dean Close, at eight twenty-seven p.m.

A full eight minutes after Andrea Velasquez's departure.

12:00 P.M. EST

Aslan230: I'm here.

TORquil: Not like you to be punctual.

Aslan230: Very funny. What do you have for me?

TORquil: Data's in the drop box. Beyond that, the mobile Dialogos is interested in is physically located in Pittsburgh, USA. Of interest to you, I suspect, the phone itself is inside a police station there.

Aslan230: A police station? How, in God's name, did you access it?

TORquil: It was still charged and it wasn't in a Faraday cage. Modern phones are greedy for data. So long as they are on and have access to a signal, they are always reaching out for the weather, or the time, or the state of local traffic. The phone doesn't care if it's in a police station or not, it still looks for data. It was easy enough to persuade it to take in hackware disguised as innocent looking information. As for not being in a Faraday cage, perhaps the American police were also poking around, or maybe they were just careless.

Aslan230: Did they detect you? The Americans are good at cyber.

TORquil: I don't think so. Dialogos warned me the phone was in police hands. I was very careful.

Aslan230: What else can you tell me?

TORquil: The phone belongs to a woman by the name of Lindsay Harris Delcade, now deceased. She was found dead some days ago inside a local school, Calderhill Academy. Murder, no less. The academy is open only to the American nomenklatura: very exclusive and extremely prestigious. Link to local media is **here**. Not a lot of coverage. Americans

kill each other a lot, I think, so maybe not very
interesting to them.

Aslan230: Thank you TORquil – payment will be as promised.
Goodnight.

Morosov leaned back in his chair and stared at the ceiling.
The short English day was already at an end, the office windowpanes splashed with streetlight. A pair of double-decker buses
rumbled by outside, one immediately behind the other, their
brightly lit interiors crammed with shoppers. Morosov paid
them no attention, his eyes fixed on the smooth plaster above
his head. Broad fingers played an absent-minded tattoo on the
edge of his desk.

'Anything interesting?' Dianna asked. She disposed of the last
possible Pittsburgh church photo with a tired swirl of the mouse.
It had been a tedious, eye-aching day.

'Possible yes,' Morosov replied. He fired over TORquil's link
to the Lindsay Delcade murder story. 'Our target has interest in
mobile phone of dead woman.'

Dianna, happy to be doing something other than looking at
pictures of orthodox churchgoers, ran quickly through the available
information. She read it out loud, her voice crisp and natural, like
an actor reading well-rehearsed lines.

Parent Found Murdered at Elite Private School.

A woman was found dead this morning in the basement of
Calderhill Academy, one of the region's most prestigious private
schools. The school, on Joseph Avenue, Pittsburgh, has been
closed today while detectives canvass the area. Pittsburgh police
department confirmed that a forty-one-year-old woman has
been found dead at the scene but refused to provide further
details. However, family members have revealed the victim to
be Lindsay Harris Delcade, forty-one, of Fox Chapel PA. Other
sources alleged that she had been stabbed . . .

Dianna's voice faded away. She consumed the rest of the article
in silence.

'Well this *is* interesting,' she said, looking up. 'At least, if your
taste runs to the lurid. A wealthy, well-connected woman done to
death inside her children's school. Ongoing investigations into a

possibly interrupted drug deal. No named suspects. Wow. This would have been real tabloid stuff if it had happened over here.'

'*Da*. But what is interest of target in this woman?' Morosov was frowning. 'Target run great risk to get information of mobile phone. Great risk. Why he do this?'

'A lover?' Dianna suggested. 'He must be close to her.'

'Possible, yes.' Morosov leered at the photograph on his computer screen. 'Good looking woman. I would – how is saying? – bend over wheelie bin.' He took no notice of Dianna's pained expression. 'But if lover, why need phone? Phone not tell him thing he does not know.'

'Lots of people keep secrets from their lovers.'

'*Da*, but target good at find secrets. In this case, if he lover, he no need phone. So he has other connection, yes?'

'It says here that *Muzz* Delcade,' Dianna pronounced 'Ms' in the British fashion and with a hint of disapproval, 'was a home-maker and mother of two. So she can't have interacted with your target professionally. She didn't have a profession. Unless . . .'

'Unless, what?'

'Well . . . the only professions that a housewife is likely to interact with are doctors and teachers – because of the children.'

'Target not doctor. Not in wildest dreams.'

'Teacher, then.'

'So. Find website of this . . .?'

'Calderhill Academy.'

'*Da*.'

Once again cursing the annoying sweater, Morosov leaned over Dianna's shoulder while she surfed the web. It took her only seconds to locate the website for Calderhill Academy, Pittsburgh. As with all American sites, Calderhill Academy's was high-gloss and full of information: page after page of sleek-looking, over-enthusiastic children and mindlessly grinning teachers. There was gushing prose about how a rounded education was more important than going to a good college, juxtaposed with long lists of the good colleges that Calderhill's children were headed to. And, on one discreet page, the cost of attendance.

'Good God,' Dianna muttered. 'How many people can afford this?'

'Plenty. Is America. Everybody rich. Find teachers now, yes?' Tired of leaning, Morosov stood up straight to stretch his back.

'Here we are. It looks to be alphabetical rather than by seniority, starting with a Mr Gregory Abimbola.'

That got Morosov's attention.

'A black man?'

'It's America. I'm sure they have lots of BAME teachers.'

'Enough with this BAME. Is black. And this American school for rich childs, yes? American black is poor. This, everyone knows. Not normal for rich American childs have black teacher. What he teach, this black man?'

'French – and Russian.'

'*Nu nifiga sebe!*' Morosov bent down again, his chin practically on Dianna's collarbone. 'Open up. Quick.'

'OK, OK. Keep your shirt on . . . Here we go. Hmmmm. He's English by the looks of it. B.A. in Russian Studies and International Relations from the University of Birmingham; M.A. from Bristol—'

'There no picture.'

'Clearly.'

'Check other teacher. See if picture.'

'Alright. Er . . . yes.' Dianna peered critically at her computer screen. 'I'll bet he's been photoshopped, though.'

'Another.'

'OK. Let's look at this one. Yep. She has one too. Photoshopped for sure.'

Dianna proceeded down the list. Every teacher they looked at had a picture on the website.

'Stop. Who this?' Morosov asked.

'Dr Demetrius Freedman. Chemistry, by the look of it.'

'He is black. Long face. Like Maasai warrior . . . Is good. I see enough. School give picture for every teacher, even black teacher who might scare away parent. Every teacher except . . .'

'Gregory Abimbola.'

'*Da.* Dianna, you wonderful woman. Buy me ticket to Pittsburgh tomorrow morning leaving. Then you go home, enjoy rest of weekend. Maybe even get under big strong man.' He clapped her on the shoulder and returned to his desk. He was almost bouncing up and down with excitement.

Dianna made the arrangements, her cheeks tinged a delicate shade of red.

09:07 P.M. EST

The day's excitement had long since worn off. Other needs had taken their place. As the day started to fade, Greg had sensed the Devil slipping into his apartment. He had put down *Desyat Negrityat* and cracked open his Bible at Paul's first letter to the Romans, reading the relevant verses again and again. But it wasn't enough. The Devil kept coming, chasing Greg out of his apartment and into the Muscular Arms, where he'd hidden behind three or four vodkas.

The Devil, this time, had not been fooled. The Devil had found him. Forced him into a rideshare. Directed the driver across the Monongahela to the Southside Flats, just off of Carson Street.

And now he was standing in front of a battered wooden door, bass notes pulsing dully through the paneling. He pushed it open, his hearing swamped by the suddenly freed music. The bar was dimly lit and not yet busy. Tired of vodka, he ordered a cosmopolitan and parked himself in a booth. Looking around, he manufactured a last, hopeful delusion.

He was too old for this place.

And he had only one eye.

The delusion held for less than an hour. A young man slid into the booth beside him, smooth-skinned, with artfully gelled hair. He found himself gazing into a pair of crystalline, blue eyes.

'Buy me a drink?' he asked.

'Sure. What are you having?'

'That looks good.' The young man pointed at Greg's glass. Greg signaled the waitress for two cosmopolitans.

'I'm Grant,' the young man said. 'You?'

'Robert.'

'Nice to meet you, Robert.'

The drink was not even finished before Grant's hand found its way to the top of his thigh. And further. Air escaped from Greg's mouth in a sibilant hiss. He leaned across, caressing the young man's hair, feeling the heat of his muscled body against his, the uncoiling desire. Their lips touched. Firm. Greedy. Mouths opened.

The Devil sat beside them, watching.

'I can't do this,' Greg gasped. He lurched up from the booth, unsteady on his feet. 'I'm sorry. Sorry.'

He weaved across the now crowded floor to the bar, paid his tab, careful to look anywhere but the booth he'd just come from. As he did so, his gaze lit upon another middle-aged man in another booth, too drunk and too enamored of his own companion to pay attention to the world around him.

The recently bereaved Bryan Delcade. Without even thinking about it, Greg reached for his phone.

SUNDAY, THE FIFTEENTH
11:10 A.M. EST

Greg didn't speak Greek. But then again, neither did most of the congregation, even if their surnames sprang from the wine-dark seas of the Aegean. A blue-robed St Andrew stared down at him from a vast, stained-glass window, while the cantor's mellifluous tones passed him by without meaning, rendered majestic by the subtle echoes of thick stone. The heady scent of incense filled his nostrils. He sat in a sparsely populated pew, toward the back of the church, overshadowed by a balcony, listening to the chanted word of God.

This was a morning where Greg Abimbola very much wanted to talk to the Almighty. But the Almighty, Greg knew, was not much interested in anything he had to say. He had given in to the Devil yet again, and God, merciful though he was, had grown tired of forgiving him. Homosexuality was wrong. Unnatural. A moral stigma that would consign the diseased soul to hell if they couldn't conquer it.

'The homosexual degrades his own sex,' his priest had told him years ago, when he'd obliquely brought up the subject. 'He thus denies to himself the self-respect that is generated from the feeling that one is in line with God's creation. He is doomed to damnation unless he can find the true path.' Greg had never brought up the subject again. And why should he? He wasn't a homosexual, or a bisexual, or anything bizarre like that. Not really. These urges he felt, the temptations to stray from the path, they weren't real. They were just . . .

Well, it was the Devil, wasn't it? Moments of weakness. God could still forgive those, couldn't he? It wasn't like he'd actually *done* anything. And he hadn't for a long time. Not since . . .

He remembered the way the English stairs had creaked under his feet as he'd climbed. The oaky smell of whisky. The warm caress of red leather in a book-lined living room.

And then nothing until the awful morning after. Head thumping in a strange bed, stomach churning, bruising on both hips – and other places. And Robert Godfrey's long, drowsy body stretched out on the sheets beside him, one arm slung across his chest. He'd slid out from under the possessive limb, thrown up in the toilet, gathered his clothes, and fled, the Devil's laughter ringing in his ears.

He closed his eyes and breathed deeply, as if hoping to drag God's mercy as well as incense to the bottom of his lungs.

He had other things for which to atone. Things that had nothing to do with the Devil. Worse things. Could a God who was somehow prepared to forgive him his venal failings also absolve him from those? Try as he might, Greg very much doubted it. Freed by the ecstatic tones of the cantor, his memory reached out across two decades and three continents, bringing back little good. Doing his job was no answer and even if it was, doing his job didn't cover the half of it. He had twisted even that thin strand of justification into something rotten. No man can serve two masters: not without being a traitor to one or both. And treachery was not a pathway to salvation. He could prostrate himself in front of glass St Andrew till his knees were bloody. There was no hope for him.

And yet he kept coming to God's house; kneeling, and praying, and breathing incense every Sunday without fail. His mother would expect it.

And because hope, perversely, was all he had left.

12:45 P.M. EST

Greg hadn't bothered to look up Demetrius Freedman's address on a map, but he was not surprised to find his GPS taking him out of Bloomfield and into the Hill District. It was, after all, a historically black neighborhood, and precisely the sort of place Demetrius Freedman would choose to live. He was driving along Bigelow, the spectacular road that ran halfway up the bluffs that rose steep and fierce from the brown depths of the Allegheny River. To his right, the landscape plunged down hundreds of feet through Polish Hill and the Strip District to the wide water below. To his left, a vertiginous wall of rock marked the lower shoulder of Upper Hill. He followed the instructions on his screen and made a hard left onto the road that appeared there, climbing so steeply he briefly imagined he was driving a fighter jet instead of a Mini Cooper.

What brought his imagination crashing back to earth was the bleakness of his surroundings. Climbing up the lower slopes of Upper Hill, the houses, swallowed up by woodland, and some of which must once have been something to behold, were rundown to the verge of collapse. Signs of poverty were everywhere: broken-down cars; a decrepit general store with every window barred; bus stops the Port Authority had never bothered to repair. Sidewalks appeared and disappeared seemingly at random, quite possibly consumed by the weeds that forced their way through uneven flagstones. And of people, there was no sign. For a city neighborhood, it was dispiritingly quiet. The world, after it had ended.

And yet, as he wound his way higher and higher, the air seemed to be getting fresher, the light brighter. The Appalachian ridges and hillsides that hemmed in the city's other neighborhoods had no place here. Upper Hill rose above it all, surrounded by nothing but boundless winter sky. Greg, a child of the great wide open, who found the city's deeply notched valleys vaguely claustrophobic, was suddenly breathing a little easier.

When his Mini Cooper finally leveled out, Greg found himself in a beautiful green square overlooked by a massively impressive water tower. The square – a little park, really – with large mature trees, was faced on four sides by grand, three-story houses; some dilapidated to the point of ruin, others rehabbed to a standard that would have fetched vast sums of money in Squirrel Hill or Shadyside. It was one of the latter, festooned with black-and-gold flags, and other Steelers regalia, that turned out to be the home address of one Dr Demetrius Freedman.

'Come in, brother. Make yourself at home,' Demetrius said, ushering him inside. Greg caught a brief glimpse of a bright living room, dominated by a huge, plate-glass window affording spectacular views across the Allegheny. He was gently shooed downstairs and into a luxuriously furnished den. No plate-glass windows here, just a TV screen so big it wouldn't have looked out of place in a movie theater. Half-a-dozen men and two teenage boys, all African American, were already present. Demetrius pressed a near-freezing bottle of Iron City into his hand and introduced him around, finishing with the two teenagers.

'And these are my boys,' he said, proudly. 'Caleb and Malik.' Caleb, the older of the two, was sixteen, if Greg remembered correctly. He was a sophomore at the Upper School, shaping up to be tall and thin like his father and, unsurprisingly, a dominating presence on Calderhill's basketball team. Malik, the younger, was thirteen and more stoutly constructed than his brother. Both of them greeted him with polite smiles.

'OK!' Demetrius exclaimed. 'It's time to play some football!'

Greg settled at one end of a deep leather couch, next to a giant of a man called Aundray Oates. Greg was not surprised to learn that Aundray had once played college ball before transitioning into adult life as a dentist. Armed with the contents of that morning's *Post-Gazette*, Greg was able to make some not-stupid observations, while Aundray expounded on what the Steelers were doing wrong and – very occasionally – right, during a low-scoring first half.

As the second quarter wound down through the two-minute warning, Aundray asked, 'So, Greg, do Brits like *American* football?'

'Some do.' Feeling a sudden upwelling of mischief, he added, 'Even if it's not really a sport.'

'What do you mean, it's not a sport?' Aundray waved good

naturedly at the television. 'Look at it! A big stadium, loud crowds, incredible athletes, points on the board. I can't think of anything that's *more* like a sport.'

Greg shook his head, an impish smile tugging at his lips.

'It's very athletic – for sure. But it's not a sport. It's more like . . . going to the ballet.'

'The *what,* now?'

'The ballet. Lots of young, lithe people in tight-fitting clothes prancing about doing pre-arranged, choreographed moves. It's dancing with a ball. Unless you're a cheerleader, of course. Then it's just dancing.'

The whole room was staring at him now. Greg just grinned.

'I guess you think *soccer*'s more manly?' Oates asked. There was a faint edge to the question.

'Well, they don't stop every thirty seconds to take a rest,' Greg pointed out. 'But no, you want a *man's* game, it's got to be ice hockey. Those guys go at it a hundred percent up and down the rink without stopping, in armor plate and holding an actual weapon. And they do it on *skates*. Did you guys *see* Friday's game?'

'You're a Penguins fan?' Aundray asked, any previous hostility wiped away by surprise.

'Big time,' Greg admitted. 'Got taken to a game when I first came here and been in love with it ever since.'

The whole room, Greg noticed, was nodding with approval. This was Pittsburgh. Anyone who loved Penguins hockey couldn't be all bad.

'Well, man,' Aundray said at last, 'you just keep watching. We'll make a Steelers fan of you yet.'

'Happy to be one,' Greg assured him. 'They already play in Penguins colors anyway.' He raised his beer. 'Go Steelers!'

That raised a chuckle. The first half expired with a whimper on the Steelers forty-yard line. Drinks and snacks were refreshed. Conversations turned to other matters. Greg, discovering that the basement level of Demetrius's house opened onto the backyard, took the opportunity to step outside for a breath of fresh air. The yard was mostly thick grass bordered by low shrubs and a couple of bare-leaved trees. It sloped precipitously downward from the back of the house but afforded a view that stretched for miles across tree-lined ridges and lesser hills, all of them clothed in white snow and the gray-brown of winter woodland. It was crisp and chill, with a hint of sun behind the thinning cloud. Greg breathed deeply, reveling in the cold.

'Are we having fun yet?' asked a voice from behind him. Demetrius.

'Very much so,' Greg said, without turning around. He was enjoying the scenery, the openness of it. 'This is simply . . . spectacular.'

'Isn't it? My ex and I fell in love with the view. It's why we bought the place. It was a complete wreck when we first moved in, but it was worth all the effort to get it the way it is now.' A slightly edgy laugh. 'Even if it did cost me my marriage.'

'I'm sorry to hear that.'

'Don't be. It's for the best. I have my boys, and she has whatever man she's shacked up with this month.'

The edge to Demetrius's tone was still there. Greg thought it safer to change the subject.

'Is the view worth the neighborhood?'

Demetrius snorted.

'The Hill District isn't a tenth as dangerous as white people think it is. And it's where our people are. If people like me don't invest in it, who else is going to? The city? Give me a break.'

Greg, realizing he was treading on dangerous ground, kept his counsel.

'The Hill District wasn't always like this, you know,' Demetrius continued. 'You've seen the houses? The architecture?'

Greg nodded.

'Up through WW Two, the big one, this place was really something. Jazz, blues, culture, you name it, the Hill District had it. But when African Americans started moving out of the South during the great migration, the only place in the city they were allowed to live was here. More and more people crammed tighter and tighter into a limited amount of housing. And no permits to build more, and just *try* getting a loan to fix things up . . . Well, you can imagine how that went. And then in the Fifties, the city basically wiped out Lower Hill. And for what? A bunch of parking lots and what's now the Penguins' stadium. Conveniences for white people and fuck everybody else. The whole neighborhood was cut off from downtown, the economy collapsed, and the Hill District is what you have today. But it's ours, and we gotta do the best we can to get it back to what it was.'

'Makes sense,' Greg said. Though, truth be told, he wasn't sure it did. Life was too short to be some kind of urban pioneer, even if the view out the back was unbelievable. He much preferred the *ersatz* counterculture of Bloomfield, with its white hipsters and Asian students; its tattoo parlors and trendy coffee shops. It's *life*.

'Demetrius, can I ask you something?'

'Shoot.'

'Last Monday night, you told the police you were in your classroom all evening, prepping sulfur hex . . . hexa . . .'

'Hexafluoride.'

'Hexafluoride, thanks, until you went home?'

'Yeah.'

'Well, have you thought about what will happen if the police look at the school's keycard logs?' Greg was still staring out at the distant hillsides. He couldn't see Demetrius's expression, but he could hear the shuffle of feet as the chemistry teacher shifted his stance.

'What are you getting at?'

'The glass doors that lead to the science department close at night. You need a card to get in and out.'

'I know that, dammit. I do *work* there.'

'Exactly. So there's a log entry every time the doors get opened. You opened the doors from the science department side at eight twenty p.m. You didn't come back in until about eight forty. And *then* you left for the night, just after eight fifty.'

'How the *fuck* do you know that?'

'I'm an incorrigible gossip. What are you going to say if the police ask you to account for twenty minutes you didn't tell them about?'

Demetrius laid a hand on Greg's shoulder and turned him around with a considerable display of strength.

'Are you accusing me of fucking *murder*?'

'No. I'm asking you to think very carefully about what you're going to tell the police if they come asking.'

'Jesus Christ, Greg, I don't *remember*! I don't even remember leaving my classroom. Maybe . . . maybe I needed something from the faculty lounge, or I went there because the restroom is nicer, or I just needed to stretch my legs. I don't fucking know. And why does it matter? Po-po's going to stick it to the Velasquez girl.'

Greg shook his head.

'I heard they've got real doubts she has anything to do with it.' He stared intently into Demetrius's angry, confused face. 'I also heard that Bryan or Lindsay Delcade did some real harm to your career.'

Demetrius stiffened.

'Where'd you hear that?'

'From Bryan Delcade. He wants his son off the hook for the "n" word thing. Threatened to ruin my career the same way he ruined yours.'

'Sonofabitch!'

'So it's true, then? Because if it is, the police are going to be giving a black man with a grudge and a twenty-minute window a much closer look.'

Demetrius glared at him, and then sighed, the sound deep and tremulous. Taking Greg by the elbow, Demetrius led him to the side of the house, away from anyone who might come out of the basement behind them. The chemistry teacher leaned in until his face was only inches from Greg's, the expression bitter. His dark eyes glittered bright with anger.

'How many white chemists with PhDs from the Massachusetts Institute of Technology end up teaching high school, Greg? How many?'

'Very few, I'm guessing.'

'Damn right. I'm a *good* chemist. Top of my class in undergrad, great doctoral program, the whole world at my fucking feet. African American. Couldn't get a tenure track job in academia to save my life, even though white classmates with way less talent and more connections did. I bummed around in a few associate faculty positions, but I couldn't make ends meet, so I ended up teaching high school. I ended up *here,* where I got passed over for the Head of Science position. Twice.'

'I'm sorry to hear that. But someone with a résumé like yours? There are other schools, surely?'

'Not many.' Demetrius nodded in the direction of his house. 'At least, not many in Pittsburgh that can give my sons a great education. Calderhill picks up their tuition. It's one of the perks.' A sardonic smile. 'One of the handcuffs.'

'And what does that have to do with Bryan Delcade?'

'Nothing. But he and his lovely wife fucked up my one chance to step up.'

'How so?'

'There was a Head of Science opening at the Edgeworth School.'

'The suburban Calderhill?'

'They wouldn't thank you for calling them that, but yes. Private, like Calderhill; great rep; free tuition for the boys. I applied for the position, everything went great, and I heard on the down-low that the job was mine.'

'So, what happened?'

'Lindsay fucking Delcade is what happened. I gave her daughter a B-plus. Lindsay hit the roof, stormed into my classroom, and demanded I regrade her. Called me an "undercover black panther" who wanted to stop her kid getting into Stayard. Stayard! Vicki's a good kid – and a genuinely talented actor – but there's no way. Anyhow, I was as polite as I could be and said no.'

'And then she went to Principal Ellis, I suppose?'

'She sure did. Ellis held the line, though. The three of us had a meeting in her office. Man, that woman ranted and raved like you would not believe. Finished up by telling me that I would regret it. And I did.'

'Really?'

'Turns out *Bryan* Delcade is an alum and trustee of the Edgeworth School. He kicked up a stink about my appointment to the Head of Science position. All of a sudden, it was "Head of Science offer? What Head of Science offer?". A "terrible misunderstanding" for which they were "so very sorry". Fuckers. They gave the job to some white guy from Chicago.' Demetrius kicked angrily at a piece of gravel stuck to the flagstones. 'And now, like you said, I'm a black man with a grudge who can't account for his time. It won't look so good for me, will it?'

'It's not great.'

'Yeah, but the cops don't know about the Edgeworth thing.' Demetrius's expression brightened a little. 'Most they're gonna get is that I was out of my classroom for a minute or two. That ought not to be enough, even for them.'

Greg shook his head.

'Bryan Delcade knows about the Edgeworth thing. And if he knows, chances are the police will, too. Sooner or later.'

'Goddamn sonofabitch!' Demetrius exploded. 'Hasn't that smug, fascist bastard done me enough harm?' He leaned into the side of his beautiful house, pressing his forehead against the cool brickwork. He took a series of deep breaths, loud in the sudden silence. 'Is there no end to this shit?' he asked. 'Doesn't it ever . . . just *stop*?' His voice was low and cracked, as if on the verge of tears.

Greg gave his host a sympathetic smile, placed a hand on his shoulder.

'Think really hard about where you went, OK? And if they ask, don't lie to them about the Delcades. Lying is what got Andrea Velasquez into trouble in the first place.'

Aundray, the dentist, stuck his head around the corner of the building.

'There you are,' he said. 'Game's started and your beers are getting warm. Get on in here!'

Demetrius straightened up and followed Aundray back inside. Greg, even less interested in football than usual, lagged behind.

Looking at the chemistry teacher's tall, rangy frame, he was dragged back to another, earlier conversation.

I'd like to line the lot of 'em against a wall, and just pull the fucking trigger.

Demetrius Freedman was a powerfully built human being. One who'd had to run the race of life knee-deep in water. There was a lot of anger there. A lot.

Maybe, in that MIT brain of his, Lindsay Delcade was a good first step.

03:37 P.M. EST

I t was cold here: far colder than London, with real snow on the ground and clinging thick to the bare-branched trees. Morosov reveled in it, winding down the window of his rideshare the moment the SUV pulled off the highway. The driver hunched into his coat but didn't say anything.

Barreling along the highway from the airport – a ride that seemed to go on forever – the driver had waxed lyrical about what a great city Pittsburgh was. He'd called it 'the Paris of Appalachia', adding that, if this was Viktor Lavrov's first visit, he was in for a treat, because Pittsburgh was the only city in the world with, as he put it, 'an entrance'.

'The entrance' turned out to be a long tunnel, bored arrow-straight through the bottom of a mountain and lined with sooty white tiles. Bursting out the other end and onto a giant yellow bridge over black water, the city of Pittsburgh lay suddenly in front of him. Morosov, who had absurdly expected to see something like Paris, France, was vaguely disappointed. A few tower blocks to one side, a couple of sports stadiums on the other, all squeezed into cracks between rearing, tree-covered hills that dwarfed every-thing else into insignificance. In fact, the geology of the place was so raw, so powerful, that the city seemed more huddled Stone Age settlement than modern metropolis, as if it was dependent on the gods of rock and deep-rooted earth for its very survival.

The city had then disappeared entirely, masked by rugged bluffs as the SUV had plunged down a dizzyingly steep ramp. Once he leveled out, the driver had raced along the banks of a wide, choppy looking river. An enormous barge, its heaped cargo of coal lightly dusted with snow, moved lazily through the water. A contented, prehistoric monster, far too big to be troubled by anything so trivial as a predator.

Only after taking the exit ramp for somewhere called Oakland had the city reappeared. The driver had joined three lanes of slow-moving, one-way traffic, allowing Mikhail Morosov, at last, to open his window. He watched with mild interest as a succession of restaurants, bars, and – oddly – medical facilities, slid into and out of view. The sidewalks were busy: young people of a certain age for the most part; from which Morosov concluded that he was in a studenty part of town.

The driver turned into a side street and pulled over.

'Here we are, Viktor,' he said. 'St Andrew's Greek Orthodox Church.'

Morosov stepped out onto the sidewalk, careful to avoid the slush piled against the curb, and waited for the driver to retrieve his roller bag from the car's trunk. The bag was barely half full and easy to carry. Morosov held it in his hand as he made his way up the church's broad steps and through the imposing wooden doors. Inside, St Andrew's was breathtaking. Built around a huge central dome, like a smaller version of Istanbul's Hagia Sophia, the church was a profusion of bright colors liberally laced with gold leaf. Apart from the fact that this church had pews, it could almost have been Russian. The faint aroma of incense hung in the air, heady in its familiarity. As for the pews, they were not quite deserted. A couple of gray-haired old ladies, dressed black as crows, sat far apart from each other, each alone with her thoughts, or, as they no doubt told themselves, with God. A couple of votive candles flickered fitfully in a small shrine off to one side.

Morosov and his bag made their way forward to the lower altar, short of the Holy of Holies, and waited. He could have sat in a pew like the old ladies, but the Russian in him resisted. He put down his bag and stood, arms folded across his wide chest, rocking gently back and forth.

Waiting.

'Welcome to St Andrew's.'

The voice was heavily accented – Greek, presumably. Morosov turned around to find himself facing a heavily bearded man in black robes. As powerfully built as Morosov himself, the man's gentle smile and worldly brown eyes gave him the mien of a kindly bear.

'Father Kyriakos, yes?'

The priest looked pleasantly surprised.

'Just so. And you?'

'Viktor Lavrov. I come long way to see you.'

'Indeed?'

'*Da.*' Morosov rolled the dice. 'I looking for cousin, Gregory Abimbola?'

'You're *Gregory's* cousin?' The priest looked confused. 'But Gregory is, ah . . .'

Morosov chuckled.

'Aunt Russian. White as snow. Visit England. Meet student from Nigeria. Very handsome. Black as ace of spades. And *boom*! Gregory. Cousin.' Morosov spread his hands as if in apology. 'The world change, Father.' He gazed appreciatively at the haloed apostles looking down on them from the ceiling. 'Even here, world change, yes?'

The priest smiled then, a little wryly.

'Yes. Even here, things change. It is the will of God.' Kyriakos took a deep, meditative breath. 'I always thought Gregory was English,' he mused.

'*Nyet.* Russian. But speak excellent English, like mother. Me?' He swept his hands down his body in a self-deprecating gesture. 'I not speak it so good.'

The priest threw him a quick smile.

'Your English is as good as mine,' he said, kindly. Father Kyriakos looked around at his church, as if seeing it for the first time. 'I wonder why Gregory chose us,' he wondered. 'If he's Russian like you say, there are a number of Russian congregations not far from here. Why settle in with us Greeks? Not that he isn't welcome, you understand. It's just . . .' The priest struggled to find the right words. 'An unusual choice.'

Morosov had to struggle to keep his expression friendly. Lies, he knew, are best told when they are mostly true. But the truth at the heart of this one made his gorge rise.

'Family fight very bad. So bad Gregory like pretend not Russian. But still religious, yes? So . . .'

'So, Greek Orthodox is still Orthodox,' the priest finished, comprehension dawning on his features. 'I see. And you're looking for Gregory?'

'*Da.* I was hoping you provide address, yes? My family loses contact with him long time ago.'

'I'm afraid I couldn't do that,' Kyriakos said, regretfully. 'You know how it is. But I could send him an email on your behalf, ask him to get in touch?'

Morosov shook his head.

'He not come. Gregory is – how to say – *black* sheep?' He couldn't resist smiling at the double meaning. 'Family fight, like I say you already, very bad, so no see for many, many years. But mother – my aunt, yes? Mother is dying. Want see son one last time. If I see face to face, maybe persuade come. Email not work.'

Kyriakos's eyes moistened. He was, Morosov decided, one of those men who cried easily.

'He comes to church every Sunday, regular as clockwork. Perhaps if you could wait . . .?'

'No, no, no. Too long. His mother very ill. Maybe days only. And flight to Russia long, yes? At home all she tell priest and doctors every day is she want see son one last time. Is dying wish.'

The priest's expression became stiff and impossible to read. Morosov worried he had laid it on too thick. But it turned out to be the final crumbling of the Father's resistance.

'Well, in the circumstances . . .' The priest dabbed at an eye. 'Gregory lives not far from here, if I remember correctly. If you'll come this way? I'll look it up for you.'

MONDAY, THE SIXTEENTH
07:27 A.M. EST

I
t was snowing again. Any more of this, Greg thought, and it would turn into a proper winter. NPR murmured soothingly out of the Mini Cooper's retro-looking radio. The sanitation strike was over, apparently. There was a short sound clip of the mayor describing the outcome as a 'victory for common sense', before they cut back to the announcer, who informed her audience that pickups would resume on a normal schedule, which Greg took to mean that the trash trucks would be picking up two weeks' worth of garbage in one go. Road conditions distracted him from the story. He kept a careful grip on the steering wheel as he rode out a fishtail. While he knew for a fact that the city of Pittsburgh had snowplows – he'd seen them on the road from time to time – he'd never seen one actually plowing. And wherever the city's snowplows did their business, it wasn't on Joseph Avenue. The Mini Cooper made it a little unsteadily to the top of the hill and slid down the other side, slipping into the last available free parking space. A mother with a minivan full of kids gave him a baleful look as she drove past.

'Morning, Stacey.'

'Morning, Mr Abimbola.' Greg walked briskly past the front desk and trotted up the stairs to the second floor, hanging his winter coat on the back of his classroom door. More or less ready for the day, he strolled over to the admin suite.

'Good morning, Emily,' he said cheerfully, leaning over her cubicle. Emily's computer monitors were bevel-to-bevel with spreadsheets. 'Are we still on for tonight? Forecast says it'll have stopped snowing by then.'

Emily, who had probably been at her desk since before seven, beamed up at him.

'Of course we are. Looking forward to it!' A sudden look of concern. 'Unless something's come up?'

'Absolutely not! I wouldn't miss it for the world.'

'Then all's good.' Emily took a sip from her cup of coffee.

'I didn't know you had a kid at Stayard.'

'What?'

'Your mug,' Greg observed. 'It says "Stayard Mom".'

'Oh, right. Yeah, my son's a senior there.'

'Congratulations! You must be very proud.'

Emily smiled fondly.

'I am. He's majoring in Art History. Absolutely loves it.'

'Good for him. Maybe next time he's home he can help me with my interior design. Between you and me, I have *terrible* taste.'

Emily giggled at that.

'You're too funny.'

'I wish. Though, on a more serious note, I'd like to have a quick word about Andrea Velasquez.'

Emily's expression became businesslike.

'Oh, I wouldn't worry about that. She's suspended until further notice. Can't have a murderer walking the halls, you know? Not a good look.'

Greg made a deprecating gesture.

'Oh . . . I don't think she's a murderer, Emily.'

'Really? Then you're in a minority of one.'

'I don't think so. The police have been tracking Lindsay Delcade's movements. Apparently, Lindsay got here almost ten minutes after Andrea left the building. Andrea was already on her way home by the time Ms Delcade got murdered, so I don't think she's a good fit for our particular little scandal.'

'Where, in God's name, did you hear that?' Emily asked, wide-eyed.

'Oh, people talk, you know how it is. You can't keep stuff like that quiet for long. Anyway, I think suspending her until this is cleared up is absolutely the right thing to do. I'm just hoping we're not planning on firing her.'

Emily pursed her lips.

'How good is this information of yours?'

'Well, it's third-hand information, if you know what I mean. But it's not the sort of thing anyone would say unless it was true.'

'Hmmm. Well, we can keep her suspended for a while, I guess. Normally, in a situation like this, we'd have to let her go. We're in damage control right now and the parents will expect nothing less. I'll talk to Principal Ellis, but we certainly don't want her fired if she turns out to be innocent. We can certainly wait a few days until everything becomes clearer.'

'You are justice personified, Ms Pasquarelli.'

'Why, thank you, Mr Abimbola.'

Greg left the admin suite, slightly alarmed that Andrea had been right after all. He'd still not adjusted to American employment practices. Calderhill Academy had been all set to throw Andrea to the wolves.

Heading toward his classroom, he ran into Principal Ellis taking quick steps in the opposite direction. The steel tips of her heels clacked on the hardwood floor.

'Ah, there you are, Greg. A word please.'

Thrown off his stride, he followed her into her office. As ever, Ellis's cluttered domain made him feel slightly ill-at-ease. What had he done this time, he wondered? There were a number of bad answers to that question, so he decided not to dwell on it. He took a seat instead, separated from the principal by the cluttered width of her desk. Unstable towers of paper, each held in place by the usual collection of heavy objects, covered the wood and leather surface.

'The last time I sat here,' he said, trying to gauge Ellis's mood, 'I was being interviewed by a homicide detective.'

Ellis grimaced.

'What an awful, *awful* business. All those questions. As if one of us could possibly have done it.'

'*Someone* must have. Or we wouldn't have had a dead body in the basement.'

'Of course, of course. But to think it was one of the faculty . . . . absurd, just absurd. As I told that overbearing detective . . . what was his name?'

'Cassidy.'

'Oh yes. Sat in this very seat and made me feel like a visitor in my own office. Practically accused me of murder. Said I'd been arguing with Lindsay the day before and wanted to know if I had an alibi, for god's sake.'

'And did you?'

'Thankfully, yes. Or I think he'd have arrested me rather than Maybelline. As it happens, I had a very pleasant, very *public* dinner with an old friend of mine, Johnathan Lorde. He's the dean of the faculty of Arts and Sciences at Stayard. Technically, he was in town to fly the flag for the college and discuss admissions policy, but it was really an excuse to catch up.' A sudden smile brightened her face. 'I couldn't have had a more respectable witness.'

'It pays to have friends in high places,' Greg joked. Somewhat to his surprise, it fell flat. Ellis's expression turned serious.

'I wanted to speak to you earlier, but you know how crazy it gets around here. I just wanted to say how sorry we are about this Chandler Delcade business. What the boy did was unforgiveable.'

So you'll be expelling him, then? Greg held himself expressionless, waiting for the other shoe to drop.

'Of course, with what happened to his mother, he's probably been punished enough, don't you think? Such a terrible, *terrible* thing. No one should lose a parent like that.'

'A tragedy,' Greg said, his voice carefully neutral. 'But the boy's going to start detention later today. What he did can't go unpunished.'

'Oh, of course not. Of course not. Absolutely right. I just wanted to know if you considered this the end of the matter? Obviously, if you choose to take it further . . . the school will back you a hundred percent.' There was a tense pursing of lips.

'I don't think that will be necessary, Principal Ellis. But I appreciate the show of support.'

The relieved slump of Ellis's shoulders spoke volumes.

'That's very gracious of you, Greg. Very gracious. Hopefully, once this is over, the boy will have learned his lesson.'

'From your mouth to God's ears.' Greg knew his smile was tighter than he would have liked. 'Is there anything else?' He made to rise from his chair.

'I don't believe so. Oh . . . wait. I completely forgot. Can you take French IV on Thursday? Claire has a doctor's appointment.'

'Of course.' Greg stood up, impatient to be free of Ellis's office and its oppressive untidiness. As he did so, however, one of the principal's makeshift paperweights caught his eye.

'Isn't that the key to the metal door in the custodian's room?'

Ellis looked surprised.

'Yes it is. How'd you know?'

'I don't think there's another lock in the school big enough for a key like that.'

Ellis chuckled.

'I guess not.'

'Aren't you afraid you'll lose it?'

'This? I never let it out of my sight. It's far too useful for holding down papers.'

Greg grinned at that and headed out into the corridor. As he did so, the cellphone in his jacket pocket started to vibrate.

'Hello?'

'Mr Abimbola, it's Detective Lev. I'm returning the voicemail you left me Saturday? I believe you have something to give me.'

G reg was not surprised to see Vicki Delcade lingering behind
while the rest of Russian III filed out. Violating instructions to treat the Delcade children the same as always on
their first day back, classmates brushed sympathetic hands across
her shoulders instead, or whispered quiet, kindly words as
they passed by, each small gesture a quiet twisting of the knife.
Vicki's eyes sparkled with tears, her usually porcelain-pale skin
the lifeless white of Greek marble. Her notebook was clasped
tightly across her chest, slim fingers marred by chips in her nail
polish. Grief, however, had not deprived her of grace. She moved
toward his desk with the sinuous agility of a cat.

'What can I do for you?' Greg asked. His voice, while not
unkind, held no hint of condolence. Just a teacher making himself
available to a student.

'I need more time to finish my assignments, sir. You know.
Because . . .'

Greg braced himself for the floods of tears. But something in
his expression or, rather, lack of it, must have drained the water
from Vicki's eyes. She smiled weakly instead.

'Mom's funeral took up a lot of time. I'm behind on pretty
much everything.'

'Take as much time as you need, Vicki. Within reason, of course.'

'Thank you, sir.'

'You're welcome.' He turned to the Russian I assignments piled
neatly on his desk. It took him longer than it should have to notice
that Vicki Delcade was still standing there, shifting her weight
gently from one foot to another.

'Something else I can do for you, Vicki?'

Vicki stood there for a moment, tongue-tied. One hand played
awkwardly with the blonde tips of her hair.

'I . . . uh . . .' Then the words came out all in a rush. 'I wanted
to apologize for my baby brother. He's an idiot but he's not, you

know, *that* kind of idiot and I don't know what got into him but it was really, really wack and I'm like totally sorry for what he did. Like, *totally*.'

She paused to draw breath, her face flushed.

Greg was strangely touched. Here was a girl who had other – awful – things to think about, and yet she'd made the time to do . . . *this*. He scratched at an imaginary itch at the edge of his patch, if only to distract himself from the prickling sensation in his other, good eye.

'You didn't have to do that, Vicki.' On impulse, he reached out and touched her wrist. 'But I appreciate it. Truly.'

Vicki heaved a sigh of relief.

'You're welcome, sir.' She made to go.

'Vicki?'

'Yes, sir?'

'Why did your mom take a rideshare here last Monday? Why not drive?'

Vicki paused at the door, looking back at him.

'She never drives Monday nights. It's . . . it *was* . . . just a thing she did.'

'Every Monday?'

'Pretty much.'

'And did she always come to the school?'

Vicki was frowning.

'Why would she do that? She just went out, is all.'

'Of course.' Greg looked at his watch. 'And I'm sorry for keeping you. Tell whomever you have next that it was "*like, totally*" my fault.'

Vicki flashed him a quick grin and disappeared. The door swung silently shut behind her. Greg stared at it for a few moments more and then, reluctantly, turned back to the Russian I notebooks awaiting his attention.

'Care to join me, Detective?' It was a ridiculous question, but Greg felt a real American would have made the offer, so he made the effort.

'No thanks.' But Detective Sergeant Rachel Lev was taking in her surroundings with something more than professional curiosity, Greg thought.

As well she might. The Nanchong Palace in South Oakland was not pretty. The tables were utilitarian Formica, the overhead lighting was harsh and fluorescent, and the floor was covered in nothing but scuffed and faded linoleum. But the food was delicious – and as close to authentic Sichuan cuisine as it was possible to get outside of China. Almost all of the tables were occupied, and the occupants were almost entirely Asian. Apart from an adventurous group of painfully Caucasian Pitt students, Greg and the detective were the only people in the room whose genes hailed from a different part of the world. The Pitt students were attempting to work their way through a massive hot pot. They were all using – or trying to use – chopsticks.

Greg spared the students a good-humored glance. Three of them were sweating already, and they had barely begun to eat.

'Do you come here often?' the detective asked, with a note of wry amusement.

'Yes,' Greg admitted. 'Ms Tsai, our Chinese language teacher, brought me here once. I like the spices. Probably the African in me.' He pointed at the students, dipping thinly sliced beef into the bubbling hot pot, and then laughing and gasping as they swallowed down the results. '*That's* what I'd really like to be having, but unless you have six stomachs there's no way to manage it alone. And certainly not in one man's lunch hour.'

That raised a ghost of a smile from the policewoman, who sat down opposite him. Flimsy metal chair legs scraped noisily on the linoleum.

'You have something for me?' she prompted.

Greg pushed over Bryan Delcade's parking ticket. He was about to explain what it was and why it mattered when he saw Lev's expression change from one of mild interest to intense curiosity.

'Where'd you get this?'

'The man littered my classroom with it during a discussion about one of his children.'

'And does he know you have this?'

'I don't know. Maybe? I'm sure he'll have an explanation but, given the circumstances, I thought you should have it.'

The police officer shot him a quick smile.

'Thank you, Mr Abimbola, you've been very helpful.'

Greg grabbed what he hoped was his chance.

'Do you mind if I ask you a question, Sergeant?'

Lev's smile turned cautious.

'You can always ask, sir.'

'Are you still looking at Andrea Velasquez? Because if you are, you're really barking up the wrong tree.'

'What makes you say that?'

'I think if you do a little digging, you'll find that Andrea left the building shortly before Lindsay Delcade got there.'

'And how would you know that?' Lev had the sort of open, direct gaze that made people with secrets uncomfortable. Greg ignored the sensation.

'Do you know how Lindsay got to the school?' he asked.

'Yes.'

There was a long, long silence. Greg took a bite of his meal, watching the detective watch him. Small, subtle signs of an internal struggle played quietly across her face. She had freckles, he noticed, surprised he hadn't picked up on that before. Maybe she'd covered them with make-up.

'We believe she took a rideshare,' Lev admitted, at last. There was the smallest hint of a sigh.

'Then you should know the rideshare arrived at Calderhill eight minutes after Andrea left the building. It's pretty obvious Andrea can't be your killer . . . Unless you're suggesting Andrea Velasquez, our junior custodian, and Lindsay Delcade, the Type-A parent, were bosom buddies who met on the street, somehow evaded the cameras, and sneaked into the school together.'

'So you're saying that Lindsay Delcade didn't get to the school until . . .' Lev's eyes rolled upward as she consulted some internal timeline, 'until, what? Eight twenty-seven?'

'Precisely.'

'And how do you know that?'

'It's when she was dropped off, isn't it?'

Rachel Lev placed her chin atop two clasped hands and leaned forward, planting her elbows on the table in front of her. The soft smile playing on her face made her look almost coquettish.

'See, here's the thing, Mr Abimbola. We have no idea what rideshare company Lindsay Delcade used, or when – or even if – she was dropped off at the school. We can't get into her phone because her husband doesn't have the password, and the subpoena for the phone company hasn't been processed yet. So, unless you were there watching, how come you know so much about something we don't?'

Shit.

Greg bent over his bowl, careful to hide his face until he had his expression under some sort of control.

'Then I suggest you process the subpoena,' he said, evenly. 'You'll see I'm right.'

'You didn't answer my question.'

'No, I didn't.'

Lev leaned back in her chair.

'Do you want me to arrest you for obstruction of justice, Mr Abimbola?'

'No.'

'So answer the question. I'm not in the mood for BS.'

Greg made himself look pained.

'Nothing I've told you is BS, Sergeant. It's the straight-up truth. And here's some more. You can pull me in if you like. By all means, add to your collection of black people behind bars.' The detective winced at that, and Greg felt mildly guilty. But it was the only brush back play he could think of. 'Know this, though: if you do pull me in, I'm not going to tell you anything I wouldn't have quite happily told you out here.'

'Which doesn't include how you know so much about Lindsay Delcade's rideshare?'

'Correct.'

Lev grunted with annoyance, an aural counterpoint to the grim cast of her eyes. She leaned forward again, dropping her voice as she did so.

'I don't think that fancy school of yours would be very forgiving if one of its teachers was arrested. It'd be a career ender for you.'

'You're assuming I care about my career, Sergeant. It's a lot less interesting than yours, let me tell you.'

Despite herself, the police officer smiled. She doused it out quickly, though. Greg took another stab at his meal, buying himself time to think.

'Look,' he said, coaxingly. 'Just follow through on your subpoena thing. You'll see I'm right. Andrea Velasquez is not your woman.'

'It's not that easy,' Rachel said. She seemed to crumple a little. The confident police detective faded into the background. Greg found himself staring into the soft eyes of a vulnerable young woman. Someone who needed his help, one human being to another. Someone hoping against hope that Greg Abimbola was not a completely irredeemable shit.

'We have a theory of the case,' she said obliquely. 'The subpoena will get done, but the nature of this theory means it's not a high priority. And the theory won't change unless you give me something to work with.'

'The parking ticket isn't enough?'

'It's a start. Maybe enough to open the door a little. But only a little.' A quiet little smile. 'It's a *real* heavy door.'

Greg, thinking of the burly Lieutenant Cassidy, found himself chuckling. For some reason, the sudden burst of humor opened his mind to another possibility. There was, after all, at least one alternative route to the same destination. A route that didn't involve a slow-moving subpoena, or Greg Abimbola revealing a hard-to-explain familiarity with Russian hackers.

'What if I were to tell you that the rideshare driver identified himself as "Jamal"?' he said, quietly, examining the contents of his bowl with exaggerated care. 'That he works for a particular rideshare company – and that he drives a 2021 Ford Escape. In respect of which, I just happen to know the license number?'

Rachel Lev pulled out her notebook.

'Now *that*, Mr Abimbola, might kick open a door or two.' A small smile played across the sergeant's lips as she started to write.

One of the Pitt students screamed with laughter. A piece of ferociously hot fish wriggled off her chopsticks and onto the linoleum.

03:30 P.M. EST

'Sir?'

An apprehensive looking Chandler Delcade stuck his head around the door to Greg's classroom.

'Come in, Chandler. Take a seat.' Greg pointed to what looked like a table covered with a large blue drop cloth, though it was, in fact, simply two desks jammed together. The damaged *Vostok* sat on top of it, surrounded by small tins of model paint, varnish, solvent, some fine-pointed paintbrushes, various cloths, and sandpaper. Seated and forced to look at the results of his earlier vandalism, the Delcade boy looked distinctly uncomfortable.

'You have your phone with you, I hope?'

'Yes, sir.' Chandler was unable to keep the surprise out of his voice. The use of phones was essentially forbidden at Calderhill Academy. Every classroom had a table where students had to deposit them for the duration of the lesson. For a teacher to *require* the use of a phone was a rare thing indeed.

'Good. I've emailed you the link to a how-to video. In this case, how to fix the damage you inflicted on my ships. You have everything you need right in front of you, so get to it.'

'Yes, sir.'

'And Chandler?'

'Yes, sir?'

'I'm sorry for your loss.'

'Thank you, sir.' Chandler pulled out his phone, looking appropriately intimidated by the nature of the task ahead of him. Greg had little doubt the boy would make a hash of the whole thing, and was resigned to sending his ships away for expensive restoration. But that wasn't the point. Chandler Delcade needed to understand how much damage he'd caused, how difficult it was going to be to put it right.

And that was just for what he'd done to the models.

'Sir?'

'Yes?'

'You've sent me two links.'

'Have I?'

'Yes, sir.'

'Hmmmm. Come show me.'

The boy approached, holding the phone in front of him as if it were a crucifix to Greg Abimbola's vampire.

'This one,' Greg said, barely looking at the screen, 'is the link to the video. And this one is about one of Pushkin's grandfathers. You've heard of Pushkin, of course.'

'N . . . no sir.'

'Only the greatest poet, playwright, and novelist who ever lived. Certainly up there with Shakespeare and –' Greg allowed himself an impish smile – 'Agatha Christie.'

'Agatha Christie, sir?' Chandler appeared to be very sure that Greg was pulling his leg, less sure about how to react.

Greg picked up the copy of *Desyat Negrityat* that was lying on his desk.

'Do you know who wrote this?'

Chandler's complete inability to read Cyrillic didn't stop him from hazarding a guess.

'Agatha Christie?'

'Exactly,' Greg said, smiling. 'This book alone has sold over a hundred million copies in any number of languages – including Russian. And it's been selling solidly, year after year, since 1939. That's a lot of years, Mr Delcade. In fact, the only author on the planet who's sold more than Agatha Christie is William Shakespeare – and he had a three-hundred-year head start.'

'Cool,' Chandler said. He was at least pretending to look impressed. 'But what about the Bible? I thought nothing beat that. At least, that's what my mom and dad say.' The boy's face clouded over. He was realizing, perhaps, that he could never say 'mom and dad' in the present tense ever again.

'The Bible sells more,' Greg agreed, gently. 'But it doesn't have a single author, like a William Shakespeare or Agatha Christie. It's more like a library of books, written by different people, hundreds and thousands of years apart.'

'God wrote the Bible.'

'People wrote the Bible, Chandler. Inspired by God, I'm sure. But I don't think God himself ever put pen to paper. I don't think

God has actual, you know, *hands.* Some of it is the word of God, and some of it is what the people who wrote it *say* is the word of God, which is not the same thing. It's what makes the Bible so tricky. You have to make some tough decisions about which parts of it you believe.'

The words twisted Greg's stomach into an unexpected knot. Was he trying to excuse his own degenerate urgings? He imagined the Devil whispering in his ear, the voice sweet and soothing, the gentle cadence of a therapist. *Ignore what that stupid old book says. It's all a lie, and you know it. The ravings of a bunch of prehistoric bigots. You can* feel *it, can't you? The dishonesty of it. The hypocrisy. What does God care about such things? God, who is so much bigger than your petty little world. Do what you feel. Be yourself. Your* true *self. Be free . . .*

He shepherded his mind onto greener, safer pastures.

'But we're not here to study the Bible, or William Shakespeare, or Agatha Christie – or even the great Alexander Sergeyevich Pushkin. In addition to fixing my ships, you will write fifteen hundred words on Abram Petrovich Gannibal, Pushkin's grandfather. Who he was, where he came from, and what he means to the world today.'

Chandler Delcade looked appalled. Sufficiently appalled to make Greg wonder if he was being too hard on the kid. And then, remembering what the boy had scrawled on the side of his ships, he pushed the thought aside.

'The link will get you started, Mr Delcade. You can hand it in by the end of the week.'

'Yes, sir.'

The boy lapsed into awkward silence. He sat down at the table, his head obscured by the *Vostok*'s high masts, and watched the video. Video complete, he started wiping the side of the vessel with a soft cloth, cleaning the surface before trying to fix it. The movements were surprisingly delicate. At least the boy seemed to be taking the task seriously.

Greg, making his way through the pages of *Desyat Negrityat,* kept a weather eye on Chandler's progress. The boy was pushing on, determined to get the damn thing over with, no doubt. He worked diligently, between bursts of texting, or whatever else teenagers did on their phones these days.

'Sir?'

'Yes?'

'I can't get the top off this paint tin.' The boy was holding the tiny can of modeler's paint between thumb and forefinger.

'Here, let me,' Greg said, getting up from his desk. He reached into his pocket for a penknife – a habit from his previous life that he'd never quite been able to shake. The blade made short work of the recalcitrant lid. The sweet, oily odor of modeler's paint wafted into his nostrils.

'Sir, can I ask you a question?'

'Sure.'

'Was Pushkin's grandfather . . . African American?' The boy's voice was hesitant, wary of causing further offense.

He'd been doing something more productive on his phone than texting, apparently.

'I don't think Abram Petrovich Gannibal ever lived in America, Chandler.' He said it kindly, though, pulling some of the sting.

'So he was . . . African?'

'Yes. An African who became Russian. And a pretty distinguished one at that.'

'I didn't know there were any . . . Black Russians.' He said the word 'Black' with the peculiar intonation of white Americans. Like he'd just stepped on a landmine.

Greg, thinking suddenly of the cocktail, gave the boy a quick grin.

'Not many. Not as many as there are here, for sure. But there are definitely a few.'

'Not a lot of people know that, I bet.'

'You got that right. Not even Russians.'

The boy grinned, bent his head down to the ship. Time slipped by in surprisingly good-natured silence, considering it was detention, and considering what the detention was for. Every time Greg glanced up from his book, he found the boy working diligently, tongue poking from his lips as he dabbed deftly at the *Vostok*'s sides. And then, minutes before detention was due to end for the day, Chandler raised his hand.

'Sir?'

'Yes?'

'I'm done.'

Greg swallowed back his surprise.

'Let's have a look, then, shall we?'

He strolled across to the table, its drop cloth now spattered with tiny flecks of paint. Bent down to examine the defiled side of the *Vostok*. Let out a low whistle.

'That, Mr Delcade, is very good work.'

'Thank you, sir.'

It really was. The boy had a knack – though whether for modeling or for following instructional videos to the letter, Greg couldn't be sure. Either way, you could no longer see the original damage. It wasn't good as new, but it was still pretty good.

'Do the same with the *Mirny* tomorrow and your debt to society will be paid. At least as far as detention is concerned. I still want the essay, though. Friday.'

To Greg's surprise, the boy looked disappointed.

'Why the long face? I thought you'd be happy to get out of here.' An ironic raising of the eyebrow. 'You can have detention all week if you'd rather.'

'Could I? Seriously?' The boy's eyes were sparkling with unshed tears.

Greg threw him an appraising look.

'Better here than home, eh?'

The boy nodded.

'Vicki's crying all the time, and Dad's just worried about politics, and people keep coming around asking how I am, which is like the most stupid question *ever*.'

'Then detention it is. Until the *Mirny* is fixed, or you want your freedom – whichever is later.'

The boy's unvarnished gratitude shone out of his face. Greg was slightly disturbed that Chandler Delcade viewed his classroom as some kind of haven. That he looked upon a teacher whom he'd racially insulted, and who had subsequently punished him, as a benefactor. Maybe it was *because* of those things that the boy felt safe here. There would be no cloying sympathy from Mr Abimbola. No pious pity. Just the banal normality of school.

'Seeing as you're going to be around for a while,' he said, 'let me ask you something. What's politics got to do with your mother's death?'

Chandler's expression darkened.

'Dad wants to run for congress. He's piss . . . he's worried that Mom's death will hurt his chances. He needs . . .' The boy struggled to find the correct words. 'Endorsements and donors. The dude spends every minute he's not at work whining and sucking up on the phone. He didn't even want me to get detention because he was worried there'd be a written record, and someone would leak it to the press. And at the funeral, he was like . . .' The words drained away. 'Whatever. It's all bull . . . It's not about Mom at all. It's just about him.'

He lapsed into sullen silence. Perhaps he was already regretting exchanging one type of intrusion for another.

'I'm sorry to hear that. Maybe it's just your dad's way of coping.'

'Yeah, right.'

'How're you getting home?' Greg asked, changing the subject. 'Or do you have sports today?'

'My aunt's picking me up. She'll text when she gets here.'

'Your dad's at work, I suppose?'

'Uh-huh. Dad leaves home early, around six, and he's never back till late, so Aunt Barb's been taking us to school and back – even though her car's like, tiny.'

Aunt Barb, it turned out, was extremely punctual. The boy's phone announced the arrival of her text message with a cheerful chirp, at precisely the moment detention was scheduled to end. Chandler grabbed his things and headed out the door, leaving it slightly ajar in his wake.

Greg stared after him for some minutes, lost in thought. Then, reaching a decision, he unhooked his coat from the door's lightly scuffed back and headed out.

05:52 P.M. EST

This, Greg decided morosely, had been a mistake. The snow was still coming down: tiny, innocent looking flakes that you could barely see. The sort that, unlike their bigger, flashier sisters, refused to melt when they hit the ground. The Mini Cooper slipped yet again on the churned gray carpet that constituted the surface of Sixth Avenue. Inching painfully downhill from Bigelow and into downtown Pittsburgh, Greg cursed under his breath. First in English, then in Russian, and finally, for good measure, French. Though why he bothered with the latter was a mystery, even to him. The French had many strengths. Swearing wasn't one of them.

Pittsburghers had to be the worst snow drivers Greg had ever seen. Worse even than the English, and that was saying something. Crawling along at a snail's pace and leaving at least two car lengths between themselves and the nearest vehicle, each block could only hold about a third of its usual volume of cars, with the inevitable result that downtown's narrow, utilitarian streets became gridlocked, choked by the non-existent traffic that failed to enter the capacious gaps between vehicles.

Greg, of course, was driving within a handful of feet of the car in front of him, hoping to shame others into driving more efficiently. It was a wasted effort. Realizing that he was not going to get where he was going on time otherwise and calculating that the Parking Authority's minions were tucked up out of the weather, he bounced the Mini Cooper onto the nearest sidewalk and abandoned it, running through the snow until he reached the chocolate-box façade of the Union Trust building. Rushing inside, Greg passed beneath the stunning Flemish–Gothic cupola without even an upward glance, so determined was he to gain the elevators before the six o'clock witching hour.

In the event, he made it through the heavy glass doors of Booth, Chanain and Hinkershil, LLP with just under a minute to spare.

The receptionist, who already had her coat on, stared at him with a mixture of disbelief and mild resentment.

'Can I help you? We're just about to close.'

'I'm here to see Bryan Delcade.' Snow was already beginning to melt off his boots and onto the deep green carpet.

'Do you have an appointment?'

'He'll see me. I teach his children.' Greg's voice had the vague air of someone who was distracted. Which he was. He was fiddling with his phone.

Hearing the word 'teach', the receptionist's expression softened considerably.

'Can I tell him what it's concerning?' she asked, stabbing at the keys of a complicated-looking telephone.

'It's a personal matter, not business.'

Greg smiled and glanced down at his boots. The carpet around his feet had turned almost black with damp. He shook the last of the flakes off his toecaps and onto the deep pile. The receptionist, meanwhile, appeared to have gotten through.

'Mr Delcade? I have a Mr . . .?'

'Abimbola.'

'A . . . Abimbo to see you.' There was a brief pause. The receptionist put down the phone. Seeing her expression, Greg fiddled once again with his cellphone.

'I'm afraid he's with a client right now. Perhaps I can make you an appointment?'

Greg smiled at her apologetically.

'I'm afraid you're going to have to call him back. Ask him to check his texts.'

'I don't think I can do that.'

'Trust me. If you *don't* do that, he's going to be very, very angry when he finds out.'

A flash of fear, almost unnoticeable and quickly suppressed, passed across the receptionist's face. A sure sign that Bryan Delcade was the sort of man who took out his displeasure on underlings. Wordlessly, she picked up the phone again.

'He's not answering.'

'Oh.' Greg was mildly surprised. 'Then I'll just wait.'

'You can't do that, sir. We're . . .'

'Greg! How nice to see you.'

Bryan Delcade walked into reception, immaculately dressed in a dark gray suit and brown shoes. The overhead lights, reflecting off the polished surface of his spectacles, made his blue-gray eyes impossible to read. He was, Greg saw, clutching tightly onto his cellphone. An even tighter smile played across his lips.

'Alicia?' he asked, turning to the receptionist. 'Is Conference Room A free?'

'Yes, it is. It's not booked out until tomorrow at two.'

'Great. Greg? If you'd follow me?'

The lawyer led him into a room immediately off reception. It had the same deep green carpet as the one he'd already stained with snow. The room itself was a modestly sized space furnished with a baroque-looking circular table – oak, at a guess – and swivel chairs upholstered in luxurious green leather. On one wall, ornate gothic windows looked out over what Greg took to be Grant Street: he could see the hideous brown cladding of the BNY Mellon Building on the other side of the road. The other three walls were floor-to-ceiling glass, one of which looked onto reception. He noticed Alicia, still in her coat, staring at them curiously from behind her desk.

Electric motors hummed suddenly to life. Beige blinds descended from recesses in the ceiling, blocking the view.

'Just what the fuck do you think you're playing at?' Delcade hissed. Hidden from Alicia's prying eyes, his fury was plain to see. Greg, as at their previous meeting, got the distinct impression that Bryan Delcade, Esq. would love nothing more than to beat him to a pulp.

Let him try. Greg had a sudden, vivid impression of Delcade writhing on the green-carpeted floor, clutching at a shattered windpipe.

As if reading his thoughts, the lawyer took a step back; made a massive, almost physical effort to calm himself.

'What's this about?' he asked, a little more quietly. 'You want money, is that it?' He sat down heavily in one of the green leather swivel chairs. 'I don't have as much as some people seem to think.'

Greg did not sit. The beige blinds had not come down over the Gothic windows. He wandered across to them, curious, and looked out. It was, indeed, Grant Street. And it was still snowing. Small piles of white had built up on the other side of the glass. Curiosity satisfied, he turned back to face the lawyer.

'I'm not here for money, Mr Delcade. Though I trust you won't be taking steps to damage the careers of anyone else on the Calderhill faculty?'

Delcade nodded, looking distinctly relieved.

'If that's the price to have this picture destroyed, then we have a deal.'

'I don't need a deal – and I'm not destroying the picture.' Greg pulled out his phone, examining the text he'd sent Delcade from the lobby of his own law firm. It was little more than the picture he'd unthinkingly snapped in that Southside bar. Delcade consorting with a young man. The young man, intense and smooth-skinned, with gelled hair and immaculately manicured hands. The lawyer, greedy for the young man's attention, sleek and attractive in his own right, his hair just so. Lithe, well-maintained muscles straining against an expensive shirt. Although taken on the fly, there was something subtly erotic about the picture's composition. The way the two men leaned into each other as they kissed, the casual beauty of their bodies, the warm framing provided by the wood and leather booth. He looked at it longer than he should have.

'I don't need a deal because I already have you over a barrel,' Greg said, at last. 'You'll stop fucking with people's careers, because if you don't, this picture will pretty much sink any hopes you have of a political future. Though, God help me, I think the voters of Western PA can do better. Do you understand me?'

'I didn't grow up in the fucking ghetto. There's no need to assume I'm stupid.'

'It never occurred to me that you grew up in the ghetto, Mr Delcade. You lack the skills. But, no worries. All I want from you today is the answers to some questions.'

Delcade looked at him warily.

'Questions about what?'

'About why you were parked down the street from Calderhill Academy the night your wife died.'

'I don't know what you're talking about.'

Greg stuck a hand into his coat pocket and fished out a photocopy of the parking ticket.

'You should be more careful about where you litter – and with what. This little beauty –' he waved the photocopy in Delcade's direction – 'fell out of your pocket when you came to see me the other day. You couldn't be arsed to pick it up. I did. And it says quite clearly that you were parked on Joseph Monday night, at eight eleven p.m. Right around the time your wife was being murdered.'

Delcade jumped to his feet. Greg tensed, certain this time that the man was going to take a run at him.

He needn't have worried. Delcade was pacing up and down, from one blind-covered glass wall to another, his rapid footsteps soundless on the deep green carpet.

'I didn't kill my wife,' he muttered. 'I didn't.'

'Fine. What were you doing?'

Delcade didn't answer. He just kept pacing. A caged animal. Greg leaned against the Gothic windows and waited. Despite the muffling effect of the snow, a faint rumble of traffic could be heard through the glass.

Eventually, after what seemed like an eternity, the pacing stopped. Delcade slumped back into the green leather swivel chair, apparently exhausted.

'I was seeing someone.'

'Who?'

'Does it matter? Someone not my wife.'

'Man or woman?'

There was a long pause.

'A man.' Delcade let out a long, confessional sigh. 'We've been seeing each other, on and off, since college.'

'So not the young man in the picture?'

'No. And fuck you,' he added, seeing Greg's expression. 'It's not an exclusive relationship. He's married, for a start.'

'So this married . . . *homosexual* is your alibi?' The word, spoken aloud, churned up something uncomfortable in the pit of his stomach. Something complicated. Poisonous. Disgust mixed with a sense of connection. A mirror held up to something he didn't want to look at.

'Yes,' Delcade confirmed, dragging Greg away from his confusion.

'And does this person have a name?'

'Not one I'm prepared to tell you.'

'It wouldn't take much to ruin your life, I don't suppose.' Greg pulled out his phone again, looked at it speculatively, fingers poised over the screen. Delcade licked his lips, suddenly apprehensive.

'Look. Even if I wanted to kill my wife – which I didn't – why the fuck would I kill her at the goddamn school? How could I even get in there?'

'Your wife did.'

'And I have no clue how she managed it!' Delcade's voice vibrated with exasperation. So much so that Greg almost believed him.

Almost.

'Or maybe, because you were already tailing her, you saw how she got inside and just followed her in. Good a place as any to kill a wife, I suppose. Why else would you be parked outside the school on a Monday night?'

'I told you, already. I was seeing someone.'

'Yes, you did. So who was it?'

Delcade reverted to tight-lipped silence. Greg turned back to his phone.

'Look,' Delcade interjected. 'Let's make a deal.'

'I don't like repeating myself, Mr Delcade. There's no deal you can make that would be of any interest to me. Tell me who you were with Monday night.'

'Hear me out, OK? Just hear me out.' The lawyer plunged on without waiting for an answer. 'If I tell you who it is, it isn't just my life you'll ruin, it's someone else's. And someone else's family. The guy I'm seeing may not be happily married, but his wife is. They have children: two daughters and a young son. If this gets out, it'll break their hearts.'

'Maybe you should have thought of that before you slept with him,' Greg said, even more roughly than he'd intended. The lawyer's words were making him uncomfortable.

'Yeah, maybe I should have, but I didn't, and the fact remains that you're asking me to throw four innocent people to the wolves. And all because you mistakenly think I murdered my wife.' He smiled thinly in Greg's direction. 'So here's the deal. If you can answer one question – just one – I'll tell you who I was with. And if you can't, you let this go. Agreed?'

Greg, imagining himself with a wife and kids of his own, said nothing.

'Great.' Delcade licked his lips, took a deep breath. 'Hypothetically, let's assume I followed my wife, intending to kill her. And let's assume that – somehow – I followed her in. Now, here's the question: who was she meeting?'

'I'm sorry?'

'Who was she meeting? She must have been meeting *somebody*. I mean, c'mon, why else was Lindsay there? She didn't get her kicks from wandering around empty buildings. Even you know that. So, whoever she was seeing would have either been there when I "killed" my wife, or would have discovered the body shortly thereafter, correct? In which case, why didn't they raise the alarm on Monday night?' He smiled in answer to his own question. 'Because *that's* the person who killed her. Not me.'

Greg stood quietly, then, thinking. Snow continued to fall into Grant Street. In the BNY Mellon Building, vague silhouettes could be seen moving past the windows.

'I'm told your wife went out most Mondays.'

Delcade let out a sigh of relief.

'She did, yeah.'

'And did she always take a rideshare?'

'Always.'

'Why?'

Delcade laughed, the sound guttural, devoid of humor.

'Because by the time she got home again she'd be in no fit state to drive. She'd either be tight, or high as a kite. Sometimes both.'

'Where'd she go?'

'No fucking clue. What she did on Mondays was her business, not mine.'

'And the same arrangement for you?'

'Not officially, but, you know, her being away for most of the evening allowed for, ah, *opportunities*, particularly now the kids are old enough to look after themselves.'

'And who did she see, do you know?'

'No, I don't. Girlfriends, I imagine.'

'Could she have been meeting a man?'

Delcade seemed to find the thought amusing.

'Maybe. But I doubt it.'

'Why?'

'Because she'd be too hammered to do it. Women don't usually get that drunk with men around, particularly if there's more going on than just dinner and a movie. Now and then? Sure. But this was a regular thing with Lindsay. She was night-out-with-the-girls drunk; not I've-just-been-laid drunk. There's a difference.'

Greg wasn't sure there was, but he let it slide.

'If she *had* been seeing another man, how would you have felt about that?'

'Relieved, actually, so long as she was discreet. Less pressure on me to . . . *perform*.'

Greg nodded. He stole one more glance at the rutted snow on Grant Street, the spaced-out traffic crawling toward the suburbs.

'Thank you, Mr Delcade. I imagine, given the time, you'll have to let me out of the office?'

Bryan Delcade did so. Opening the heavy glass doors with his keycard, he let them swing slowly shut behind Greg's back. They had not, however, completely closed when the lawyer spoke again. The words, not intended for Greg's ears, reached him anyway.

'Fucking nigger.'

Greg pressed the elevator call button as if nothing out of the ordinary had happened.

Because, in one sense at least, nothing had.

07:45 p.m. EST

'**M**y, aren't you punctual? I like that in a man.'
Emily Pasquarelli smiled up at him. Even under the too-bright lights of her apartment building's lobby, she looked gorgeous. Her strawberry blonde hair sparked with still-youthful iridescence. Underneath a brown, knee-length coat, she was wearing a belted sweater that stretched down over her slim hips. The sweater covered the top of dark, pleated pants that ran down to black, ankle length boots with soles serious enough to handle the heavy winter weather. Her brown leather gloves, expensively elegant as always, and complementary to the coat's slightly darker hue, were the lightest part of her ensemble, at least if you didn't count the small diamond earrings and matching necklace.

'You look terrific,' he said, and meant it.

'Thank you!' A small sigh. 'I really needed to hear that today.'

'Bad day at the office?'

'At home. Mom's been just . . . cranky. She's put her glasses down somewhere and lost them – and now she's accusing me of hiding them from her.'

'Are you?' Greg asked, deadpan. 'Because that would be, you know . . . *cruel.*'

They both chuckled.

'No, of course not. But the more she forgets things, the more paranoid she gets about it. She's just getting old, is all.' Emily peered past him into the darkness outside. 'Is it still snowing?' She wasn't wearing a hat.

'No. It's stopped, thank God. The roads are a bit dicey, but it's not like we're going far. Shall we?' He pointed to the Mini Cooper, which he'd parked right outside the lobby entrance. 'I'll do my level best to keep us safe, although it would help if the city would actually plow something now and then.'

Emily giggled. He opened the passenger door for her to get in. She slid in gracefully and Greg wondered if it would be possible to have a life with her. It was too late for kids, but he'd accepted that long ago. Someone like Emily by his side, and the Devil banished to a safe distance, would do just fine.

Or would he just drag her to hell with him? No one deserved that. As the Mini Cooper started up and slid out of the parking lot, he thought about Bryan Delcade and his sordid secrets. He wouldn't do that to anyone. And certainly not to Emily. But for being caught red-handed at her computer, he wouldn't even have asked her out. Drinks, dinner, and nothing more. It was safer that way.

Emily's apartment block was a modest, four-story affair in what was technically Shadyside, but felt more like studenty, neighboring Oakland. It was about a ten-minute drive from the school. Greg, though, drove in the opposite direction. He eased past the over-flowing dumpsters in the parking lot and out onto the streets, cutting across Bloomfield before climbing up and then down the perilously steep slopes that led to Lawrenceville and Butler Street. With the snow negligently unplowed, the road down was more like a ski run than an actual street, and the little Mini threatened to slip dangerously out of control. Greg, however, was well used to driving on snow and they made it down without incident. Leveling out on Butler Street, he parked right outside the wide, plate-glass windows of the Restaurant Alleghalto.

The Alleghalto was one of those slightly edgy American-cuisine restaurants, opened by an up-and-coming millennial chef for the benefit of up-and-coming millennial customers. Much to management's bewilderment, however, the actual clientele skewed significantly older; so much so that Greg and Emily were, if anything, a little on the young side. The two of them, having declined the use of a coat check, followed a smartly dressed maître d' with a heavily tattooed neck to a window table. Outside, flakes of snow were falling again, blurring the streetlights. Emily draped her coat over the back of her chair. Creature of habit that she was, she placed her gloves to one side.

'I've always wanted to come here,' she said. 'Thanks so much for bringing me.'

'My pleasure.'

Their waiter, an enthusiastic woman by the name of Kelly, whose own tattoos ran the length of both forearms before disappearing under crisp white sleeves, guided them through an evening that, even if forced on Greg by circumstance, turned out to be a lot of fun. Emily

was good company, was well read, and had a steady supply of interesting stories. One of which explained something that had piqued
his curiosity ever since he'd observed her typing it out on her
keyboard: *Ba$ra01*, the password to her computer.

'I didn't know you were a vet,' Greg said, genuinely fascinated.
'How long were you in Iraq for?'

'Just the one tour. A lot of it doing liaison with the Brits.'

'My peeps? And how did you find them?'

'The Brits? I stepped off a C-one-thirty transport and there they
were.'

Greg chuckled.

'Seriously,' Emily went on, 'they were good people. Knew what
they were doing. But I swear to God –' she'd had a couple of
glasses of wine by now, otherwise Greg was pretty sure she'd
never have said it – 'they were the whitest army units I've ever
seen in my life.' She frowned in recollection. 'I loved Iraq – and
hated it. It's so different from here, so *old*. But totally screwed
up. And we didn't do them any favors. By the end, I realized I
didn't agree with the mission. I got out not long after. Had Scott.'

'Your son?'

'Yes. It didn't work out with his father, but I wouldn't give
Scott up for the world.' Her eyes sparkled in the Alleghalto's soft
light. 'I'm *so* proud of him.'

'Stayard is a big deal.'

'It is. But I'd be proud of him wherever he went. He's a good
kid. Kind.' Another frown. 'Not like me at all.'

'I don't believe that for a minute,' Greg said, gallantly.

'Believe it. I can be quite difficult to live with, apparently.' She
pointed to her leather gloves with a wry smile. 'Too army. A place
for everything, and everything in its place. My ex found it . . .
oppressive.'

'I'm a bit of neatnik myself,' Greg confessed. 'Tidy is *good*. It
makes the world easier to deal with.'

Emily smiled at him then, looking strangely relieved. She raised
a nearly empty wineglass.

'Here's to neatniks.'

'Hear, hear.' Greg topped her up.

'And what about you?' she asked. 'Any children?'

Greg shook his head, ignoring the small swirl of regret in the
pit of his stomach.

'Never found the time – or the right person.'

'Siblings?'

'No. Just me.' A small hesitation. 'My father left us when I was very little. I don't really remember him, to be honest. It was just me and my mum after that. She never married. I think, after my father, she was damaged goods.'

Emily looked horrified.

Greg grinned at her, trying to lighten the load.

'Don't worry about my mum, Emily. She's a very strong, upbeat person. Happy. You'd like her. She's a professor – *was,* I mean. She's retired now. Taught foreign languages at university.'

'Russian?'

English.

'She taught me all the Russian I know.'

'Wow. I'd love to speak a foreign language. It's so . . . so *glamorous.*' A small frown. 'But I'm just another of those ugly Americans who's too stupid and lazy to learn.'

Greg shook his head.

'You're not stupid – or lazy. But you already speak the one language everyone else wants to learn. It's hard to learn someone else's language when so many foreigners speak your own.' He leaned forward conspiratorially. 'You'd have to be a little twisted.'

'Like you?' Emily giggled.

'Like me.'

'Well then.' Emily raised her glass. 'I guess I'll have to settle for being a monolingual, hard-to-get-along-with neatnik.'

'I guess so.' Greg raised a glass in return. 'Though you can't be *that* hard to get along with. Sorry to speak ill of the dead, but how many other people could be friends with Lindsay Delcade?' Greg pulled a face. 'Demetrius couldn't stand her.'

'Yeah, well. Demetrius had good reason. She and Bryan really did a number on him.'

'Over Edgeworth, you mean?'

Emily looked at him in surprise.

'Exactamundo. When it came to Vicki, everything had to be perfect, and no teacher, least of all Demetrius, was going to get in the way of that. He needed to be taught a lesson, you see, so that Vicki could have the life that Lindsay never did. She was going to Stayard, and then Harvard Law, and then she was going to be a partner in some big-ass New York law firm – or maybe a congresswoman.'

'Vicki wants to be an actor. At least, that's what she told me.'

Emily chuckled.

'Not if Lindsay had anything to do with it. She thought it was way too insecure – and low rent. "I'm not having my daughter shacked up in some cockroach-infested attic, with a greasy-haired, loser boyfriend hoping for a *big break*".' Emily's imitation of Lindsay's harsh diction was spot on. She gave Greg a wry shake of the head. 'No way. Lindsay wanted her daughter in a big corner office with a Stayard diploma on the wall. *That's* why she kept freaking out about Vicki getting less than an A. It put Stayard at risk. You have *no* idea how many A grades she bullied out of people.'

'Really?' Despite himself, Greg was shocked.

'Really. Think about it. We're talking teachers here, not al-Qaeda. Once you've been on the wrong end of a Lindsay Delcade tongue-lashing, are you really going to put yourself in line for another one? And given how vindictive she can be, and how connected Bryan is, do you really want to put your career at risk the way Demetrius did? Or *you* for that matter.' Emily was looking at him shrewdly.

'Me?'

'I don't think telling you to "go teach in the ghetto" was a sign of Lindsay's affection.'

'You heard about that?' Greg asked, wryly.

'Certainly did. She was *livid* about that B. I don't think it was something she was going to let go.'

'Then I'm glad I didn't have to talk her down from her son's detention. If her husband's reaction was anything to go by, she'd have had me run out of town on a rail.'

Emily chuckled.

'I doubt you'd have had to worry about that. When it comes to school, it was Vicki that Lindsay really cared about – oh, she loved Chandler, don't get me wrong – but it was Vicki who was going to live the life she gave up when she married Bryan. She was *way* more invested in Vicki's education than her son's. Mind you, the father isn't someone you'd want to cross either. You be careful with him.'

'I will do my best.' Greg hesitated before adding, 'To be honest, it was a bit dispiriting to have him make light of what happened. I'd hoped for better, coming from a parent.'

'Well, good luck with that,' Emily snorted. 'The only thing Bryan Delcade cares about is Bryan Delcade. He's obsessed with making it in politics. From what I hear, he's got a good shot at it, too. But if what Chandler did ever leaked out, it would probably sink him. Not that his voters actually care about that stuff, but it's not a good look, you know?'

Greg nodded, swamped by a brief wave of depression before coming out the other side.

'It sounds like you're not one of Bryan Delcade's biggest fans.'

Emily shook her head. Took a large sip of wine.

'The guy's a shit. Always was. I never did see what Lindsay saw in him. Well . . . that's not true. She was very political, like him. The idea of being a congressman's wife really turned her on. It was the only reason they were together, in the end. He needed the family man image; she wanted to go to DC.'

'Not a happy marriage, then?'

'Once, maybe.' Emily leaned across the table, letting her hands rest on his. 'Between you and me, I think she'd had enough. Congress or not, I think she was ready to end it.'

Greg knew he should have pulled his hands away, but he didn't. He liked it too much. The humanity of it. The warmth.

'You two must have been very close for her to be telling you stuff like that.'

Tears sparkled in Emily's eyes. Greg found himself staring into them, unable to look away.

'We were. We really were.'

'But you're very different people.' The words came out more tentatively than he'd intended.

Emily looked at him quizzically.

'I mean you're . . . *you*,' he ventured, struggling to find the right words. 'Whereas Lindsay is . . . *was* a . . . a . . .'

'An angry, racist little bitch?' Emily finished for him. Her hands were still in his, warm and soft, her smile good humored and a little dreamy.

'Well . . . yes,' he agreed, relieved not to have caused offense.

'She wasn't always like that, at least, not that I remember. In high school she was one of those girls you wanted to be or wanted to be with. People were drawn to her – I know I was. She was smart, she was funny, and if you were her friend she could be very, very kind.' Emily's gaze became unfocused, drifting back across the years. 'I guess, even then, she had a sharp tongue. God help you if you *weren't* her friend and you got crossways with her. But I never noticed. We just got on really well. And when you have high school in common like that, you overlook . . . other things. Things that become more apparent as you get older.'

'Such as?'

'She was always super, *super* competitive, you know? And it didn't matter too much when she was winning – she was prom queen at high school, valedictorian, and got into a great college, so she had a pretty upbeat attitude about life. But life . . . life's more grinding than that, isn't it? The losses pile up as you get older. She married Bryan, gave up her career. Not that she thought it was a loss at the time. She was financially secure for the first time in her life, with a great-looking husband on his way to DC. But I think her world got very small – just Bryan and the kids, so every little thing became life or death. And somewhere along the way she stopped being so much fun.' Emily leaned forward, dropping her voice to a conspiratorial, slightly slurred, whisper. 'She just *hated* it that Scott got into Stayard. *Hated* it. 'Cause now Vicki had to get in as well or I'd somehow have beaten her. It was eating her alive.'

'She doesn't sound like much of a friend.'

Emily smiled wryly.

'Only a man would say that. Girl friends are . . . complicated. We're all frenemies at some level. But we need each other. We need the support. The love. Lindsay was always incredibly loyal. If you were in any kind of trouble, she would always have your back. And all that anger would be turned on whatever the problem was. She was kind of awesome that way.'

'Maybe that explains why she was always out on Monday nights.'

Emily looked at him sharply.

'What?'

'Monday nights. Bryan Delcade says that Monday night was girls' night.'

Emily was frowning now.

'I don't think that's right, Greg. *I'm* a girl friend, and I don't ever recall seeing Lindsay on a Monday night – not regularly, anyway. Most of my evenings involve keeping an eye on my mother.'

'Maybe she had other friends?'

'I guess. I think she has a sorority sister in town somewhere, but I don't think she has a ton of friends here. Her old high school buddies are either out of town or she fell out with them – and her college friends are almost all in New York and DC.'

'She has newer friends, surely?'

Emily shook her head.

'I don't think so.' Greg must have looked skeptical because she felt compelled to add, 'Women aren't like guys. Guys make new friends all the time. Women aren't like that. It's one thing to know someone from high school or college and stay close to them. It's totally different when you're older. When you get older, it's more difficult. It's harder to form that bond of trust, you know? No shared history: no mutual screw-ups, no calling each other at two a.m. because some boy's broken your heart and you'll never make it to morning. Plus, grown-up Lindsay was definitely an acquired taste.' Emily's smile returned. 'Honestly, if I'd met Lindsay for the first time a few weeks ago, I don't think we'd have hit it off. Like you said, we're both very different people. *Were* very different,' she corrected herself. And then, suddenly and without warning, tears bubbled to the surface, threatening to streak her make-up. 'I'm sorry,' she sniffled, reaching into her purse for a tissue. 'Here you are taking me to this wonderful place and all I can do is cry.'

'Don't worry about it,' Greg said. 'Losing a friend is hard. Always.'

He signaled the waitress for the check. Emily looked up at him, her face thoughtful.

'You know, Greg, Lindsay was a good-looking woman. If she was out every Monday like you say, I'd bet you money she was seeing someone.'

'You think so?'

'For sure. It makes sense. I'm certain she didn't have another gal pal. Has to be a guy.'

'Did she ever mention one to you?'

'No. But she might have been working up to it. Like I said, I got the distinct impression she was about done with Bryan.'

The check arrived, putting an end to Emily's speculations.

'Thank you for this, Greg. It's been wonderful.' She pulled on her coat in anticipation of departure. Then her gloves.

'Ow!'

'Something wrong?'

'Oh, it's nothing.' Emily looked slightly embarrassed. 'I just snagged my wrist on a stupid bit of plastic. Should have cut the damn thing off already.'

She showed Greg the translucent little loop. Presumably, it had once had a price tag attached to it. Greg dug deep into the pocket of his coat and pulled out his penknife.

'Allow me,' he said. A quick snip with the penknife's little scissors and the plastic loop was no more, lying broken on the tablecloth.

'You're a useful guy to have around,' Emily said, smiling. Whether the wine had made her genuinely unsteady on her feet or not, she contrived to lean against him. Her body was warm under his arm, the faint hint of perfume caressing his nostrils. 'I think you should take me home.'

And Greg did. He stepped out of the car, opened the door for her, and escorted her to the entrance of the building. Light from the lobby spilled out into the night and bounced off the snow, bathing Emily in a soft glow that made her look almost ethereal. She held him by both hands, her chin tilted up to face him, her eyes wide and sparkling.

'I'd invite you up,' she said, in a breathy whisper, 'but my mother . . .' An apologetic shrug. 'You know how it is.'

'I do,' Greg said. He bent down to kiss her, but only on the cheek, missing her expectant mouth. 'See you tomorrow,' he said, ignoring the disappointed look on her face. 'Have a good rest of the evening.'

He turned on his heel and was gone. He didn't look back once.

10:37 P.M. EST

Morosov hated surveillance. Always had, always would. He was not a patient man. The prospect of having to wait all night to lay eyes on the man calling himself Gregory Abimbola vexed him almost beyond measure.

It shouldn't have been this way, he thought, gritting his teeth in frustration. But nothing, absolutely nothing, in the previous twelve hours had gone as planned.

He'd spent the night holed up in the faded magnificence of the Omni William Penn hotel, his sleep shallow and easily interrupted due to jet lag. He'd risen the next morning utterly unrefreshed, and well aware that the slightest setback would blacken his mood irreversibly.

The setbacks weren't long in coming. An apologetic text from Dianna informed him that she was too sick to work that day, and that she wasn't checking messages. So his overnight voicemail asking her to arrange a rental car for him was still sitting in her inbox. And then it turned out that finding a rental car with the heavily tinted windows he wanted was not as easy as he'd thought. It was beyond the ability of the various sales clerks he tangled with on the phone; interactions that had not been helped by their apparent inability to understand his accent.

'We don't keep information about tinted windows,' had been a typical response.

'Is easy. Go outside. You check. Come back. Tell me, yes?'

'I'm afraid that won't be possible, sir.'

By the time he'd secured a suitable car, a Hyundai sedan completely devoid of character, it was already mid-morning. Morosov had then driven to Calderhill Academy, but his attempts at reconnaissance had been stymied by geography and chaos. The school, he discovered, had three entrances, a main one at the front and two at the back. Opting for the main entrance as the most likely place to pick up his target, Morosov had been unable to find a good vantage point. Parking directly across the street was illegal, and the closest he could manage was over a hundred meters distant. The telephoto lens on his camera made short work of the gap, but the angle was bad. And when school let out a little after three o'clock, the mass comings and goings of parents, children and their attendant vehicles made it impossible for Morosov to cover everybody. If the man Morosov believed was calling himself Greg Abimbola had left school by way of Calderhill Academy's broad front steps, then he, Mikhail Sergeevich Morosov, had missed him.

Morosov had then driven along snow-choked streets to Parkside Hill, hoping to acquire the target at his home. He soon discovered that Parkside Hill – like every other street in Pittsburgh, it seemed – was an actual hill, and a ferociously steep one at that. Patches of cobbled brick bled red through slushy ruts in the road as he urged his reluctant car forward. The street serpentined as it went, leaving only a limited number of spots with a good view of number 236, all of which were occupied.

Afraid that his quarry might spot him if he kept passing by looking for a parking space, Morosov returned only intermittently. It was almost eight p.m. before he finally found what he was looking for, a stretch of curb perhaps thirty meters from the front door to the building, a shabby row house long since converted into apartments. If Greg Abimbola had settled in for the night, Morosov had no chance of picking him up before morning. He settled deeper into his seat, scratching irritably at the back of his neck, and waited. Flurries of snow continued to come down, forcing him to use the windshield wipers to clear a view. With the engine silent, the interior of the car quickly chilled to freezing. Morosov didn't mind. He liked the cold. A refreshing change from London's insipid winters. He stared out into the snowflaked night, letting his mind drift.

Termites.

Greedy, unseen fuckers, gnawing and gnawing away until the chair had lost its integrity. Any other fucking chair and none of it would have happened. But they'd tied the man calling himself Gregory Abimbola to a chair eaten hollow by the little bastards. It had collapsed, catching everybody by surprise except the man himself. He remembered the giant African moth swinging around the bare, overhead light; the burning smell of spilled acid; and Polukhin's face, comical in its dropped jaw amazement, the last thing he saw before a hastily swung chair leg had smashed into his temple. The termites had left enough wood to knock him out cold. By the time he came to, the bastard *negr* was disappearing into the harbor, and from there into thin fucking air so far as GRU was concerned. Target presumed dead. Case closed. And a giant blot on his record.

Not Polukhin's, though. His boss, whose connections had protected him, simply climbed higher and higher in the organization. Not that Morosov minded – much. Polukhin was good for business. Had set him up in his security consultancy, ready to be called upon when needed.

Bright headlights were sweeping up the street from behind him, the glare bouncing off the wing mirror of his car. Moments later the vehicle responsible had slipped smoothly past. A Mini Cooper, absurdly tiny compared with the giant American automobiles jammed nose to tail against the winding curb.

And British.

Morosov sat upright in his seat. Reached for his camera.

The Mini Cooper was slowing down, looking for somewhere to park. It passed the entrance to 236 and then, tiny as it was, it backed into a space its neighbors could not even imagine fitting into. The engine died, the lights vanished.

An elegant silhouette emerged onto the sidewalk, backlit by a distant streetlight.

It's him! Traitorous black bastard.

Morosov pulled the camera to his face, focusing on the figure walking toward him. Optimized as it now was for night shooting, the SLR had no trouble picking out the monkey's familiar, ridiculously handsome features. With a start of surprise he noticed the eye patch and grinned, remembering how the fucker had screamed when the first searing drops had hit his face.

Not so good looking now, are you?

He pressed the shutter, a whispered *click-click-click* as it stored irrefutable proof that the *negr* was alive.

The target had reached the entrance to his building, was fishing in his pockets, presumably for a key.

Goosebumps prickled on the back of Morosov's neck.

The shit was taking far too long. And he was standing at an angle to the front door. Enough so that he could see Morosov's vehicle without appearing to turn his head.

Moving very slowly, so as not to draw attention to himself, Morosov laid down the camera, moved his finger over the rental car's ignition button.

Hands thrust into the pockets of his coat, the target was moving away from his front door, strolling casually along the sidewalk in Morosov's direction. Morosov's breath moved quickly through a suddenly dry throat. This was America. It was entirely possible the *negr* was armed.

Morosov pushed on the ignition button. The car's engine rumbled into life. He turned on the indicators as if everything was normal, and pulled gently out into the street, careful to turn his head away as he passed through the monkey's one-eyed gaze. Within seconds, the cobbled contours of Parkside Hill moved him out of sight. Dimly lit buildings loomed above him on either side, the cracked wood of their windowsills freighted with snow.

'*Zhizn' ebet meya*!' he roared, pounding the rental's dash in frustration.

The traitorous fuck knew he was being watched.

11:10 P.M. EST

Greg Abimbola's mind was awhirl, bouncing between Emily Pasquarelli and the unknown car, refusing to let him sleep. He lay unhappily in bed, staring unseeingly into the darkness, his only illumination the glow from a digital clock and a wisp of stippled street light that had squeezed past the tightly drawn curtains.

He shouldn't have left her like that, he thought, with a quick kiss on the cheek and a rapid departure. She deserved better – and certainly not to be left with the feeling that the evening had been a failure, that maybe *she* had been a failure, when the problem was all him.

But what else could he do? Lead her on? That would have been far worse, surely, in the long run. But, then again, that only made sense if he didn't want to take it further. Emily Pasquarelli was beautiful, and clever, and funny. He enjoyed her company, and she clearly enjoyed his. There were worse things to build a relationship on. This was his life now: America, Pittsburgh, Calderhill. It would be infinitely more bearable if he had someone to share it with.

He tossed uncomfortably on a judgmental mattress.

Bearable for him, maybe. What about for her? What would happen if Emily wasn't enough, if the Devil somehow slipped through the keyhole and found a way into the blissful life he was imagining for them? He thought about Bryan Delcade, about the dark undercurrents that must have ripped at the roots of his marriage from the very beginning. Why would he put Emily, or anyone else for that matter, through that?

And there were things in his past worse than the Devil. Darker. More violent. Things that might, even now, be slinking toward the present. A sudden image of Emily, strawberry blonde, petite and beautiful, invaded his mind. She was stretched out on a suburban carpet, her neck casually broken. A lifelessly elegant porcelain doll.

He could do that to her, too.

His thoughts turned reluctantly to the car that was all wrong.

He'd almost missed it, distracted as he was by the way he'd left things with Emily. Only when he'd started to reach for his keys had he noticed that the car was different from its neighbors. Its roof and hood were covered in snow, as you would expect from any vehicle parked out in winter weather, but the windshield had been wiped clear. A clear windshield might make sense if the car had only just arrived. But, in that case, there would have been no snow on the hood: the heat from the engine would have melted it off. And if the engine was cold enough to allow snow to settle on the hood, the same snow should have settled on the windshield. Which basically left one alternative: someone was inside the car, staring through the windshield of a vehicle that had been parked up for hours.

He'd taken his time retrieving his keys, all the while looking at the vehicle for the slightest sign of life. He thought he might have seen a hint of movement, a barely visible glow, maybe from the screen of a digital SLR, but he couldn't be sure. He'd walked casually toward the automobile instead, hoping for a better look.

But then it had pulled away. Not in a panicky, I've-been-made manner, but the way someone might if they'd just got in and cleared the windshield to go somewhere normal and mundane.

He'd tried to get a look at the driver as the vehicle swept past, but the windows had been hard to see through and the occupant had averted their head. He was, however, able to get a look at the plates. Alabama. Either the driver was an unfeasibly long way from home or, far more likely, it was a rental. Who would pick up a rental, park it in an obscure part of town, and then drive off the moment he approached it?

He didn't care for the answer. This was Pittsburgh, Pennsylvania, not London, or Moscow, or DC. It shouldn't be happening here.

'Pittsburgh will be perfect,' they'd said. 'It has everything you'd want from a bigger city. Culture, sports, things to do, places to visit. Beautiful countryside, we're told. Plus, it has one other thing going for it, which is absolutely priceless.'

'And what's that?' he'd asked, listlessly. He'd been beyond bored, he remembered, rain pattering against Georgian windowpanes.

'No one'll think to look for you there in a million years.'

And they'd been right. He'd settled into a new life. Sedate, but safe, untroubled by anything from his past except nightmares, the only danger an irate parent who didn't care for his grading.

'Don't try and re-enter your old life,' they'd told him – repeatedly. 'That's how they'll acquire you.' Yet, driven by curiosity and, he needed to be honest with himself here, thrilled by the danger, he'd done precisely that. He'd known the risks when he'd reached out to TORquil, and he'd done it anyway.

And now the risks had been made manifest. In the form of a rental car from the Deep South.

With a sigh of resignation, Greg rolled out of bed and headed to the living room. If reaching out to TORquil was going to get him a bullet in the head, he might as well see what he was paying for. His hands glowed ghostly faint as he peered at the characters on his computer screen. It was a struggle to make sense of Lindsay Delcade's text messages. TORquil had managed to retrieve a good number of them, but their presentation left a lot to be desired, swamped as they were in a torrent of meaningless characters and symbols. Frowning, Greg tried to remember the word TORquil had once used to describe the sea of nonsense washing across his laptop.

Mojibake. That was it. Japanese, maybe. For character mutation.

Nevertheless, *mojibake* or no, the messages were in there somewhere. There were patterns to be discerned if you just looked hard enough. A whole word here, a predictable letter substitution there. Sleep was hours away. Time to do something useful.

Greg relaxed, letting the pixels float in front of him without making a conscious effort to read them, trusting his brain to pick out the patterns for him.

And it did. Step by slow, uneven step, Lindsay Delcade's texts revealed themselves. Arrangements made and remade with a pilates instructor. Cancellation of a piano lesson for Vicki. Orders to Chandler about being on time for something.

There were texts with Emily Pasquarelli, too. Coffee in Aspinwall, an art house movie in Sewickley, shopping at the Ross Park Mall.

And then, finally, an exchange with her husband. From Friday, the sixth, three days before her murder.

I checked with the bank. Not there. Where is it?
1:22 PM

> Not coming. I told you. 1:39 PM

WTF? You said you would fix! 1:40 PM
> I said I would TRY. Not possible. Sorry. 1:51 PM

This is totally f***g unacceptable. Can we get by Monday? Monday is last possible day. After that too late!!!!!!!** 1:53 PM

> No. 2:00 PM

Not good enough. This is ALL your fault!!!!! Sort this by Monday or we are done!!!!!! 2:01 PM
> I can't. Not possible!!!!!! 2:02 PM

Find way. Speak to your so-called friends. But get it done. 2:02 PM

> I can't!!! 2:03 PM

You'd better. Otherwise I'm going to Channel 2 and you will be f***d!** 2:04 PM
> Do that and I will fucking kill you. I mean it. 2:05 PM

Maybe I'd be scared if you were a REAL man. Monday. Channel 2. Your choice. 2:06 PM

Greg Abimbola leaned back in his chair, staring into the darkness. Bryan Delcade had played him for a fool.

TUESDAY,
THE SEVENTEENTH
02:00 A.M. EST

'**A**llo?' Polukhin's voice, a little fainter than usual because of the encryption, sounded in Morosov's ear.

'*Da, zdravstvuyte*, Comrade General. It's Mikhail Sergeevich. Good morning. I have news.'

There was a pause on the other end of the line. Morosov imagined Polukhin closing the door to his office, or maybe lighting a cigarette before putting the mobile phone back to his ear.

'The line is secure?' he asked.

'Yes, Comrade General.'

'Then, please, Mikhail Sergeevich, tell me your news.'

'I've found Petrov. He's alive.'

The pause at the other end was even longer.

'You're certain?'

'Check your email.'

In distant Moscow, winter beating uselessly against the grimy windows of his office, Morosov had no doubt Polukhin was doing exactly that.

'*Nu ti dajosh*! How the *fuck* did you get this?'

'The picture is good, no? Bastard's lost an eye, too, so even better.'

'The picture is good, Mikhail Sergeevich, very good. So, where is he?'

'The line is secure, Comrade General. It's not *that* secure.'

Polukhin let loose a dry chuckle.

'Time was, Comrade, you would have provided the information without thought of reward.'

'Times change, Comrade General.'

'They do indeed. Ten thousand US for the location.'

Morosov just laughed.

'I've spent more than that just finding him. Half a million.'

'*US?*' Polukhin sounded outraged.

'Is there any other currency?'

'There are rubles. You take rubles.'

'I have no interest in *Derevianni rubli*. I'm only interested in dollars.'

'Petrov isn't worth dollars, never mind half a million of them.'

'Fuck you, Comrade General. Half a million is cheap and you know it. Do you not remember the networks he rolled up? The operations he compromised? The Americans saved their fucking elections!'

'Networks fail from time to time, as you very well know. As for operations, the Americans saved shit. They're at each other's throats over election fraud, so no harm there, eh? In any event, the little shit's not worth anything like as much as you say.'

'And Pavel? Is Pavel not worth as much as I say, either?'

Silence. For a moment, Morosov thought the line had gone dead.

'We don't know that Petrov had anything to do with that.'

'He had *everything* to do with it. Pavel *ran* those networks. You think his body turned up in Djibouti by coincidence?'

'I know he was your brother, Mikhail, but . . .'

'They cut his *balls* off, Comrade General. His balls! And they left him . . .'

'I know where they left him. I was there, remember?'

Another pause. Longer this time.

'If you want dollars, you can't have what you're asking. I have committees to answer to. Fucking *accountants*.' He practically spat out the word. Morosov thought he heard a little squeak, as if Polukhin was tipping back his chair. Morosov had seen him do it a million times. 'If you want that sort of money, you'll have to bring him in. Can you do that?'

'No. I don't have the resources.' Morosov hesitated before adding, 'Also, time is short. He may have seen me.'

'You fucking *Zjulik*! You want a fortune for nothing! Why should I pay you anything for this shit?'

'Because I found him when the whole fucking GRU gave him up for dead, that's why. Because I was the only one who cared enough about Pavel to chase the fucker down. Because the British made you their fucking bitches and you didn't even know it! You want Petrov, pay me. Otherwise, go fuck your own ass with a cactus.'

'You can't give me Petrov, you already told me that. And if he made you, he'll be gone long before I can put together an operation. So again, I ask you, what am I paying for?'

Morosov took a deep breath.

'We can finish him on site. Send a message. Get me a weapon and I'll do it myself.'

'You're not armed?' Polukhin sounded surprised. And then: 'You flew somewhere, yes? So not in Europe?'

'Not in Europe,' Morosov admitted, albeit reluctantly.

'No matter. We don't want bullets for this anyway. Too ambiguous. Anyone could have shot the fucker. Criminals. A jilted lover. Anyone. No! The world needs to know that it was *us,* the goddamned, fucking GRU. A message to the other traitors. They need to know that no matter how much protection our enemies promise, it will never be enough. Never.'

'What are you proposing?' Morosov asked, although he had a queasy feeling he already knew the answer.

'Novichok. The nerve agent. Made in Russia and *only* in Russia. This way, everyone will know it was us, even though we will deny everything. Western conspiracy, rogue terrorists, whatever. But the people who matter – MI5, CIA, their fucking traitor assets – *they* will know exactly who did this – and why. They'll be shitting in their boots.'

'The last time we did this, it didn't go so well,' Morosov reminded him.

'Salisbury? *Pah!* You will do better, yes? No fuck-ups.'

'No fuck-ups,' Morosov agreed. 'If you pay me.'

'You'll get your money. But half in rubles.' Anticipating Morosov's objection, Polukhin pushed on. 'It's the best I can do in the time available, Mikhail Sergeevich. There's no time to fuck about with accountants and committees. Petrov will become a ghost, and we may never reacquire him. Understand?'

'*Da,* Comrade General. But you pay the dollars into my account today. Rubles when the job's done.'

There was another long pause.

'Agreed,' Polukhin said at last. 'Now, where is our man?'

'The United States.'

'Care to be more specific?'

'No.'

A chuckle at the other end of the line.

'How quickly can you get yourself to Washington?'

'I can be there in less than ten hours.'

'Good. Plenty of time. Go to Washington, see Dmitri. Be there by noon, eastern. He'll have what you need.'

Morosov hung up. In his mind, he was already wearing a pair of heavy latex gloves, and the man calling himself Gregory Abimbola was frothing his life out on the floor.

05:56 A.M. EST

Fox Chapel, an endless wasteland of gigantic houses with no discernible center, provided many opportunities for surveillance. The roads were steep and gently curving with fat, grassed edges, many of which were overhung by mature, drooping trees considerably older than the suburb itself. In the pitch black of early morning, it was a simple thing to park unobtrusively and just watch. There were no sidewalks because no one walked, and the traffic, apart from rush hour, was desultory. If a passing driver paid any attention to Greg's darkened Mini Cooper, they would assume that the owner had gone for a run along one of the various bucolic paths, or, if he was a real glutton for punishment, was riding a bike up some horrific, alpine-like grade. Covert observation would be the last thing on their mind. This was Fox Chapel. Apart from the oversized mansions, there was nothing even remotely interesting to look at.

Greg, irritable with lack of sleep and too angry to wait for another opportunity, was observing the entrance to a driveway. Surfaced in smooth asphalt, it poked through a low brick wall topped by immaculately coiffured hedges. In the winter dark, Greg's Mini Cooper, with its headlights off and in the deeper shadow of a bare-branched tree, was almost impossible to see. His view of the driveway, however, was unimpeded.

All of a sudden, beams of light were reaching out of the driveway and onto the road beyond, splashing everything they touched into sudden, vivid color.

Greg glanced at his watch. Almost exactly six o'clock. Chandler Delcade was right. His father was a creature of habit.

With the ease of someone who had done this sort of thing many times before, Greg gunned the Mini Cooper across the road. He barreled down the driveway in the opposite direction to the approaching vehicle, his headlights on high beam.

The sound of Delcade's horn was deafening. His car, a sleek BMW sedan, came to an abrupt stop, as did Greg.

Delcade was already out of his vehicle.

'What the fuck do you think you're doing?' he roared. He headed angrily toward the Mini Cooper, forced to squint against the glare of Greg's headlights. He was unable to see that Greg, too, had exited his vehicle.

Though, even if he had, he would have been unable to prevent Greg from seizing him by the lapels of his soft, cashmere coat, and slamming him backwards onto the hood of his own automobile.

'Stop! Wait . . .' The shift from fury to fear was almost instantaneous.

'You and I need to have a chat, you slimy piece of shit.' Greg pressed down hard, driving the lawyer's shoulders into the hood with so much force that the metal flexed. He could feel Delcade's body squirming beneath him, the heat of the man's breath against his face, arms spread uselessly to one side.

Something in his own body twitched, threatened to distract him.

'I already told you what you wanted to know!' Delcade screamed. 'Let me alone! We had a deal!'

'I never said we had a deal, you fuck. And even if we did, it's off. You told your wife you were going to kill her the Friday before she died.'

'Wait . . . what? I never . . .' His voice was cut off by the pressure of Greg's forearm against his throat. The lawyer's well-toned body was spread-eagled beneath him, wantonly angelic.

Blood was rushing below Greg's waist. He pressed harder.

'You texted your wife Friday afternoon. You told her: "I will fucking kill you. I mean it". Ring any bells?'

Delcade's body went limp, signaling surrender. Greg lifted his forearm but found himself still pressed against the man's thigh. He felt dizzy. Elated.

'How'd you know that?' Delcade gasped. 'No one knows that!'

'The police do. The only thing I don't understand is why they haven't hauled your arse into the station.'

'No, they *don't*. I deleted my texts. Lindsay's cell is password protected and they can't get in. Not yet, anyhow.'

Greg finally took a step back. The lawyer prised himself off the hood of his car, his coat and hair badly disheveled. He looked wildly beautiful, his skin glowing in the Mini Cooper's headlights.

'You deleted your texts?' Out of physical contact, the distraction started to ease. Greg heaved a soft sigh, unheard by the other man.

'Yes I did. How the hell . . .?'

'You threaten to kill your wife. She winds up dead. You delete the texts in which you threaten to kill your wife. Not a good look for you, I'm thinking. So, why, exactly, did you kill her?'

'I didn't kill her!'

'Do better. What were you fighting about?' Greg took a small, menacing step forward.

Pinned in the glare of halogens, Delcade looked, if anything, more frightened than when Greg had been at his throat.

'It's not relevant.'

'You said you'd kill your wife, and you put it in writing. You don't get to decide what's relevant anymore. Talk. Or I'm taking the texts to the police and you can—'

'No! Don't do that. Please. I can . . . I can explain.'

Greg sat on the hood of his Mini Cooper. To Delcade, blinded as he was by the high beams, he'd be little more than a menacing shadow. The lawyer's squinted eyes watered in the glare. He licked his lips. Opened his mouth once, and then twice. But, still, there were no words.

'I'm waiting, Mr Delcade.'

'This can't go any further, you understand?'

Greg said nothing.

'It was a row about money,' Delcade said, at last. 'A lot of money. Money I didn't have.'

'And what was the money for?'

'Vicki.' There was a long, anguished pause. 'To get her into Stayard.'

Greg fought to keep the surprise out of his voice.

'Stayard? How?'

Delcade mumbled something inaudible, shook his head.

'Talk, Delcade, before I start breaking fingers.'

Delcade shrank back against his car.

'Don't. Just don't.' He held up a placating hand. 'Give me a minute, OK?'

The lawyer took a series of long, deep breaths, trying to calm himself. It was the best part of a minute before he spoke again, his voice low and close to cracking.

'The dean of the faculty of Arts and Sciences, Johnathan Lorde,

is a classmate of Principal Ellis's. They go way back. As dean,
Lorde gets some discretionary picks as to who gets admitted. It's
a way to bring in kids who will do well at Stayard even if their
grades aren't the best.' He wiped at his mouth with a nervous
hand. 'Ellis and Dean Lorde have . . . an arrangement.'

'Which is what, exactly?' Greg had heard the name before.
Ellis's dinner partner the night Lindsay had been murdered.

'For a fee, Dean Lorde will exercise his discretion in favor of
a Calderhill student. Maybe one or two a year.'

'And how much is this "fee"?'

'Five hundred thousand dollars.'

'*What?*' The expostulation escaped into the air before Greg
could do anything about it.

'Oh, don't look so shocked,' Delcade fired back, nettled.
'Everybody does it.'

'I don't think they do.'

Delcade snorted with derision, looking more like his old self.

'You think all those buildings that go up on college campuses,
the donors who hand over all that money, are doing it just so they
can see their fucking names etched in limestone? You think they're
paying out of a love of learning, or a sense of – what – *gratitude*?
Give me a fucking break. They get favors, Abimbo: *influence.*

'A kid or a nephew who's dumb as a box of rocks suddenly finds
himself in a goddamn Ivy League dorm room. Some scrawny klutz
who couldn't pick up a javelin, never mind throw one, suddenly
gets a full-ride sports scholarship. It happens all the time. You don't
actually think that all those billionaire children, the senatorial spawn
at Stanford and Yale and Harvard, got there because they were at
the ninety-ninth percentile in *smarts*?'

The lawyer answered his own question with a short, cynical
laugh.

'Yeah, well, some of us can't afford a ten-million-dollar donation to get our kids into the Ivy League. Five hundred grand to a
college dean is a goddamn *bargain.*'

'But you didn't have it?'

'No,' Delcade agreed, ruefully.

'But Lindsay thought you did?'

'She wanted to go to Washington. She wanted to be the wife
of a congressman, and then senator, and then maybe even
goddamned president of the United fucking States. That costs

money. A lot of money. For favors, endorsements, a word in the right ear. And sometimes just to convince people that you have enough of your own resources to kickstart a campaign. She watched me spend it. She fucking well *encouraged* me to spend it. And it worked.' He held thumb and forefinger half an inch apart. 'We're this close to sealing the nomination.' Another laugh. Bitter. Disbelieving. 'And then the bitch is outraged when there isn't enough left for Vicki. Who doesn't even *want* to go to college!'

Greg let the lawyer's anger pass him by.

'And what was so important about that Monday? Why was Lindsay so insistent she have the money by then?'

'That was Ellis's deadline. If we couldn't raise the money by then, she and Lorde had another family lined up.' A twisted smile. 'The man didn't care which kids he waived in, so long as he was paid.'

Greg's mind drifted back to that Monday morning. Lindsay Delcade screaming at Principal Ellis. Principal Ellis trying to keep it civil.

They're not my rules, Ms Delcade. It's how this admission process works. The deadline's passed, I'm afraid. But next year is still a real possibility . . .

She'd been begging – or bullying – for more time to pay. And Ellis had said no.

'You know that Lindsay went to see Principal Ellis on Monday to ask for an extension?'

'Yeah. Lot of fucking good *that* did.'

'And she was furious, of course?'

'Of course.' A wry smile.

'Furious enough to out you?'

The smile disappeared.

'No. Lindsay said stuff like that all the time. She never followed through.'

'And yet you still felt the need to threaten her life?'

Delcade wiped his mouth again.

'I was angry, alright? I was tired and pissed. I'd had a long week, my weekend was shot because of fucking work, and Lindsay was dancing on my last nerve.' Struck by a sudden thought, he managed a small smile. 'And she knew I didn't mean it. If you've read our texts then you know she didn't take it seriously.' He looked upset again. 'She was laughing at me. She demeaned me.'

Maybe I'd be scared if you were a real man.

'Men have killed women for less, Mr Delcade.'

The lawyer looked like he'd been punched.

'But I didn't,' he said, pleading. 'I absolutely didn't.'

'So you keep saying . . . Who were you with that Monday night?'

'I can't . . .'

'*Who* were you with?'

'Corey McGill.' The voice was little more than a whisper.

The name rang a bell, but Greg couldn't quite place it.

'He's the deputy mayor. He lives on Joseph Avenue: four seventy-seven. His family was out for the evening. I went to see him. Left around nine.'

'And he'll confirm that?'

'I'm begging you, Greg. Don't do this. It'll ruin everything.'

The man was shaking.

The uncomfortable feeling that had surfaced in Delcade's office slithered suddenly back to life. A vile sense of connection. A mirror in the corner of his eye. One he wouldn't – couldn't – look at.

'I think,' Greg said, slowly, 'that you should tell the police. They already know you were parked illegally on Monday night. Sooner or later, they're going to get into your wife's phone. I'd get ahead of it if I were you.'

'They'll hang me out to dry.'

'You have an alibi, remember?'

Delcade's eyes were watering badly, and not just because of the glaring headlights.

'I can't tell them who I was with. I can't tell them I was with a . . . a *man*. It'll be the end of me.'

The thread of connection snapped.

'Then you'll be spending quite a bit of time with the sort of lawyer who doesn't practice out of swanky offices in the Union Trust building. Let me know how it goes.'

Greg Abimbola got back in his car and reversed out of Bryan Delcade's long, asphalted drive. The attorney just stood there, shoulders slumped; beautiful and stricken and starkly illuminated in the Mini Cooper's retreating beams.

06:38 A.M. EST

Greg made good time from Fox Chapel. The roads were mostly clear of traffic, and the snow of the past few days had melted off the roads, without, so far as he could tell, the slightest help from a snowplow. NPR chattered amiably in the background, having shifted from a perky description of the plight of Middle Eastern refugees, to an equally perky presentation on the merits of mashed-up insect larvae as a replacement for butter.

Greg listened to it all with only half an ear. Having crossed the Allegheny by way of the Highland Park Bridge, he'd climbed up from the river, down into Bloomfield, crossed over to Shadyside, and was now moving smoothly up the steep gradient of Joseph Avenue on his way to school. He had a vague plan about taking a quick nap in the early-morning quiet of his class-room, but he was mostly fixated on Lindsay Delcade. How had she gotten into the custodian's room? Someone must have let her in, which, reluctant as he was to admit it, continued to rule out her shit of a husband, alibi or not. But, of those who did have keys, Andrea had left the building shortly before Lindsay even arrived, and Ellis and Emily were long gone, one to dinner, the other to home, with no possible reason to come skulking back to the custodian's room. And there was no sensible scenario in which Demetrius Freedman, who *was* there, could have persuaded Lindsay to meet him in the school basement. She couldn't stand the man. And if she *had* wanted to meet him, she would surely have marched up to the front entrance and demanded his presence from the security guard.

Beyond that, what had made Lindsay Delcade change her Monday night routine and go to Calderhill in the first place? A grungy janitor's lounge was neither the place for a girls' night out, nor a suitable tryst for a man on the side. For a brief, disorienting moment, Greg entertained the possibility that Demetrius Freedman *was* the man on the side, but then rejected it. Demetrius was militantly African American. The idea that he would have relations with a racist or near racist like Lindsay Delcade was absurd.

Or was it? Greg scratched at his eye patch. Maybe, like Bryan Delcade, Demetrius had a secret side to his sexuality, something he was ashamed of. Something completely antithetical to his public persona. And once he got involved with someone like Lindsay, it was all too easy to imagine her pushing him over the edge . . .

'This is ridiculous!' Greg muttered. He pounded out his frustration on the thick padding of the Mini Cooper's steering wheel. Everywhere his mind turned, it lost traction, skidding into a brick wall of internal contradictions and missing information. *Someone* had killed Lindsay Delcade. And yet no one *could* have. He couldn't shake the feeling he was overlooking something right in front of his face, that he was just too stupid to see.

Also, too stupid to tell the time. He stole a quick glance at the dashboard clock. Stacey wouldn't open the front entrance until seven a.m., almost twenty minutes away. No wonder the road was so empty. He crested the top of the hill and headed down toward the school, picking the closest of the available free parking spaces. As he got out of the car, he heard a familiar roar coming up the road behind him.

A decrepit, burnt orange Chevy pulled up alongside. The driver lowered their window, grinning.

'Good morning, Mr Bimbo!' said Andrea Velasquez. 'Early for you, yeah? What's the matter, couldn't sleep?'

'Something like that,' Greg replied, drily. 'And why are you here? I thought you were suspended.'

Andrea's cheerful façade crumbled away.

'I am,' she admitted. She looked at him, suddenly worried. 'You won't tell on me, will you? I need my college books. Thought I'd sneak in before anyone got here.'

Greg smiled at her reassuringly, grateful to make small amends for bringing the subject up in the first place.

'Me?' He pointed playfully at himself. 'No way, lady. I ain't no snitch. But on one condition. You bring me in with you. It's *way* too early for Stacey.'

Andrea grinned at that.

'Deal,' she said.

Once she'd parked, the two of them made their way into Dean Close. Approaching the loading bay, Greg noticed that the overflow from the dumpsters was threatening to block vehicular access. It was a good thing the strike was over, he told himself, because there was no way the school could have handled a second week.

He glanced up at the security camera, apparently all-seeing, but blind where it really mattered. A rime of icy snow clung to its housing. The piece of packing case that he'd used to jump down from the ledge the previous Saturday was still there, like a make-shift step.

Greg stopped, staring up at the camera, his face blank.

'What?' Andrea prompted.

'Look at that,' Greg said, pointing. 'What do you see?'

'Well, *duh*. A security camera.'

Somewhere in the depths of Greg's coat, his cellphone was ringing. He let it go to voicemail.

'Right,' he agreed. 'A security camera. You can't miss it. Half the point of a security camera is that people know it's there. Just knowing about it *discourages* people from trying to sneak in. Because they know they'll be seen.'

'But they *weren't* seen,' Andrea pointed out.

'That's exactly my point. Think about it. Before anyone could let Lindsay Delcade into the school, she managed to reach the custodian's room door without a single pixel of her hitting the security footage. Which means she must have *already known* that the security camera, even though it's pointing right this way, couldn't see her. Which means someone must have told her. There's no way to tell just by looking at it.'

'OK, but why? And who? It still don't make no sense.'

Greg sighed.

'You've got that right, Ms Velasquez. In spades.' He followed the junior custodian deeper into the loading bay, and then up the steps to the gray metal door. Andrea's key rattled in the lock. As before, Greg was expecting the slow creaking of a horror movie, but the door swung open smoothly and silently on well-lubricated hinges.

'I won't be a minute,' Andrea said. She strode across the room to where the custodian's television sat atop the rickety old book-case. She crouched down to retrieve her textbooks. Greg closed the big metal door behind them. As he did so, something caught his eye.

'Andrea?'

'Yeah?' She was still fixated on the shelves.

'Where's your key?'

'In my pocket. Where else would it be?'

'Up there.' Greg was pointing at the nail by the door. As there had been since Vern Szymanski cleaned up after the police, two keys nestled against each other: mute, and metal, and heavy. 'I thought one of them was yours.'

'No way, man.' Andrea stood up and turned around, a pair of IT textbooks tucked under one arm. She patted a pocket with her free hand. 'My key's right here.'

'But on Saturday,' Greg protested, 'when we came down here, you opened the door with one of those.' He was pointing at the nail again.

'Sure I did. It was *Saturday*. I didn't have my own key on me. I used the spare.'

Greg scratched at his eye patch, frowning.

'Right. *The* spare. Not *spares*, plural. When I came down here the day after the murder, there was only one key on that hook. Then Vern found another one, in a bucket of bits and pieces, which he said was yours—'

'But it isn't.'

'—and put it on the hook with the "real" spare. Which begs the question . . .'

'Whose key is it?'

'Exactly.'

Andrea shrugged her shoulders.

'Maybe it's no one's. Maybe it's just—'

'*Zhizn' ebet meya!*'

Greg felt slightly nauseous, as if the ground was shifting, making him seasick.

'What the hell does that mean?'

'It means I think I know who did it.' The words were little more than a whisper, squeezed from between dry, cracking lips. And even though he'd said the words out loud, they still didn't feel real. More like a dream – or a vodka-fueled fantasy. And maybe, just maybe, Greg thought, he was wrong.

Except he knew, with absolute certainty, that he wasn't.

'So, who is it?' Andrea was hopping up and down with barely contained excitement.

Greg didn't answer. He was staring through the thick panes of the glass-brick window. Dim light seeped through it from the loading bay.

'Mr Bimbo! Who is it?'

'What?'

'Who. The fuck. Did this?'

'If I tell you, you have to help me out with something unpleasant.' He looked at his watch. 'We might not have a lot of time.'

'Sure. What is it?'

'You need to go dumpster diving. There's a lot of stuff to go through before the garbage trucks get here.' Seeing the look on her face, he broke into a wry smile. 'No take-backsies.'

The cellphone in his pocket rang again. This time, more to keep Andrea in suspense than for any other reason, he took the call.

'Hello?'

'Gregory? It's Father Kyriakos. Good morning. How are you today?'

'Good morning, Father.' Greg could feel his eyebrows arching into his forehead. Andrea Velasquez, meanwhile, was looking at him with a curiosity that had nothing to do with the identity of Lindsay Delcade's killer. He pointedly ignored her. 'What can I do for you?'

'Sorry to call at this time of the morning, but I know you're an early riser, and I hadn't heard anything, so I thought I'd call to see if I could perhaps talk you through a few things, you understand, with time being so short.'

'Slow down, Father,' Greg said, smiling. 'You're going to need to start at the beginning. I have no idea what you're talking about.'

'I'm talking about your cousin, Viktor – and your mother, of course.'

'My cousin?' There was nothing he could do to stop the blood draining from his face.

'Yes. He came to see me Sunday, with bad news about your mother.' There was a sudden, anxious, pause. 'He *did* find you, didn't he? I hope I haven't just put my foot in it. These things are too delicate for the phone. If I've spoken out of—'

'No worries,' Greg interrupted, smoothly. His voice betrayed no connection to the pounding in his chest. 'Viktor found me. But he didn't tell me he'd been to see *you*. What did he tell you about our situation?'

Greg listened, expressionless, as Father Kyriakos relayed the

earlier conversation with his 'cousin'. When he was done, Greg
said, 'I have two cousins called Viktor, Father, both of whom came
to see me. But which one came to see you?'

'Two?' Father Kyriakos chuckled. 'This one was big, like a
bear. But not fat. A little over six foot, with brown hair and
a touch of gray. Nice man. Laughed a lot.'

Morosov.

'Thank you, Father.' It was all he could do to stop his hands
from shaking, to refrain from pacing back and forth across the
custodian's room like the trapped animal he was. Andrea, after
all, was still watching him.

'Gregory?'

'Yes, Father?'

'It's not for me to tell you what to do, but God will guide you
to the right decision if you'll let him.'

'Thank you, Father. I'll do that.'

He hung up.

'Something wrong?' Andrea asked. She seemed genuinely
concerned. Greg, despite himself, was touched.

'You could say that,' he replied. 'I need to make some calls.
And you, young lady, need to start looking in dumpsters.'

'And what am I looking for, exactly?'

Greg told her. Then, unable to minimize his distraction any
further, he pulled out his cellphone and marched out of the room.

'Hey, wait!' Andrea called after him. 'You still haven't told me
who . . .'

But it was too late.

11:10 A.M. EST

When Colonel General Polukhin had told Morosov to 'see Dmitri' he did not intend for Morosov to do any such thing, and Morosov knew it. Arriving at Reagan National on the first direct flight of the morning, Morosov had taken three different cabs to various parts of Washington DC, before taking a fourth taxi across the Potomac to Alexandria, Virginia. Morosov, who'd spent a modest amount of his career in the DC area, still had trouble getting his head around the idea that Alexandria was a separate city, in a separate state. It looked and felt like little more than one of Washington's upscale local neighborhoods. In the absence of DC's traffic jams, it was only a fifteen-minute ride from Capitol Hill. It was like driving to Khamovniki District from the Kremlin, or to Soho from the Houses of Parliament. For Alexandria to be its own city was, quite simply, ridiculous.

Someone had once told Morosov that for most of the American Civil War, Confederate soldiers had occupied Alexandria, unable to push on into the capital, but apparently safe from the depredations of Union forces. It must have taken a spectacular level of incompetence to arrive at such a state of affairs, Morosov thought. Unfortunately for Russia, America's armed forces had improved quite a lot since then.

It was this chain of thinking that brought a wry smile to Morosov's lips as he got out of the cab. He was a couple of blocks short of his intended destination, a UPS store on Pendleton. It was a fine, crisp day, and Morosov left his coat open to the weather as he strode along the sidewalk. He was careful, however, to put on a pair of gloves. A gentle breeze caused the coat to billow like a cape as he walked.

Stepping in from the outside, the interior of the UPS store felt warm and stuffy. Overhead fluorescents gave the corporate-beige color scheme a washed-out pallor.

'Can I help you?' The woman at the desk was young and black, with loud pink hair extensions.

'I wish to make complaint,' Morosov announced. 'Where is manager?'

'Lou!' the woman called.

A stooped old man appeared from the back of the store.

'What seems to be the problem?' he asked.

'I send package to my niece in Buenos Aires from this store. It not arrive.'

'I am so sorry to hear that,' the old man said, though he didn't look sorry at all. He was staring intently at Morosov's face. 'What was your niece's name?'

'Silvia Delmuro. She live at Agustín Caffarena One, La Boca.'

A slight pause.

'I see. I seem to remember there was a problem with the labeling. Wait one moment.'

He disappeared to the back of the store, returning with a small parcel.

'Here it is. I'm afraid we don't deliver to this address. Someone should have told you at the time. I'm very sorry.'

'Sorry heal no hurt. Now I have make other arrangement.' He took the package from the old man with apparent ill grace and stepped out into the fresh air. Turning it over in gloved hands, he checked the package showed no signs of leaking. Satisfied, he walked all the way to City Hall before picking up the first of three cabs back to the airport.

Once back at Reagan, he ducked into a men's restroom. Still wearing gloves, he opened up the package. Inside was a much smaller box, commercially labeled as a bottle of contact lens solution. Hampered by his gloved hands, Morosov opened up the smaller box and peered inside. Sure enough, the contents appeared to match the labeling: a small bottle of contact lens solution, complete with a trademarked logo and directions for use.

Discarding the packaging, Morosov placed the bottle back in its box, placed the box in his pocket, and headed for security. The screening line was short. When he got to the front, Morosov placed the novichok into a plastic security dish, together with his watch, phone, and wallet, and placed the dish onto the conveyor belt for X-ray scanning. He watched with satisfaction as the nerve agent passed through without incident. He stepped into the people scanner, only to be met by an annoying beeping sound.

'Random check,' the TSA officer informed him. He was a tall, black man, his dark-blue shirt immaculately pressed. 'If you'll step this way, sir.'

Morosov had no choice but to do as instructed. He extended his arms while the officer scanned him with a wand, and then submitted to the minor indignity of having his hands swabbed for traces of explosive.

'Just one moment.' With an apologetic smile, the TSA officer placed the swab into a machine for sampling. After a moment or two it emitted a strange buzzing sound. When the officer turned around, he was no longer smiling.

'The reading is positive, sir. You'll need to come with me.' Already, pursuant to some unseen signal, Morosov could see an armed police officer approaching. He fought to stay calm.

'There must be mistake,' he said, and immediately wished he'd kept his mouth shut. His heavy Russian accent was unlikely to endear him to an American security officer.

'The machine *does* make mistakes,' the officer agreed. His nametag identified him as 'Lewis'. 'But you'll still need to come with me. Are these yours, sir?' He was pointing at Morosov's coat, and the security dish with the novichok and his various belongings.

'Yes,' Morosov admitted. He was careful to keep his eyes on the coat, so that his gaze gave nothing away to the people watching him.

'Do you want to pick them up and come with me, sir.'

It took Morosov a moment to work out that it wasn't a question. He put on his coat and emptied out the security dish, casually dropping the novichok into his pocket.

'This way, please.'

With the police officer at a discreet distance, Morosov was led to a small interview room. A security camera stared down at him from the ceiling.

'OK, sir,' Officer Lewis said. 'You've tested positive for nitrates. I'm going to pat you down all over. Can you take your coat off please?'

No sooner had Morosov done so than Lewis handed the coat over to another TSA officer who had just entered the room. The man walked out with it.

'My coat . . .'

'We're just going to run some tests on it,' Lewis said. 'Can you turn around for me and put out your arms?'

Morosov endured the ensuing pat down. Lewis was nothing if not thorough.

'Now, sir. I'm going to swab your hands one more time and do a re-test. Have you been handling explosives?'

'No!' Morosov didn't have to fake the incredulous laugh that accompanied the statement.

'Have you used hand lotion today, anything like that?'

'Yes,' Morosov lied. Some hand lotions, he knew, contained glycerin, which produced the same chemical signature as actual explosives. 'Accident this morning. Top come off bottle. Lotion everywhere. Big mess.'

'I see. OK, wait here. I'll do a re-test and consult with my supervisor. I shouldn't be gone too long.'

Lewis left, leaving Morosov with only the security camera for company. Conscious that he was being watched, he played the part of the delayed but innocent passenger to perfection. Not calm, like a criminal accepting the game was up, and not wildly disturbed, like the same criminal desperately looking for a way out. Just agitated. Annoyed. Resentful of the bureaucracy. A businessman whose journey had been unnecessarily interrupted.

And he was, he reminded himself, actually innocent. He hadn't been touching explosives. There was nothing in his (admittedly false) background that would raise any red flags when TSA ran his name through their computers. In the end, he knew, the Americans would have to let him go.

Unless, of course, someone was stupid enough to break open the seal on a brand-new bottle of contact lens solution. The thought caused his fingers to beat out a brief but anxious tattoo on the interrogation room's desk.

In the end, they kept him for less than an hour. Officer Lewis returned with his coat and a broad smile. Morosov would very much have liked to smash his teeth in. Officious *negr* bastard.

'You're free to go, sir. Sorry about the inconvenience. I've phoned down to the gate, they'll hold your flight until you get there, OK?'

'Thank you,' Morosov said, gruffly. He put on his coat and

allowed the officer to guide him back to the public part of the terminal. Walking a couple of steps behind the TSA man, he casually sank his hands into his coat pockets.

The novichok was exactly where he'd left it.

E mily Pasquarelli pushed open the door to Greg's classroom.

'Hey,' she said, all smiles. 'What is it you wanted to . . .?' Her voice trailed off in a puzzled uptick. Greg, despite the end of the school day, was not alone. Andrea Velasquez was sitting at the back of his classroom, the heel of one ratty looking sneaker tapping absently against the floor. And sitting beside *her* was the woman police detective, Rachel Lev. Lev was absolutely still, her face expressionless, her eyes drifting from Greg, to Emily, and back to Greg again.

Emily closed Greg's door with exaggerated care, sealing them off from the outside world. When she turned back around the smile was still there, but tighter now, not quite reaching her eyes.

'What's going on?' she asked. Her voice was bright, perky even.

'You killed Lindsay Delcade, biatch,' Andrea blurted out before Greg could say anything.

Emily's response was half gasp, half laugh.

'Don't be ridiculous,' she said dismissively. She looked over to the detective. 'Is this some kind of sick police joke?'

Lev shrugged.

'If it is, it's nothing to do with me, ma'am – or the department.' She pointed a finger firmly toward Greg. 'Mr Abimbola, here, has a theory of the case. It's not the department's theory –' she glanced sideways at Andrea – 'but Mr Abimbola was most insistent that I be here to hear it just in case the department has it wrong. So here I am.' She stretched in the chair like some recalcitrant student, sparing Greg a glance that was something between amusement and exasperation. 'I hope he's not wasting my time.'

'Greg?' Emily looked a little unsteady on her feet. She placed an immaculately manicured hand on Greg's desk, bracing herself against it. 'You don't actually think I had *anything* to do with this, do you? Not after you and I . . .' Her voice trailed off, stilled by whatever it was she saw in Greg's face.

Greg was glad he didn't have a mirror. If his expression reflected even half of what he was feeling, he had no interest in seeing it. His heart thumped slowly in his chest, pumping thin, listless blood into a still-resisting brain. He desperately wanted to be wrong, to reset to that magical evening at Alleghalto, with a beautiful, intelligent woman whose skin had gleamed in the soft light, whose hands had meshed so easily with his. Compatible gears in the same machine. A possible future.

But he wasn't wrong. Because God had no future in mind for people like him. It was what he deserved. What he had *always* deserved. The first hints of a headache pounded at his temples.

'Maybe you should take a seat,' he suggested, not unkindly.

'I'd rather stand.' The words were cold, now. The sort people reserved for those who would do them harm.

'Fair enough. And I want you to know, I understand why you killed her. I might have done the same in your position.'

There was a sharp intake of breath from the back of the room. Lev, Greg guessed.

'I didn't kill anybody.'

'Yes, Emily, you did.'

Emily laughed without humor, the sound ringing dismissively in Greg's ears.

'All of this,' Greg said, '*all* of it, is about two things. Stayard College, and Lindsay Delcade's inability to take no for an answer.'

He smiled at her sadly.

'You must have been so happy when Scott got into Stayard. He's a bright, clever young man, and now he's at one of the best universities in the world. With a degree from Stayard, all things are possible: doors that you didn't even know existed suddenly swing open. Your son's future is assured. And you, his mother, are rightly proud of his achievement. And proud, happy mother that you are, you share your joy with Lindsay Delcade, your good friend from high school.

'Lindsay was kind to your face, I'm guessing. But, as you told me yourself, she was very, *very* competitive. You knew it was killing her to think that Scott could get into Stayard when Vicki Delcade couldn't. You told me the other night that it was "eating her alive". Vicki, as we both know, is a genuinely talented performer, but not particularly academic. And as Vicki moved through high school, her mother must have realized that she wasn't getting anywhere near Stayard without help. Never mind that the poor kid had no real interest in going there, Lindsay Delcade did. She terrorized the teachers into giving Vicki As that weren't deserved, and ruined the career of a chemistry teacher who had the temerity to give her a B.'

'Which makes Dr Freedman far more likely to have killed Lindsay than anybody!' Emily interjected. 'He was there that night, you know.' She was looking at Detective Lev, seeking her support. 'He could easily have gotten her into the custodian's room and killed her right there. He *hated* her.'

'I thought about that,' Greg agreed, dragging Emily's attention away from the police officer, 'but it doesn't make any sense. If Demetrius Freedman had lured Lindsay into the custodian's room, it would have been because he had a plan. Demetrius is a planner. He was here half the night rehearsing for some damned experiment, because that's the kind of man he is. If he'd planned to kill Lindsay for what she did to his career, how come he forgot to bring a weapon? Whoever killed Lindsay stabbed her with the first thing that came to hand: Andrea's screwdriver. Demetrius would have brought a knife, or a gun, or a rope to strangle her with. He would have been *prepared*. And besides, if Demetrius hated Lindsay Delcade, the feeling was entirely mutual. No one *dragged* Lindsay Delcade into the custodian's room. She must have intended to go there of her own free will. And there's no way Lindsay Delcade would agree to meet someone she couldn't stand in a school basement, after hours, to smoke *marijuana*.'

Greg saw the shot hit home. Emily flinched. Detective Lev shifted in her seat.

'Vernon, the custodian, told me that the police found pot at the crime scene, and an ashtray that he said didn't belong there. Which means someone brought that ashtray with them. No one was dealing pot down there, Emily. Pot dealers don't bring ashtrays. Lindsay and her killer were smoking it together. Demetrius *could* have let her in, I'll give you that, but they weren't friends. Quite the opposite, in fact. There's no way on God's green earth that those two would've been sharing spliffs.'

Emily, at long last, decided to take a seat.

'But the ashtray would have had prints on it, or DNA,' she said, defiantly. 'And if it did, I'd have been arrested days ago, wouldn't I, Detective?'

'There were no usable prints on the ashtray,' Lev said, after a moment's hesitation. 'The DNA was all Ms Delcade's.'

'From her blood, I suppose?' Greg asked. 'Vern did say the ashtray was covered with it.'

Lev nodded.

'And here's the other thing,' Greg continued. 'What kind of person brings an ashtray – a *Stayard* ashtray, no less – just to smoke pot? Someone who's neatnik tidy. Perhaps army tidy, and with innate good taste on top of it, so she couldn't bear to use something as hideous as a coffee mug or an old tin. And maybe someone who wanted to send a message: my child is at Stayard, yours isn't.'

'That's cold, man,' Andrea interjected. 'Cold.'

'It is,' Greg agreed. 'But it was Emily who told me that women's friendships are complicated. What was it you said? Oh, yes: "We're all frenemies at some level.".'

Almost despite themselves, Greg noticed, Emily and Rachel were nodding. Only Andrea seemed unconvinced.

'When all's said and done, there are only four people who looked like they might have killed Lindsay Delcade: Andrea Velasquez—'

'I didn't do it!'

'—who couldn't have done it, because she'd already left before Lindsay even got here; Lindsay's husband, who, even if he followed her here, couldn't have killed her without the murder being discovered by whomever Lindsay was meeting; Demetrius Freedman, whom Lindsay wouldn't have been seen dead with, if you'll excuse the expression; and you, Emily: a tidy, tasteful woman, who brought an ashtray to send a message.'

'This is nuts!'

'Is it? Apart from her children, the only person in the world who ever had a good word for that woman was you. She and her husband were at daggers drawn, you yourself told me she had no close friends. And yet she went out every Monday night, regular as clockwork, to see *someone*. And that someone was you.'

'I never said that! I *told* you she was seeing someone – some *man*. A guy.'

'A guy that your good friend somehow never got around to telling you about. And a guy that even her husband, who has no warm feelings toward his wife at all, doesn't believe exists. He was adamant that she was having nights out with the girls. His only mistake was his use of the plural. There was only one girl. You.'

'Right, like I'd come down to the school basement for a girls' night out.'

'What better place to smoke pot? You can't smoke at home with your mother there, I suspect, and Lindsay, I'm guessing, wouldn't smoke in front of her kids, or anywhere she might be seen in public. She wanted to be a congressman's wife, remember? The custodian's room is perfect. It's completely private, it's comfortable in a grubby kind of way, and no one would ever think to look for you there. And the two of you did it regularly. So regularly, you didn't even have to text about it. You both just turned up; same time, same place. That's why you had an ashtray specially for the occasion, and it's why Andrea and Mr Szymanski often smelt marijuana down there the morning after.'

'I thought it was Vern,' Andrea murmured. 'That it was medicinal or something.'

'And he thought it was you,' Greg said, smiling. 'He called you a pot head.'

'Ornery old bastard.'

'But it was Lindsay and Emily the whole time. And for a long time.' He turned to face Emily again. 'I don't know when you figured out that you could get into the custodian's room without being seen, but you turned it into a routine. There's an old packing crate outside the loading bay. You placed it there so you didn't have to clamber up a four-foot-high ledge, just a couple of big steps and you were up. And once you figured it out, you told Lindsay. You even gave her a key.'

Emily Pasquarelli was looking very pale, now.

'A key?'

'A key,' Greg repeated. 'I should have seen it before, but I was too stupid to notice. There are meant to be five keys. Ms Ellis has one, you have one, Vernon and Andrea have one each, and there's a spare kept on a hook in the custodian's room, just in case. If I went to your cubicle right now, I'd find *your* key, wouldn't I?'

'Yes,' Emily admitted, reluctantly.

'And I know for a fact Ms Ellis's is holding down one of her ridiculous piles of paper. I saw it there yesterday.'

Emily looked, if anything, even paler.

'Andrea and Vernon both have theirs, which means there should be only one key in the custodian's room. But there are *two*. Vern found it last Wednesday, while he was cleaning up the crime scene. It had fallen into a bucket of odds and ends. Vern thought it was Andrea's, and I did, too, for the longest time. Until Andrea put me right, that is.'

'So whose was it?' Rachel Lev asked. She'd pulled out her notebook and was scribbling furiously.

'Lindsay Delcade's. You had it made for her, didn't you, Emily? So she could get in as soon as she arrived. Couldn't have your friend hanging around a loading bay where some passerby might see her if you were running late, could you?'

'I have no idea what you're talking about.' Emily Pasquarelli's voice was little more than a whisper.

'If you say so. I doubt it's been used much since Monday before last. There's a good chance Detective Lev will find Lindsay's prints on it, even now.'

'I'll take my chances.' Emily's bright eyes glittered with defiance.

'When I realized there were too many keys, I knew it had to be you. Bryan Delcade didn't have access to a key to copy it. Ellis could have, of course. And Demetrius, I suppose, could have sneaked down to the custodian's room and borrowed the spare long enough to make one. Problem is, like Andrea, there was no reason on earth why either of them would copy a key for Lindsay Delcade. The only one close enough to Lindsay to *want* to give her a key, was you.'

'Circumstantial.'

'I don't think circumstantial means what you think it means, Emily. Circumstantial evidence is still evidence. And if there are prints on that key, you'll never be able to explain it away.'

'*If* there are prints on that key, Columbo, come talk to me then. Better yet, talk to my lawyer.' She stood up abruptly. 'I've had enough of this . . . this . . . *witch-hunt*. I'm leaving.'

'I think you should stay,' Rachel Lev said, suddenly. 'And it would be better for everybody if I didn't have to make you.'

Greg tried to shoot the detective a grateful look, but she wouldn't meet his eye. Emily sat back down, perched awkwardly at the edge of her seat.

'I'll be quick, Emily, I promise. Quicker, anyway.

'As you very well know, but I didn't until Bryan Delcade told me, the relationship between Calderhill Academy and Stayard College is corrupt. Stacey joked with me the other day that you're the one who runs the school, not Ms Ellis. While that's not strictly true, you told me yourself that you handle all the school's finances. I've seen the spreadsheets on your computer. You've got a spreadsheet for everything. You know every cent that goes in and out of this place – and why. And a good chunk of that money greases the wheels in the Stayard admissions office. Sure, there are kids, like your son, who get in honestly. But there are a whole lot more whose parents pay bribes to a guy called Johnathan Lorde, Dean of the Faculty of Arts and Sciences at Stayard. Bribes brokered by the school principal. Vicki Delcade is no Scott Pasquarelli. There was no way she was going to Stayard without Johnathan Lorde's very illegal assistance. Assistance that cost half-a-million dollars, and which had to be paid no later than the Monday on which Lindsay Delcade died. Lorde was in town that night, having dinner with Ms Ellis. I'm guessing they were finalizing the details. It'd be nice to think that she slid him the money in a big brown briefcase, but I'm guessing it got wired to some dodgy account somewhere. Boring but practical.

'In any event, Lindsay didn't have the money. Her husband had already spent it smoothing the path of his political career. Lindsay came in that Monday morning to beg Dean Ellis for more time.' Greg found time for a wry smile. 'I say "beg", but that wasn't really Lindsay's style, was it? "Berate" was more like it. I heard some of the histrionics myself, but I didn't understand the context until much later. Anyway, Ellis held the line, and Lindsay saw her daughter's shot at Stayard slipping away.

'But Lindsay, as we all know by now, was not the sort of woman to take no for an answer. She took a rideshare that evening for her regular girls' night out, arriving here, with the key she shouldn't have had, at eight twenty-seven p.m. Maybe you'd already got here, maybe you arrived a bit later: only you know, of course, because you knew how to get through the loading bay without being picked up on camera.

'You brought the ashtray, and either you or Lindsay brought the pot. Lindsay was still steamed about the Stayard thing, and I daresay the ashtray didn't help her mood. It was cold, too, because even though Andrea had fixed the furnace by then, it hadn't had a chance to warm the place up. Lindsay kept her coat on. So did you, I imagine. You were certainly wearing your gloves because, like you told me, you can't stand having cold hands.

'And then Lindsay, who can't take no for an answer, started leaning on you to help her out, didn't she? Because, if there was anyone at this school who could work a miracle for her, it would be you. It's you who knows where all the money goes. It's you who knows everything there is to know about the Stayard admissions scheme. It's you who Lindsay hoped would know about any loopholes. And Lindsay, who can't take no for an answer, and doesn't know how to beg, did what she does best. She *threatened* you. She would blow the lid on the whole, rotten scam. The school would be ruined. *You* would be ruined. You'd never work again. You might even go to jail. And Lindsay Delcade just kept piling it on because that's what Lindsay does. She would have been right in your face about it, screaming and abusive. And at some point, you just snapped, grabbed that big old screwdriver and stabbed her. Again, and again, and again. You're ex-army. You know how to kill someone, even if this was your very first time.'

'And then what happened?' Emily asked. Her voice had become somehow unmoored from her stiffly held body. It sounded light and carefree – curious, even. As if she genuinely wanted to know.

'Killing someone is . . . hard to process. It's difficult to think straight. Your heart would have been going a million miles a minute, your hands would have been shaking, you'd have been gasping for breath. You dropped the screwdriver. You'd been wearing gloves because of the cold, that's why your prints aren't on the handle, only Andrea's. But now the gloves were covered in blood. You cleared away the joints you'd been smoking, but when you tried to pick up the ashtray, you couldn't hold it. It was too heavy, and your gloves were slick. You let it lie where you dropped it. During the attack, Lindsay's key had fallen into a bucket full of bits and pieces, and the unsmoked marijuana had rolled under the sofa. I don't know if you tried to find them before you fled or not, but flee you did. Your smooth-soled shoes left a couple of bloody footprints on the way out, and your gloves deposited Lindsay's blood on the door handle when you opened it. After that, you were gone. No one suspected you. You were "at home with your mother". And your mother would have backed you up, I'm guessing. Either because you asked her to or, more likely, she was confused and assumed you were home. You almost got away with it.'

'Almost?' Emily's laugh was laced with derision. 'None of this is going to hold up in court. You've got a key that might have Lindsay's prints on it. So what? I let her have the key as a favor so she could come in here and get high. *I* never joined her. I wasn't here and there's absolutely nothing that says I was.'

'Pity about the sanitation strike.'

'The what, now?'

'Trash cans are cleaned out on Tuesdays, both here and at your apartment. But for the strike, they'd have been emptied the day after the murder.' Greg took a step toward his desk. 'But they weren't.'

'Strike's over,' Emily reminded him. 'They were emptied today.'

'But not before Ms Velasquez over there went dumpster diving. Turned out the police had gone through the school trash after the murder—'

'Of course we did,' Lev interjected. 'We're not idiots.'

'—but Andrea made it to your apartment building before the garbage trucks. She found these.' Greg reached into a desk drawer. Pulled out a bulging Ziploc bag. 'The leather gloves you had at dinner last night looked exactly like your old ones. But last night's were brand new. You hadn't even removed the little plastic loop that held the shop label. *These*, the ones in the bag, are your old ones. They were soaked in blood. Enough that you couldn't pick up the ashtray, that you left marks all over the door handle. Even though you probably weren't at your best, having just killed your best friend from high school, you knew enough not to throw them away outside. You dumped them at your apartment building instead. And you know what? They're *still* soaked in blood – caked, really. They'll be loaded with Lindsay Delcade's DNA – and yours.' He shook his head, genuinely saddened. 'I don't think you'll be talking your way out of that one any time soon.'

Emily Pasquarelli gasped, the blood draining from her face.

'Jesus fucking Christ,' Detective Lev muttered. 'You didn't think to *lead* with that?' She stood up, produced a pair of flex cuffs from her overcoat pocket.

'It wasn't like that,' Emily said. She said it so quietly no one was sure she'd spoken until she said it again, more loudly. 'It wasn't like that at all.'

The room was suddenly very still. Even Lev stopped moving, the cuffs hanging poised and translucent in her hands.

'It wasn't about the school,' Emily Pasquarelli said. 'It wasn't about me. It was about Scott.'

'Your son?' Greg prompted. He said it gently, like a priest. He'd seen the look on Emily's face many times before, in musty basements and corrugated-iron shacks in Africa, and Asia, and Central Europe. Capitulation. The recognition that there was nowhere to go, nothing to fight over. Only a last, final need to be understood.

Emily nodded.

'Lindsay was furious Ellis hadn't given her more time to pay. But she could have gotten Vicki in next year if she'd been prepared to wait. Ellis had told her that. She'd make sure the kid was still on Lorde's list next time around. *I* told her that, too. It would give her a chance to get the family finances in order – or to get a divorce settlement out of Bryan. And it would give Vicki a year out to try her hand at acting like she wanted.'

Tears were starting to leak from Emily's eyes.

'But Lindsay wasn't having any of it. She wanted Vicki in right now. She said Vicki would have gotten in already if it hadn't been for ghetto teachers like you and Mr Freedman screwing with her GPA. And Ellis had approached *her* with what she called a "side way in", so Ellis had a moral obligation to make it happen.'

Emily took a long, stertorous breath.

'Then she said it was up to *me* to persuade Ellis, because the principal always listened to what I had to say. I tried to tell her that there was nothing I could do, that it really was too late, but she wouldn't have any of it. She would go to the press, she said, and the police, and it was my son who would pay the price. After she was done, *no one* would ever believe Scott got in honestly. He would be thrown out of Stayard without graduating, along with every other Calderhill alum. His face would be all over the internet, on TMZ. He'd be disgraced. No other college would take him. His whole future would be ruined, and he'd spend the rest of his life as an anonymous nobody, just like his mother.'

Emily jammed a fist into her mouth, held her breath for a moment.

'I . . . I just lost it. The screwdriver was right there, and she was screaming at me to stop and I just couldn't. And then it was too late. It was too late . . .'

She broke down, then, sobbing. A deep, primal wailing

interrupted by jagged gulps of breath that filled the whole room. She seemed insensible to Rachel Lev moving alongside her, looping the flex cuffs around her wrists.

'Emily Pasquarelli, I am arresting you for the murder of Lindsay Harris Delcade. You have the right to remain silent. Anything you say can be used against you in a court of law. You have the right to have an attorney . . .'

Minutes later, as Rachel Lev transferred her prisoner to the custody of two uniformed officers, Emily managed to shoot Greg a watery smile.

'We would have made a good team,' she said.

Greg was too churned up to say anything. He watched her go, face and body rigid. So lost was he in his own thoughts that the gentle tap on his shoulder made him jump.

'Thank you, Mr Abimbola, for all your help,' Detective Lev said. The smile was wide, and genuine, and made her look far less severe than normal. 'I'd like to say that we'd have got there eventually but, hand on heart, I'm not sure we would have. You and Ms Velasquez get down to the station as soon as you can. For statements and all that good stuff.'

And with that she was gone, taking long strides out of the room in her sensible shoes and slightly scuffed pantsuit. Her overcoat billowed behind her as she walked.

'You did it, Mr Bimbo! You did it!'

Andrea hugged him so hard it almost squeezed the breath out of him.

'So we did,' Greg agreed, smiling.

'You think they'll give me my boots back, now?'

'I'm sure they will. But take the receipt, just in case.'

Andrea let go of him, looking slightly worried.

'Now I have to go to PCC and do some *serious* brown-nosing. I don't want to get flunked out because of the, you know, furnace thing. I got an appointment with the dean of students at four thirty.'

'Well, good luck with that. If there's anything I can do there, let me know.'

'Thanks, man.'

Greg found himself casting a speculative eye over the assistant custodian.

'Andrea? How would you like to put that IT training of yours to good use?'

WEDNESDAY,
THE EIGHTEENTH
06:13 A.M. EST

Morosov had changed his rental car. On his return from Washington, he'd swapped the Hyundai sedan for a Chevy Silverado pickup, something totally different from his previous vehicle. And more in tune, he thought, with the city's distinctly blue-collar vibe. Pittsburgh's tightly spaced housing, clinging limpet-like to every hillside, was clearly designed for industrial workers, even if the industry itself was long gone. Morosov had no idea what that industry had been, nor did he very much care. But having been moving around the city since Sunday, he had little doubt a pickup would fit right in. Within minutes of taking possession of his new vehicle, he'd driven it onto a derelict patch of land, the fat wheels churning up mud and patches of snow until the sides of the Silverado were covered in pale brown dirt. This time, when he returned to Parkside Hill, he was determined to blend in. The mongrel bastard wasn't going to pick him up a second time.

He'd pulled into Parkside Hill around two a.m. and found a decent place to park with a good view of the *negr*'s apartment. Then he'd set the alarm on his phone for five in the morning and sunk into a deep, exhausted sleep. When the alarm had gone off seemingly moments later, Morosov had cursed the target's annoying habit of getting up early, rubbed at his tired eyes, and waited.

Now, sure enough, the door to the target's apartment building was swinging open. Petrov was standing at the top of the steep steps that led down to the sidewalk, dressed in running gear. He looked as trim and fit as ever. Morosov, conscious that he was getting soft around the edges, felt a stab of envy. No matter. The prick would be a hell of a lot less fit after he got home.

Petrov headed downhill at an easy pace, disappearing around a bend in the street within a few seconds. Morosov waited a couple of minutes and then got out of his truck. Crossing the street in

long, purposeful strides, he trotted up the steps to the front door
of the apartment building. Peering at the front lock, he pulled what
looked like an electric toothbrush out of his pocket. To be fair, it
was an electric toothbrush. Morosov had just modified it a little.
He pulled off the brush head to reveal a thin sliver of metal that
looked like, and operated as, the business end of an electric lockpick. Using his right hand, he inserted the makeshift pick into the
top of the lock. Then, with the other, he pushed a small, L-shaped
piece of metal taken from a hairgrip into the bottom. The noise
from the toothbrush's electric motor sang far too loud in his ears,
but it was only for a few seconds. The L-shaped piece of metal
turned in his hand.

The front door to the apartment building swung open.

Morosov climbed the rickety, creaking stairs, looking for the right
apartment number. By the time he got there he was out of breath
– and angry at Petrov for choosing to live at the very top of the
building. Oddly, there was a set of free weights neatly stacked on
the landing outside the apartment door. Undoubtedly the target's,
vain asshole that he was. He thought about smearing the novichok
on either the weights or the apartment's door handle but rejected
the idea. There was no telling when the weights would be used
again. If his handlers extracted him before then, he might never use
them, or some American operative might pick them up for the
move to a new safe house. And other people would doubtless open
the apartment door, not just the target. Killing the monkey was one
thing. Sickening an American agent, or the local *politsiya,* or
some emergency worker, was something else entirely. He needed
to place the novichok somewhere that was absolutely guaranteed to
be fatal, but that no one else would think to touch.

He made short work of the apartment door and found himself
in a living room, unsurprised at the contrast between the upscale
décor and the rest of the building. He'd always had airs and graces,
this one. As if that would ever change what he was. An ape in
Pushkin's clothing.

He glanced through an open door into the spotless kitchen, its
every surface polished to gleaming. He could see part of a straight-
backed dining chair, its wooden legs dark and rich and
expensive.

There'd be no termites in that thing. Anyplace the monkey
bought furniture would be too upscale for that.

Suddenly, he wasn't seeing the apartment. There was a lightbulb swinging from a corrugated-iron roof, Polukhin's dropped jaw, a chair leg slamming into his temple. He remembered his knees giving way, the dirt floor flying up to meet him.

Fucking baboon. Now, he was going to pay.

Reaching into his coat pocket, Morosov fished out a face mask and a pair of latex gloves. Pulling them on with an efficient snap of rubber, he found his way into the *negr*'s bathroom. Every surface gleamed, like an operating theater. And sure enough, to one side of the sink, there was a spotless electric toothbrush. Morosov grinned at the irony. It was the same make as his lockpick.

He pulled out the small bottle of novichok disguised as contact lens solution; held his breath; carefully unscrewed the cap with latex-gloved hands; squeezed a handful of drops onto the brush head and a few more onto the handle. Finally satisfied, he screwed the cap back on and stepped out of the bathroom.

'For Pavel,' he murmured.

The monkey was as good as dead.

Careful not to touch those parts of the gloves that had been in contact with the novichok, Morosov peeled them off and dropped them into a plastic shopping bag emblazoned with the words 'Giant Eagle'. The face mask followed, together with the novichok itself. Morosov made sure the top of the bag was tied tightly before heading out. He would dispose of everything safely. Not like those GRU fuck-ups in England, who'd fled for home leaving behind apocalyptic levels of poison. And in dangerously deceptive packaging, too. What did they think would happen? That the first Englishwoman to come across an abandoned bottle of perfume *wouldn't* use it? The resultant death had been horrible, and public, and unnecessary. Even worse, the actual fucking target had *survived.* The entire op botched from backside to tits, the whole of Russian intelligence made to look like a bunch of brain-dead *kulaks.*

Not this time. Petrov – and only Petrov – would die. Mikhail Sergeevich Morosov would have his revenge – and be $500,000 richer into the bargain.

Smiling broadly, he opened the apartment door and headed out.

For a moment, he thought he was back in Djibouti. There was the same bare lightbulb hanging from the ceiling, there was the monkey, angry and fearful, swinging hard at his head. But there was no Polukhin this time, no dirt floor, and no chair leg. The monkey was swinging a dumbbell. It was the last thought he had before the cold metal connected with his temple.

06:47 A.M. EST

Greg Abimbola was drenched in sweat, his muscles aching from recent effort. Mikhail Sergeevich was heavy, significantly more so than Greg. It had been an effort lugging the limp, ursine mass back into the apartment. Morosov's unconscious form, the whole left side of his face a swollen, bruised mess, kept sliding off the straight-backed dining chair he'd chosen for the purpose. It took several attempts to get the man sufficiently balanced for Greg to secure him with every last roll of duct tape in his kitchen cupboard. He tried not to think of the damage he was doing to the varnish.

Greg brushed a drop of sweat from his one good eyelid, noticing almost dispassionately that his hands were shaking. He was too old for this.

Too out of practice.

He'd barely started his run that morning when the phone had rung. It was Andrea. He could hear the muted growl of her Chevy's busted muffler in the background.

'Mr Abimbola? That nanny cam and motion sensor you had me install? I got an alert, like, thirty seconds ago. I'm looking at the feed right now. Some guy's just gone into your apartment.'

The roar of blood rushing past his ears had been almost deafening.

'Thanks, Andrea.'

'You want me to call the po-po?'

'That's OK. I'll handle it. And Andrea?'

'Yeah?'

'You have a real future in computers.'

He'd turned and jogged back up the hill, heart thudding far too hard for the effort required.

Staring at Morosov's unconscious form, Greg stuck his hands into the waistband of his leggings in an attempt to steady himself. Part of the reason he was shaking was that the sweat was cooling on his body, making him feel a chill. He desperately wanted to change out of his running gear, but having seen the contents of Morosov's Giant Eagle carrier bag, he hadn't dared run the risk. Even retrieving the duct tape had been a gamble. He'd taken off his sweatshirt to do so, using it as a makeshift barrier between himself and any exposed surface. Thus protected, he'd retrieved an unopened pair of rubber gloves from his pantry. Only after he'd pulled the stubborn elastic over his hands had he accessed the yards of gray tape needed to hold Morosov down. Task done, he'd instinctively headed to the sink to wash his hands with soap and water but stopped himself just in time. Whatever was in the Russian's innocent looking bottle of contact lens solution – and Greg would have bet dollars to rubles that it was some kind of skin-absorbed poison – there was a very good chance Morosov would have smeared it on the faucets. It's what Greg would have done if the shoe had been on the other foot.

His cellphone emitted a small, plaintive chirp. A text message.

On our way. Do nothing.

He deleted it without bothering to reply. Still wearing the rubber gloves, he placed the bottle of contact lens solution on his coffee table, sat on his sofa, and waited.

Morosov groaned. The Russian's left eye was swollen shut, but the right eye managed to find its way around the room, taking everything in before focusing on Greg with undisguised malevolence. He was already straining at the duct tape, testing its strength.

'*Zhopu porvu margala vikoliu,*' he growled.

Greg subconsciously rubbed his eyepatch.

'This is Pittsburgh, Mikhail Sergeevich. We speak English here. Of a sort.' He couldn't resist a mischievous smile. 'I'm English, now.'

'*Ty chertov predatel. Tya mama huyem v rot ebala!*'

Stung by the insult, the smile vanished from Greg's face.

'English, Mikhail Sergeevich.' Morosov was at least as slippery as he was greedy. But he was no great linguist. And dissembling in a foreign language would be more difficult for him.

'*Idi v zhopu.*'

Greg leaned across to the coffee table, picked up the bottle of contact lens solution.

'OK, OK, English,' Morosov grunted. 'You are fucking traitor. Your momma fuck you in mouth with big cock.'

'Your English is still terrible, I see.'

Morosov glared at him out of his one good eye.

'Who sent you?'

'I send me.'

Greg chuckled.

'Last I heard, GRU officers don't give themselves orders.'

Morosov spat on the carpet, his bloody spittle making a watery red stain. Greg managed not to wince.

'Because of you, not GRU anymore. Private practice. Security consultant.'

'So who paid you?'

A stony silence. Greg stared meaningfully at the little plastic bottle on the coffee table. Morosov shrugged.

'GRU pay me.'

'How much?'

'Half million, US'

Greg raised an ironic eyebrow.

'Good as a place at Stayard College.' He ignored Morosov's puzzled expression. 'And where did you leave my present?'

'I not understand.'

Greg picked up the plastic bottle with a gloved hand, shaking it gently. There was a liquid, sloshing sound.

'The nerve agent, or whatever it is you've got in here, where did you put it?'

Morosov grinned.

'Fuck you, Petrov.'

Greg started to unscrew the cap on the bottle.

'Go ahead. I dead man anyway. I know where you live.'

I . . .

Not 'we'.

Greg's fingers came to a halt. He'd been about to tell Morosov that if he talked, he would live. There was no point in killing him otherwise. Because if Morosov knew he was alive and in Pittsburgh, so did the GRU. Killing Morosov because he wouldn't talk was one thing. Killing him to protect his location was quite another: it solved nothing.

But Morosov should *know* that. And yet, putting himself in Greg's shoes, he had decided he was as good as dead. Which could only mean the GRU didn't know where he was. They must know he was alive, obviously, or they wouldn't have agreed a price for

him. But, if Morosov didn't trust them to pay, he would have kept
Greg's actual location a secret.

Maybe.

'There are easier ways to die, Mikhail Sergeevich, than by
poison. Are you sure this is the way you want to go?'

'Bullet, breaked neck, novichok. Is all same to me.'

Novichok.

Well . . . shit.

'I'd have thought, after Salisbury, GRU would have had more
sense. America is not Britain, you know. You fuck up and kill Joe
Public by accident over here, the consequences will be serious.'

'I not fuck up.'

Greg had to laugh.

'You're tied to a chair in my living room, Mikhail Sergeevich.
If that isn't a fuck up, I don't know what is.'

'Maybe chair have termite and break. Then I kill you with bare
hand.'

Greg smiled.

'Did you see Polukhin's face?' he asked. 'When the chair
collapsed? I saw it like that only once before. In—'

'Nairobi,' Morosov finished. 'When he put hand up woman
dress. Discover not woman at all!'

Incongruously, the two men burst out laughing. When the
laughter died down, Morosov asked softly, 'Why did you become
traitor, Grigoriy Adamovich? You good officer. Loyal. Why you
become British bitch?'

The rumble of London traffic, the creaking of stairs sounded
loud in Greg's ears, as if it were happening right now, instead of
a decade ago.

'My circumstances changed.'

'*Chush' sobach'ya!* I dead man, anyway. Tell truth before I die.
Why not?'

Greg was still on the creaking steps, following Robert Godfrey,
junior diplomat, into his flat. He was sitting down on the deep
red, leather Chesterfield, making small talk, intent on cultivating
the man as a possible source. But the next thing he knew, he was
waking up on a gray English morning, raindrops spattered on the
windows, the same British diplomat naked in bed beside him. He'd
grabbed his clothes, thrown up in the toilet, and rushed out of the
house before the man had awakened.

Only to have an envelope of lurid photographs thrust into his hands a few days later.

The agents from the Security Service had been unfailingly polite, as if embarrassed to have raised the topic at all.

We're all men and women of the world here, Mr Petrov, and God knows, far worse things happen at sea. We don't judge. What would be the point, eh? Disapproving of homosexuality is like disapproving of . . . rain: it happens anyway. Always has, always will. Of course, our Russian friends are not so forgiving, as I'm sure you know. Still stuck in the 1950s, if you don't mind my saying so. I have to be honest with you, Grigoriy – can I call you Grigoriy? This is a career ender for you. And your family is bound to be vilified. I don't mind saying, I feel for your poor mother. Not her *fault, of course, but unkind people will think otherwise, won't they? And then there's the Church. It's hard to believe they still excommunicate people for same-sex attachments, but there it is . . .*

It had gone on and on. If he'd been a real man, he'd have laughed in their faces and told them to fuck off. But he hadn't, not when they'd asked for so little in return, and he got to spare his mother heartbreak and keep doing the job he loved. It wasn't even confidential information they wanted, just public domain stuff you could lift off the internet.

At first. Soon enough they began to ask for small secrets, and then bigger ones. He'd been dragged in deeper and deeper, until the only way out involved a bullet to the back of his head.

He'd thought about it, too. The catharsis. The welcome relief. A slate wiped clean with blood and brain matter. He'd thought about it a lot. Because at the end of the day, he'd never found a way to forgive himself, not for any of it. For letting the Devil win; for betraying his country; for slamming Morosov in the head with a chair leg instead of taking the punishment he so richly deserved. And even now, with Morosov stalking him across a brand-new continent, he'd still refused to do the right thing: to surrender to his fate; to meet his maker and the eternal damnation that went with it.

Because he was weak.

The stairs creaked in his head again, even louder. It was only Morosov's expression that told him he wasn't imagining things. These creaks were real. Someone was climbing the steps.

Morosov's sneer was made uglier by the fact that only half his face was working.

'You not man enough kill me on own? You need others hold your hand?'

Greg ignored him. Headed to the door instead. He reached for the doorhandle.

'Why you kill Pavel?'

His hand dropped away.

'I didn't kill Pavel.' A sudden drying of the throat.

Morosov's bark of a laugh was mixed with spittle and blood.

'Do not lie to me, Grigoriy Adamovich. Not now. We find him dead, my *brother* dead, in Djibouti ditch, two day after you vanish like ghost, his balls cut off. His fucking balls! You kill him clean, like professional, OK, maybe I understand. He one who discover you traitor. But like that? Like some . . . *animal*? Pavel was your *friend*, you monkey bastard. He deserve better.'

Greg stared at the door, trying to gather himself, to control his breathing.

'It wasn't me,' he said. 'I knew something was up. Pavel had gone missing and suddenly you and Polukhin were flying in from Moscow. But I didn't know I'd been made, not till later, till it was too late. Almost too late. And I didn't know it was Pavel who'd figured me out . . . I swear to you, I didn't know he was dead.'

Thinking himself more composed, he turned to look Morosov in his one good eye. But he still couldn't meet the other man's gaze. His stomach twisted with newly acquired guilt.

The one good eye narrowed shrewdly.

'*Da idi ty!* Maybe you not kill him, after all. But you know who did. You sell him out to British as top handler for network. And British sell him out to some *negr* fuck gangster in Djibouti. Keep colonialist hand clean for tea and scones and make GRU think Pavel death just bad luck so we not kill one of theirs.'

'I didn't know, Mikhail Sergeevich. By all that's holy, I didn't know. I—'

Soft voices outside the door.

Greg's cellphone chimed. A text.

We're here.

He turned back to the apartment door. Looked through the peephole. Satisfied, he opened it up. A tall man in a dark-blue, woolen overcoat stepped across the threshold. He had carefully gelled dark hair and matching shoes. He was accompanied by a casually dressed woman wearing jeans and a black leather jacket over a light wool sweater. Her high-heeled suede boots, like the rest of her attire, were better suited to spring than a below freezing winter morning. She was trying very hard not to shiver.

'*Suka!*' Morosov strained so violently against his bonds that his chair threatened to tip over.

The man in the dark woolen overcoat extended a firm hand. Greg shook it.

'How you doing, Greg?' The man's friendly American accent, matched by an easy smile, had a hint of the south about it.

'Better now that you're here, Deputy Werner,' Greg answered. There was an ambiguity in his tone that made the marshall look at him curiously. Greg's gaze, meanwhile, slid toward Werner's companion. 'Who's your colleague?'

'Dianna Aldis,' the woman said, extending an immaculately manicured hand. 'Pleasure to meet you.'

'*Suka!*'

Aldis had the sort of crisp, upper-crust English accent that Americans associated with Jane Austen, or Masterpiece Theater. She did not, Greg noticed, explain whom she worked for. Not that *that* required any great leap of imagination. MI5. His mind was still churning over what Morosov had told him.

'You're not my usual case officer,' he said, quietly. 'And what are you doing here, anyway? You're on the wrong side of the Atlantic.'

Aldis smiled disarmingly.

'Perhaps I'm here as a liaison.'

'Liaisons are based in DC. I texted WITSEC less than half an hour ago.'

'Time and a place,' Werner warned, looking at Morosov.

'I think it's a bit late for that,' Greg said. 'Mikhail Sergeevich is going to be in your custody for a very long time, I imagine. And given that Mr Morosov and Miss Aldis are clearly already acquainted, I don't think I'm going to learn anything he doesn't already know.'

Aldis nodded in agreement.

'It was all a bit of a scramble,' she said, ignoring Werner's frown of disapproval. 'Part of my job is – *was* – to keep an eye on Mr Morosov—'

'*Suka!*'

'—but my particular section didn't realize he was targeting one of our own until the very last minute. Your case officer's team was out of position, so to speak, so I came along to handle it.' She glanced appreciatively at the tall American. 'Not that we could have done anything without Mr Werner's assistance, of course. Which was *invaluable*.'

Werner, despite himself, smiled a little at the compliment.

'WITSEC prides itself on keeping its charges safe,' he said. 'Even if, strictly speaking, we're doing someone else's work.'

'Yeah, well, not *that* safe.' Greg picked up the small plastic bottle on the coffee table. 'Mikhail got to me before you did. And he's managed to drop enough novichok to kill a city somewhere close by, so I would be *very* careful about where I put my hands.'

'May I see?' Werner asked.

'Do you have a pair of gloves? I'd direct you to my kitchen, but I honestly don't know where he dumped the stuff. Wouldn't want to get you killed by accident.'

'I can assure you, I'm perfectly safe.'

After a moment's hesitation, Greg handed over the bottle.

'You've got more faith in antidotes than I have,' he muttered.

Werner unscrewed the bottle cap. Before Greg could stop him, he squeezed a few drops onto the back of his hand.

'What the . . .?'

'Good old American H2O,' Werner said, grinning. 'After a lot of running around, we managed to acquire Mr Morosov at Reagan National. Swapped out his very deadly package for something a little more eco-friendly, if you catch my drift. You're welcome, by the way.'

'*Suka!*'

Greg could feel his mouth gaping open. He strongly suspected that he looked like Polukhin in Nairobi.

Minutes later, after Morosov was removed from the apartment by another pair of deputies, his cuffs tactfully hidden under a woolen scarf, Werner allowed himself to relax into Greg's sofa. Aldis perched primly beside him on the sofa arm, as if distrustful of the comfort it might otherwise offer.

'When did you realize Morosov was onto you?' Werner asked.

Greg hesitated before replying.

'Yesterday morning,' he admitted, reluctantly.

'And you didn't think to call us then? Why the hell not?'

Greg, moved by the genuine concern in the marshall's voice,

tried to formulate an honest answer. That he deserved what was coming to him. That whatever happened, happened. That it was the will of God.

'I thought I could handle it.'

'It's not your job to handle it, Greg, it's *ours*. Let us do our jobs, OK? It's what we get paid for. On top of which, these antics of yours have only gone and caused us a shitload of trouble.'

'Why? Because I did your job for you?'

'Because you *interrupted* our job,' Aldis said.

Greg looked at her curiously.

'Our friends in MI5,' Werner explained, 'planted a bug in Morosov's cellphone months ago.' Aldis nodded her head at this, happy to take the credit. 'So when he called your old boss, Polukhin, we knew they were going after you with novichok. The plan was to intercept Morosov at Reagan, replace the novichok with water, and let him carry on with his mission. That way . . .'

'He would think he'd killed me,' Greg interjected.

'Exactly. A few stories planted in the press, some calculated leaks to Russian Intelligence and you'd be dead – again. Morosov was the only GRU goon who doubted your original death. He must have been kicking over the traces for years. This time, because *he'd* "killed" you himself, there'd be literally no one looking for you ever again. Instead—'

'Instead,' Aldis cut in, 'you fucked things up royally. No more dumbbells for you.'

FRIDAY, THE TWENTIETH
12:20 P.M. EST

There was a tense, hunted air in the faculty lounge. No one was talking. Someone had drawn the shades against the street outside, protecting the interior from the prying lenses of photographers and the TV news crews. No one had been much interested in the murder of a private-school soccer mom, but a college admissions scandal was something else entirely. The *New York Post* had run a color triptych of Principal Ellis, with her gray-flecked auburn hair; Lindsay Delcade, beneath her ginger mane; and Emily Pasquarelli, her strawberry blonde hair coppery in the sunlight; all over the headline: 'Varsity Reds'. The *Pittsburgh Post-Gazette* had settled for the more prosaic 'College Admissions Scam Leads to Murder'. Either way, the school was the subject of an uncomfortable amount of media attention.

Greg, concerned that he might be caught on camera and identified by his former colleagues, had taken to wearing a hastily purchased snorkel parka with the hood fully zipped up. He looked ridiculous, but it was impossible for anyone to capture his face on film.

Of course, continuing to go to school was a problem entirely of his own making. Deputy Werner and Dianna Aldis had pointed out in no uncertain terms that his location had been compromised. If Morosov had found him today, someone else from GRU would be there tomorrow. It was time, they said, to move on: right this minute, in fact. Calderhill Academy would have to find a new foreign language teacher.

Greg had refused. Even now, he wasn't quite sure why. It was a reasonable supposition that Morosov, greedy for the money and distrustful of his paymasters, had refused to give them Greg's location. But it was only supposition. What if Morosov had been upfront and told them where he was? And even if he hadn't, was it such a stretch to imagine that GRU, or even FSB, had followed Morosov anyway, and tracked him into Appalachia's crumpled foothills? Worse yet, Morosov would be spending the rest of his life in a supermax prison. It was not beyond the ability of someone with Morosov's training to get the word out to Russian intelligence *somehow*. Choosing to stay behind was, as Aldis had said, 'ill advised', or, in Werner's more colorful vernacular, 'goddamn fucking insane'.

But here he was, sitting in a slightly threadbare armchair, on the opposite side of a coffee table from Demetrius Freedman. The chemistry teacher was assiduously reading the faculty's hard-copy version of the *Post-Gazette* and saying nothing to anybody.

Greg had balked at his handlers' instructions for much the same reasons he'd decided to deal with Morosov on his own. If GRU found him, GRU found him. Maybe next time, he would be man enough, honorable enough, to pay the debt owed. Whatever God willed.

And there was another factor, too. One that had caught him completely by surprise. The more Werner and Aldis had talked about leaving Pittsburgh, the more he realized he would miss it. Dull though it was, he had a life here, a chance to be a normal person for as long as God allowed. His whole adult life he'd moved from station to station, never settling anywhere for more than a year or two, never making friends, severing and re-severing connections. He didn't want to move again. He'd grown to not dislike the so-called Steel City, with its ridiculous hills, and claustrophobic neighborhoods, and dark, slow-moving rivers. If life ever allowed him to put down roots, it might as well be here. There were far worse places in the world – and he'd no desire to see any more of them.

I must be getting old.

'Who do you think will replace Principal Ellis?' he asked Demetrius, trying to make conversation. The chemistry teacher lowered his newspaper just enough to give Greg a slightly wary look. Greg didn't blame him. After the grilling he'd received at Greg's hands, it would be a long time before Demetrius Freedman invited him to watch football.

'No one from the school, that's for sure. Governors were right to fire Ellis on the spot, even though I'll bet you most of them knew what was going on. They'll want someone from outside, who isn't tainted with this whole Stayard admissions mess.' Demetrius could not resist a knowing smile. 'This whole thing is so *white*, man. They

go on and on about everyone playing by the rules – so long as the
rules are slanted in their favor. And when the rules aren't slanted
enough, they done go pull shit like this.'

Greg chose not to reply. Demetrius cast most of the newspaper
aside, deciding to concentrate on the sports pages. The rejected
sections landed on the coffee table with a hiss of friction.

Almost against his will, Greg leaned over and picked up the local
news section, drawn by a small headline from below the fold.

'PITTSBURGH, PA – Officials are working to identify a
man's body that was found on the north bank of the Allegheny
River late Thursday night.

According to officials at the scene, the body of a roughly
45-year-old Caucasian man was found floating in shallow
water near the Rachel Carson Bridge. He had apparently been
shot multiple times.

A passerby walking his dog discovered the body.

The case is being investigated by Pittsburgh homicide
detectives. According to sources, no one has been reported
missing in that area, and for reasons that have not been
disclosed, the as yet unidentified body is believed to be that
of a foreign national, perhaps British, or Russian.

The body was turned over to the Allegheny County Medical
Examiner's Office for further inquiries.'

There was no picture.

A small knot formed in the pit of Greg's stomach. He had little
doubt the body in question was Morosov's. But American intelligence was not in the business of summary executions. And even
if they were, they would know better than to dump a corpse into
the nearest river carrying clues about its identity.

So . . .

He wandered across the lounge to the kitchen area and poured
himself a coffee. He stood quietly by the sink, staring unseeingly
over the seated heads of his colleagues.

The bell rang for lessons.